Bury Her Sweetly

Bury Her Sweetly

Linda Amey

A LION PAPERBACK
Oxford · Batavia · Sydney

Acknowledgments

Special thanks to Marci Henna for her invaluable contributions to this book and to my editor Bob Klausmeier for his encouragement and expertise.

Published by
Lion Publishing
1705 Hubbard Avenue, Batavia, Illinois
60510, USA
ISBN 0 7459 2389 5
Lion Publishing plc
Sandy Lane West, Oxford, England
ISBN 0 7459 2389 5
Albatross Books Pty Ltd
PO Box 320, Sutherland, NSW 2232,
Australia
ISBN 0 7324 0581 5

First edition 1992
All rights reserved
Library of Congress CIP Data applied for

A catalogue record for this book is available
from the British Library

Printed and bound in Great Britain
by Cox & Wyman Ltd, Reading

DEDICATION

For my husband, John Amey,
Who planted in my imagination
The seed from which this story grew.
All my love.

And for Celtic,
My precious little friend.
How I miss you.

1

Lenny set the discreetly wrapped carton containing Jewell's ashes on the front seat of the car between him and April. She probably wouldn't think of Jewell as her mother anymore— not with Jewell dead and April knowing the truth now. Part of it anyway.

Wind gusts whipped the old Buick across the bridge spanning the Chesapeake Bay, then tugged at Lenny's shirt as he trudged along a deserted stretch of beach. He carried the carton with one hand like a six-pack of beer. Down at his side. Brushing against his jeans.

April trailed alongside him. Sand spilled over the cracked and peeling tops of her imposter Reeboks. She stopped suddenly when Lenny waded knee-deep into the chilly water, watched silently as he tore back the flaps of the carton. From inside it, he removed a plastic bag secured at the top with a twist-tie. With a flick of the hand, he tossed the empty carton at April's feet.

Fearing that the wind might whip his wife's ashes into his face, Lenny turned his head to the side and cautiously opened the bag. To his surprise, the contents of the bag looked more like coarse sand than ashes—charcoal colored sand, mingled with crushed bone fragments instead of shells.

Fifteen years he had stumbled through with Jewell. It had begun the day he paid her for a six-pack and asked what time she got off work. Weeks later they had moved into a shabby little apartment in south Dallas. Their combined income from the liquor store and what Lenny picked up laying brick hardly had kept a roof over their heads and food on the table. So Lenny had started dealing a little.

At some point, he and Jewell had married. Lenny wasn't sure why they had bothered, but he was glad they did. If Jewell hadn't been his wife, she could have testified against him at his trial for drunk driving. That would have been one heck of a mess. The way Lenny figured it, if the prosecutor had been allowed to put Jewell on the stand, Lenny Bond would have been the only first- offender in the Lone Star State to die by lethal injection. "Your heart's always in the right place, Jewell," he had told her. "Too bad your brain's just along for the ride."

It was while he was serving time in Huntsville that Jewell had neared death the first time. "Hemo-what?" Lenny had asked the warden. "I ain't never heard the word, and now I'm getting an emergency furlough because my wife's threatening to die of it." On the way to the hospital, Lenny had joked with the sour-faced old guard. "If that's not a kick in the teeth. My wife's bleeding to death 'cause she wanted French fries for supper."

In all the years they had known each other, Jewell had not told Lenny she was a bleeder. Maybe if he had asked her why she couldn't have babies, she would have told him about her disease, but he hadn't. That was one of the crazy things about Jewell, he recalled. She had told him about every jerk and moron that staggered in and out of the liquor store, all the way down to what bill they gave her and what they were saying while she counted back their change. But she had not bothered to tell him she had a disease that was almost unheard of in women, and that one wrong move with a potato peeler and he could find her name in the obituaries the next morning.

8

Lenny felt the weight of April's stare and inched forward in the water, handling the plastic bag with the caution of an explosives expert. Jewell had told him she wanted to be carried by the waves into the ocean where she had taught April to swim.

Two years old, Lenny. She's a baby and she swims like a fish.

The request had sounded simple enough, kind of touching in a way, so Lenny had agreed to do it. But now he didn't much cotton to the notion of feeding his wife's burned-up body to a bunch of scavenger fish. Pushing the thought aside, Lenny inhaled deeply, then flared the top of the bag with nicotine-stained fingers. He gave the contents a sideways glance, then held the bag in front of him, arms fully extended. With uncertain hands, he tilted the bag forward, gradually raining the cremated remains of thirty- eight-year-old Jewell Bond into the Chesapeake Bay.

Before the bag was empty, the densest fragments of Jewell's remains began to sink in the shallow water, but the lighter residue washed toward Lenny's legs. Some pieces clung to his jeans. Wide-eyed and startled, he splashed backwards out of the water, slapping frantically at his pants legs. Cursing the tide, he watched helplessly as uncooperative waves deposited the floating residue on the sand where shells discarded by razor clams and mussels cracked and faded, where clumps of stringy kelp decomposed in the winter wind.

With his heart still thumping against his ribs, Lenny turned to April. "Let's get outta here."

The sand was like weights around his ankles as Lenny trotted up the beach, with April trailing behind. Minutes later, the old Buick appeared in the distance. The tires were slick. The right fender was rusted through in spots. What was left of the paint was the color of the hair swatch the skinny dude at the crematory had swooped over his bald spot—black losing the battle with gray.

The car door creaked when Lenny opened it. Before sliding behind the wheel, he stole one final glance down the beach. Fading away without a fuss was a fitting end for a woman like Jewell, he decided. No grave. No chiseled tombstone. No eulogy for a life that was miserably short on accomplishments. The pitiful fact was that, except for one bizarre exception, Jewell had tread life's murky water for over a third of a century and caused nothing more than three-ring ripples. But, Lenny admitted, she sure churned things up that day in Texas. Eleven years later, he still couldn't fathom Jewell blowing in and out of some strangers' backyard and making off with their kid.

Lenny released a long sigh of resignation, then looked across the hood at April. "Get in the car. Time to hit the road."

2

The weather took no pity on the Fritts family and the other mourners. The sun refused to show its pale face. Wind tore at the walls of the canvas tent like an intruder. Blair Emerson stood within easy reach of the casket spray in case a gust tried again to toss the flowers onto the nearby mound of soil. She turned up the collar of her coat and swore there was no place colder in central Texas than a cemetery on a winter afternoon.

The minister's benediction was a particularly welcomed blessing. With cold-stiffened fingers, Blair removed boutonnieres from the lapels of six shivering pallbearers and stepped aside. One by one the men placed their single white carnations among the casket flowers. Awkwardly they sidled into the narrow space between the green-skirted lowering device and the first row of chairs. Each whispered hasty condolences to the family, pressed trembling icy hands and nodded thanks to the black-robed minister.

After hugs and pecks on cheeks, the handful of mourners trickled from the tent to their cars. Finally only the family and pastor remained. Blair was relieved when he suggested they leave before the casket was lowered. Sleet had begun to fall.

When the cars were out of sight, the cemetery crew descended on the grave site. Blair and Wayne, a part-time

11

employee of Emerson Funeral Home who had driven the coach, stepped aside while the handful of men did their job in silence. The casket was lowered. The vault lid was slid into place. Artificial turf and chairs were stowed in an enclosed trailer. Then the tent was disassembled. From nearby, a backhoe rolled next to the mound. Skillfully, the operator skimmed the pile of dirt with the bucket and rained soil onto the silver lid of the vault.

The well-choreographed procedure took less than twenty minutes. Blair thanked Wayne for working on such a miserable day, then picked her way across wounded winter grass to her car. From there she called the funeral home. It was almost five o'clock. She told her secretary she was finished for the day. "My feet are frozen. My fingers are numb. My lips are purple. And I'm so hungry my leather gloves are starting to look appetizing."

"Then you'll be glad to know that Liz called about dinner. She got in and out of her doctor's office in record time and is on her way to meet you at Katz's." In her usual precise manner, Jane Prescott then relayed a message from the manager of the funeral home's second location. "He needs to use one of our limousines on a funeral in Liveoak tomorrow. Can we have it there by nine for a ten o'clock chapel service?"

"No problem." Blair eased the heavy car onto the freeway. "Call in a driver. Tell him to leave Austin no later than eight-fifteen. Allowing for traffic, he should be in Liveoak in thirty minutes. Anything else?"

"Nothing that can't wait until tomorrow. You and Liz enjoy your dinner."

Friends since the early seventies, Blair and Liz had met on the University of Texas campus. They had run into each other in the Academic Center—literally bumped heads at a water fountain. Within weeks they were roommates, sharing clothes and class notes and dreams. Even during those turbulent, confusing times for women, Liz had held firm to her own private goals. Despite societal voices shouting otherwise, she had aspired to be the well-educated wife of an honorable man and the mother to three well-adjusted children.

Blair, too, had aspired to be well-educated, but that was where the parallel had ended. A degree in business. An associate degree in mortuary science. Then a career in funeral service—a partner with her father in the Emerson family funeral homes. The notion of a husband and children had seemed burdensome then.

All that changed two short years later. First Myles. Then Brandi. As she had done for years now, Blair closed the door on regrets and black memories, then pulled to a stop on West Sixth Street.

Inside Katz's Delicatessen she asked if a gorgeous pregnant woman had been seated. Hearing that the lady had stepped into the rest room did not surprise Blair. Liz was due in less than two weeks.

Blair took a corner booth and ordered coffee. Minutes later, as the after-work crowd began to trickle in, Liz weaved her way across the dining room. Hair the color of warm honey. Just enough lipstick to highlight her perpetual smile. And gentle blue-gray eyes that widened when she spotted Blair. A quick kiss on the cheek and Liz squeezed into the booth. She noted Blair's tousled hair. "You look a tad ragged, Madame Funeral Director." Her smile became mischievous. "I would say you look *dead* on your feet but..."

Blair raised a cautionary eyebrow. "But then I would be tempted to counter with a preggy joke."

"Such as?"

"Such as: Did you make that maternity dress yourself, or did some circus leave a tent behind?"

The waiter stepped into their laughter. Blair ordered a corned beef on rye, then looked across the table at Liz. "And what are the two of you having?"

Liz blushed slightly as the waiter smiled down at her protruding middle. "Just chicken salad, I think."

Some women looked beautiful pregnant. Liz was one.

Blair, on the other hand, had felt like she'd swallowed a beach ball that slowly inflated over nine long months. A corned beef sandwich would have been out of the question for her then. She had retained water like a sponge. "So what did the doctor say?"

"She moved my due date. One more week, Blair. Ten days at the most." A delighted smile swept across Liz's face. "Ten years Bill and I have prayed for this day. If it weren't for this"—she patted the mound beneath the folds of her wool jumper—"I still wouldn't believe it."

"Have you had the new parents' tour at St. Mary's yet?"

"Bill and I went Friday."

"Large group?"

"Twelve couples, I think."

"How did it go?"

Liz picked up her water glass and took a sip. "It went fine."

"That's it? It went fine?" Several seconds passed before Blair realized why Liz was holding back. "Might I happen to know someone else in your group?"

In exaggerated imitation, Blair tossed imaginary strands of thick hair over her shoulder and flashed a toothy smile. Blair's voice became a breathy, dragging drawl: "Perhaps Charmaine Lauzon Lakeman? And her baldin' husband, Myles?" Her smile tightened. "I'm surprised they didn't get a private tour. The birth announcement will probably make the society column, like her wedding did."

A hint of envy put an edge on Blair's voice but she didn't care. Liz understood. She had seen Blair through it all. The affair between Myles and Charmaine. The divorce that had followed.

"How'd Charmaine look? Still thin and gorgeous? Designer maternity dress, right?"

"Yes, but Myles looked tired. I heard him say something about being at Charmaine's father's house half the night. Do you know what's wrong with Dr. Lauzon? He resigned his place on the board of regents, you know."

The waiter returned in record time with their plates. Blair

14

nodded thanks. "Excuse me, Lizzie, but I haven't eaten since breakfast." She dug into her sandwich with vigor. "Athero-sclerosis," she said with her mouth half full. "Hardening of the arteries in the brain. A few months ago, we buried a man who had it. His daughter said he started acting really bizarre toward the end. Irrational accusations. Angry outbursts. Apparently that was totally out of character, and it just broke her heart."

Liz tasted her chicken salad. "Has Dr. Lauzon been hospitalized?"

"Several times. Some nurses I know said he was a pain. They drew straws to see who had to answer his buzzer. He was downright mean to some of them." She stopped before adding that he had hit one nurse across the back with his cane. It was something she had overheard when making a death call at the hospital and should not be repeated, even to her best friend.

"I had Dr. Lauzon for French at the university." Liz shrugged her shoulders. "I thought he was nuts back then."

"Must run in the family. Look who his daughter married." Blair picked up the other half of her sandwich, then offered the pickle to Liz. "Are you still craving these things?"

Liz's expression was amused but long-suffering. "Yes, but only à la mode." She took the pickle and resumed picking at her chicken salad. "Did you make it to the party at the club last night?"

The question made Blair smile inside, but she simply nodded and continued to chew. Recently Liz had observed that Blair's social life was lacking, specifically, men. She had insisted that, for four consecutive weeks, Blair accept all reasonable dinner invitations and that she make an appearance at every function she was invited to that could be even loosely defined as a lawful assembly. Knowing the agreement would mean laughs, Blair had consented, drawing one hard line of exception. "I refuse," she had stipulated, "to go out a second time with Pat What's-His-Name."

Liz had cackled. "Exception noted. No more Homer

Simpson with a Porsche."

So for three weeks now, Blair had made the rounds. Parties at the country club. Holiday celebrations. Fund raisers. ("Both political and worthwhile," Liz had insisted.) After two weeks, Blair had sworn that if she saw one more barbequed chicken wing or another block of cheddar sculpted in the shape of Texas or its Lone Star, she would run screaming into the streets.

"So? How was the party?"

"It was lovely. The ballroom looked festive. Beautiful Christmas tree. Ice sculptures on the buffet tables. And the food was out of this world."

"Meet any new people?"

"Oh, sure. The club's getting lots of new members." Stringing Liz along was a favorite pastime of Blair's. And Liz never failed to take the hook. "In fact, I met two more people to play golf with this spring."

Liz's eyebrows rose. "And...?"

"They both have high handicaps like me." Blair picked up the last of her sandwich. "Should be fun."

After a moment of silence, Liz popped the tabletop with her palm. "Come on, Blair. Do they play from the front tees or the back?"

A wadded napkin hit Blair between the eyes. "Ouch." She spoke through laughter. "All right. One plays from the front. The other the back."

"Well, that's better." Liz smiled broadly, then stiffened with regained composure. "Now. I won't bother to ask if you like the woman. You always do. But what about the man?"

Blair folded her arms in front and sighed deeply. "I'll start out by describing him so you won't have to interrupt with: 'Wait. Tell me what he looks like first.' By the way, do you have any idea how shallow that sounds?"

"It's not shallow. I'm a visual person."

"Yeah. Right." Blair smiled. "Let's see. He's in his late forties. Wavy brown hair. Kind of unruly—his hair, not him," she added. "Droopy eyes. Good listener, but he does

16

this when you're talking to him." She squinted her eyes and tilted her head to one side. "Friendly enough, in a bumbling sort of way." She paused. "What else?"

"Well dressed?"

"Acceptable suit. But his trench coat looked like it had been in the trunk of his car."

"Wait a minute." Liz held up a restraining hand. "You've just described that detective Peter Falk played."

"Lieutenant Columbo." Blair collapsed in a fit of laughter. "I knew he reminded me of someone."

"Homer Simpson and Lieutenant Columbo." Liz rested her forehead in her palm and spoke miserably. "Well, you are really striking out in the dating scene."

It was true. Blair hated dating. Dating was for other people—people under forty. Not for those whose curfew was self-imposed, whose workday required at least seven hours of good sleep.

Blair pushed aside her plate. "That was excellent." Liz had stopped picking at her chicken salad and was staring at Blair with a strange smile. "And what are you grinning at, Elizabeth Elrod?"

Liz carefully put her fork down on the table. "I have something to ask you, Blair. Bill and I have discussed this, and maybe I should have waited until the three of us were together to bring it up." Liz leaned forward as far as her considerable mid-section would allow and touched Blair's hand. "Now you don't have to give me an answer tonight, but . . ." she squeezed her hand, " . . .we want you to be the baby's godmother."

"Lizzie." Blair's free hand sprang to her lips. "But what about your . . ."

"My sister has children of her own, Blair. And Bill's an only child. Besides there's no one in the world I would trust more with our little Elizabeth William than you."

3

The old Buick rocked and swayed along an interstate highway somewhere in Arkansas. It was Monday. They had been on the road for two days, and April was bored out of her mind. She picked at frayed threads across an eye-shaped hole in the knee of her jeans. She avoided looking at Lenny, particularly at the disgusting tattoo of tracks on his inner forearms.

She had known for years that Lenny and Jewell were not her natural parents, that she had been adopted when she was about two years old. Jewell had claimed to know nothing about April's natural parents—something about sealed documents. But *that* part had been a lie. April knew that now. Jewell had admitted it the night before she died. The problem was that now April had to count on Lenny for the rest of the truth.

Maybe she should have been upset or confused to learn that she was adopted, but she hadn't been. In fact, for over a year she had been calling Lenny and Jewell by their first names so that people would think she was adopted. Allowing anyone to think that Jewell was her natural mother would have been okay. But Lenny was a different matter. Even when he tried to get it together—which wasn't very often— Lenny was still a loser.

Influenced by recently acquired knowledge about AIDS, April worried that Lenny might be a carrier. She had learned about high-risk lifestyles from the television public-service announcements and from a speaker who'd talked at her school. She wasn't sure that Lenny slept around, but she was dead certain he did drugs. And he was such a dope that, if he was short on money, he wouldn't think twice about sharing a needle.

Lenny didn't seem to show any symptoms—at least none that April could recognize—but she kept her distance anyway. The celebrities in the public-service announcements said the virus could not be transmitted by casual contact. That was easy for them to say. April would bet money that not one of them was living with a carrier.

She was extremely cautious when touching anything that belonged to Lenny, particularly anything that had come into contact with his spit. She wore rubber gloves when she emptied his nasty ash tray or did the laundry. And for over a year now, she had had her own plate and a four-piece place setting of stainless in a pattern different from Jewell's. The bottom of her glass was marked with her initials, written with a permanent marker so they wouldn't wash off.

Keeping her utensils separate from Lenny's and Jewell's had meant that April had to set the table and wash dishes after every meal. During the school year, she had sneaked all her utensils back to her bedroom before leaving the house. That had freed her from having to scald them before dinner in case Lenny touched them while she was at school. It had been a real pain, but what choice did she have?

When Lenny pulled her out of school Friday, April had been as shocked as her teacher. During math class, Miss Walker had spoken to someone on the intercom and then walked April to the office. "Your father is here, April," she explained. "I'm not sure what he wants."

Immediately, April's stomach had started to churn. By the time she reached the office, she was nearly sick with anxiety.

Lenny was perched on the corner of the secretary's desk.

Laughing. Talking loudly. Holding an unlit cigarette in his fingers. His dingy blonde hair fell onto his forehead and over his shirt collar. His faded plaid shirt was unbuttoned, revealing a beer company logo across the tee-shirt he wore under it. Two girls sitting outside the principal's door had giggled and whispered when they spotted April.

Lenny had hopped off the desk and strutted up to Miss Walker. "Me and April are going to be moving to El Paso," he'd blurted out. "Got a job opportunity out there that won't wait. Gettin' in the Mexican import business. *Comprende?*"

"But, Mr. Bond, the semester is almost over. Couldn't you . . . I mean . . . wouldn't it be better if you waited until . . ." Miss Walker had stuttered a few other sentences which Lenny interrupted. Finally, she told him to have the school in El Paso request April's records. The hug she had offered April had been rejected. Granted, April did not like being touched, but mainly she had wanted to get out before Lenny said something really stupid. But Lenny's big mouth had lurched ahead.

"Hey, babe," he had said, looking Miss Walker up and down. "If they've got teachers in El Paso lookin' as good as you, I might just enroll myself."

Her face burning with shame, April had dashed to her locker to grab her backpack. No time for goodbyes—not even to her best friend, Becky. She had just wanted to get out of there.

She missed Becky already, almost as much as she missed Jewell. She and Jewell hadn't really talked that much—not about things that were important to April anyway. Lenny had always gotten in the way. But it was different with Becky. She understood. Her father was an alcoholic, so she knew what it was like to feel ashamed, to pretend, to cover up. But now Becky was gone. That stupid Lenny had ruined everything. Why hadn't he left her in Virginia Beach? Becky's mom liked her. She could have stayed with them.

There were times when April actually hated Lenny. And now he was all she had. No brothers. No sisters. No grandparents or aunts. Just one adopted uncle at the top of the gross-out scale who lived in Arkansas and actually killed deer and squirrels and ate them. A bitter taste rose in April's mouth. She managed to swallow over it while rolling down the window several inches. The cold, damp air soothed her hot face.

"Roll up that window. You lost your mind?" Lenny shook his head in disbelief. "I swear, kids ought to come with an owner's manual."

The paperback April pulled out of her backpack had a circular water stain on the cover. She had bought it at a used-book store with money she had swiped from Lenny's pants pocket over a two- week period.

That was how she had gotten the money to buy her plate and glass and flatware, too. Lenny always emptied his pockets when he got home. Coins, wallet and pocketknife were dropped into his "Elvis plate"—a chipped, cracked souvenir he had picked up in Memphis. Since he kept the plate on the dresser in his and Jewell's bedroom, taking money from it was a snap.

At first, April had felt a little guilty about the stealing. But she convinced herself that Lenny was getting only what he deserved. After all, it was because of his stupid AIDS risk that she had to buy her own dishes in the first place.

After a while, swiping money from the "Elvis plate" had become routine, like washing dishes and doing homework and guarding against contamination. Like those things, stealing was not just a pointless habit. She used the money for important things, like the time she had needed seven dollars to go with her class to the theater. She'd known Lenny would just laugh if she asked him for the money. He'd have said something about the theater being a stupid waste of time. But April knew it wasn't. And she had known how to get the money without asking Lenny.

The next few miles were spent reading and rereading the back cover of her book. Concentrating was impossible. She kept thinking about Jewell. A week ago she was sitting at the kitchen table making out a grocery list. Now she was dead.

April had called Jewell at the hospital immediately after her car accident. Jewell had told her not to worry, that it was a minor accident. But for a person with hemophilia, no accidents were minor. She had talked to Jewell on the phone twice a day after that, so it wasn't as if April hadn't cared. It was the hospital. She hadn't been able to go there. Bacteria. Viruses. Protozoa. Microorganisms were on everything you touched, in every breath you took in hospitals.

Nevertheless, Lenny had dragged her there. "She's dying, nitwit, and all she wants is to see you. Jewell may not be your real mother, but you're the only kid she's got. Now get your rear in the car."

Even while her lips were moving, Jewell had looked dead. Cold skin the color of chalk. Blue-black lips that matched the circles under her eyes. Hands limp and lifeless. Touching her almost had made April gag. But now she was glad she had done it. Jewell had tried to be a good mother and, for the most part, she had been. The times that she had let April down had been Lenny's fault. Worrying about him took so much of Jewell's time, she had had little time left for anyone else.

Jewell's voice had been so weak that night—little more than a whisper. April had made herself lean in close. Still, with her ear only inches away from Jewell's lips, April thought she had misunderstood. "What, Jewell? What did you say?"

"Your mother. I lied." Her lids had fluttered down, then up again. "If you ever want to know who she is, ask Lenny. He'll tell you. He promised me."

Lenny squinted in the glare of the afternoon sun. He held a cigarette between shaking fingers, nervously thumping ashes on the floor. He started letting the wind suck them out the vent window when the little cluster on the floor mat reminded him of Jewell.

It was just like that crazy woman to have a sudden burst of

death-bed conscience and leave him saddled with the biggest foul- up of her life. What the hell was he going to tell April if she ever asked about her real mother? Holy cow. What a mess. If he could figure out a way to do it without landing in jail for the rest of his natural life, he would ship April off to her parents in a New York minute.

When his cigarette had burned down to the filter, Lenny thumped it out the window. He immediately lit another and exhaled smoke with a prolonged sigh. Life sure had a way of kicking you in the tail when you were bent over trying to pick up the pieces. With the money-making opportunity of a lifetime glinting in his eyes, he was saddled with a teenage girl who, as far as he could tell, didn't know how to do one thing but poke her nose in anything that had pages. But, he reminded himself, he had plenty of time to mull the mess over in his mind and come up with a plan. Miles meant hours, and there was plenty of both between here and El Paso.

"Your disgusting cigarette smoke is poisoning my lungs." April cracked the window and breathed in the frosty air. Without looking at Lenny, she said in a flat, inflectionless tone, "I need to get back in school immediately."

"Hell's bells, April. You talk like Jewell on her death bed. Quit your mumbling and speak up."

"School." April forced the word from her mouth. "I can't be missing school."

"That's right, April," Lenny mocked. "The great principal in the sky might strike you dead if you miss a class. And you'll be damned for sure if you slip up and make an A minus." Lenny pulled a beer loose from a six-pack and popped the top.

Lids drew down over April's brown eyes.

"All right. All right. I'll get you back in school. I don't want the law after me." He took a long swig, smacked his lips loudly and grinned at April. When she ignored him, he said, "April Bond. The human tranquilizer."

April resumed picking at the threads across the hole in her jeans. Finally she said, "I want to go back to Virginia Beach.

23

To Becky's."

"Whaddya say?"

"You heard me," she snapped. "I don't want to live in El Paso. I won't like it there. I won't know anyone. And you don't need me around."

Lenny swigged his beer. It was true. She would just be in his way. And what the heck did he know about raising a teenage girl? A girl that age needed a mother.

"So, can I?" April pressed.

Lenny didn't answer. He stared straight ahead, his eyes fixed and unblinking. His mind was racing. Yeah. A girl April's age needed her mother. *Her mother*.

"Lenny, answer me. Can I go home?"

Lenny bobbed his head up and down slowly. "Maybe." He didn't look at April when he spoke. He was still staring out the windshield. "Maybe you can go home." A grin twisted his lips. "I might just be able to arrange that."

Miles later, Lenny told April to get him another beer from under the seat. He always thought clearer when he had a beer in his hand. And he had some serious thinking to do. Grudgingly April popped the top on the can and handed it to him.

"You're as good at that as Jewell was," Lenny teased, feeling almost playful now that a plan was forming.

"She had enough practice at it, living with you." April wiped her hands on her pants legs, than paused a full minute before speaking. "Jewell made me a promise before she died."

"I guess that's the best time to make one—right before you die. Then you won't have to keep it."

"She promised you'd tell me who my natural mother is." April stole a glance at Lenny, then quickly turned away.

His pulse quickened. "What you wanna know that for?" Lenny thumped another butt out the window and rolled it up. It didn't take much wind noise to drown out April's voice. It was as skinny as she was. "You gonna play detective and track her down?"

24

"Maybe I will," April snapped. When Lenny only laughed, she asked again. "So who was she, and why did she give me up for adoption?"

Thanks a heap, Jewell, Lenny thought to himself. I'm not as good at lying as you. He had to laugh when he remembered the story Jewell had told her mother about how they'd adopted April. Holy cow. That poor old lady must not have had two brain cells to rub together if she bought that cock-and-bull story. Now he would see if April was in the market for a lie.

"Jewell met your mother when we lived in Texas. The woman was broke and her old man had skipped, so Jewell asked her if we could adopt you. Your mother said yes."

"How old was I?"

"Almost two, just like Jewell told you." Lenny rolled down the window and stuck out his thin arm. His turn signal was broken and there was a state trooper behind him. He pulled into a service station and parked near the rest rooms. Time for a pit stop. When the cruiser whizzed on past, Lenny reached over the back of the seat for his duffel bag. His stash was getting low, but he was just a few states away from some big bucks.

Smuggling parrots out of Mexico. Who'da thought it? Lenny grinned and shook his head. When his buddy had first mentioned the smuggling operation, Lenny had thought *parrots* was some code word for cocaine. But no. He meant real parrots.

"Scarlet Macaws. Yellow-Headed Amazons. Big, expensive dudes, Lenny," his friend had bragged. "Birds that'll bring eight to twelve hundred bucks from bird-brain yuppies in the States. Don't those idiots *wonder* why my birds are a couple hundred dollars cheaper than those in the pet stores? Not once, not one single time, has any of those fools asked about the name of the breeder or even mentioned anything about disease. Hell, they deserve to get parrot fever for being so stupid." Then he had snorted and said something about all the suckers out there that were just begging to let you make

25

money off of them. "But, Lenny, like they say. You got to spend money to make money. And if you can get yourself a few grand together, you'll be makin' more with me in a week than you can in a month laying brick."

"Lenny."

April's voice snapped him out of his thoughts. "Yeah? What?"

"Do you . . . do you know my mother's name?" She spoke haltingly. "Or where she lives?"

Lenny considered the question. His plan wasn't clear in his mind yet. But what could it hurt to toss a few crumbs April's way. "She used to live in Austin, Texas." Chances were the Lakemans still lived in the same house, the one with the alley running alongside their fenced backyard. He doubted that the sandbox was still next to the steps, though. They probably trashed that sucker after their kid disappeared.

"Her name, Lenny. What was it?" April pressed.

"For crying out loud, April, let me think. Jewell took care of all the legal stuff," he lied again, more easily this time. Lenny opened his door, stepped out and stretched his arms and legs. April met him in front of the car, hugging her backpack to her chest. Lenny spoke through a yawn. "I can't remember your mother's last name. But it seems like her first name was Barb or Blake. Something like that."

4

A familiar sinking sensation settled in on Blair as she drove home from the delicatessen. On the car seat lay a brown leather portfolio embossed with the words *Emerson Funeral Home*. Had her life been different years ago, the lettering now would read *Emerson and Emerson, Funeral Directors*. But chaos had reigned, starting just after two o'clock that dreadful April afternoon when Brandi disappeared.

Three years later, her father had said, "Blair, since Brandi disappeared, your life has been an absolute hell. Maybe Myles is right. Los Angeles might be just the change you two need. Take the job at Forest Lawn, honey. Promote one of your funeral directors to acting manager. I can handle things in Liveoak. Then in two short years, you'll be home. We'll have the rest of our lives to work together."

But two years had rolled into five. By then, her marriage to Myles had been limping badly. He had returned to his law practice in Austin. Months later, Blair reluctantly followed. Then, within a year, she had lost Myles to Charmaine Lauzon and her father to heart disease.

Thoughts of Myles and Charmaine and the baby they were expecting next month ignited sparks of pain and loss. And resentment. It seemed unfair that Myles should have a second chance at being a parent. After all, it had been Myles who had given up the search for Brandi in less than a year, knowing full well that hope alone had kept Blair's heart beating.

Brandi. For days now, the memories had come crowding back, bringing with them a deep, dull ache that left Blair restless and lonely. It happened every December. The day after Christmas was Brandi's birthday. This year she would be thirteen years old. Or would have been.

At home, she slipped a paper napkin from beneath a plate dotted with toast crumbs and wiped slush from her heels. The message light on her answering machine blinked red. It sat on a small oak desk that her grandmother had left her. Blair noted its cluttered top. Bills. Reminders to herself. Mail that remained unopened for fear that another invitation lurked there. *The Austin Society of Proctologists invites you to a seminar . . .*

She rewound the tape, then played the messages. The first caller had waited a full ten seconds before hanging up. The second message was from Myles. A look of half-startled wariness swept across Blair's face.

"Blair, someone called our house late this afternoon asking for Blair Lakeman. Charmaine told him that your name was now Emerson and gave him the number of the funeral home. When he said he didn't want to bother you at work, she gave him your home number. He didn't give his name but I guess you'll be hearing from him. Bye."

"I'll bet Charmaine loved handling that call," Blair said to the machine's beep. "She'd like to forget there ever was a previous Mrs. Myles Lakeman." Blair picked up the receiver and dialed the funeral home, letting the evening attendant know she was home and finding out which of her two funeral directors was on call for removals and embalming tonight. "Remember to call me if you get any death calls, Wayne. I might want to go myself if I know the family."

The remainder of the evening crept by. Blair found herself longing for a heart-to-heart with her father. Since that was impossible, she opted for the next best thing and dialed her family home in Liveoak. Curled on the sofa, she smiled when a tobacco-roughened voice said, "Emerson residence."

For a month now, Eldon Sumner, a treasured family friend and the dearest man Blair knew, had been caring for her mother. Maryruth suffered from Alzheimer's disease and was unable to live alone. Eldon's move into the family home was temporary. In June, Blair's sister and her husband would return to Liveoak after a six-month stay in New York where Charlotte's husband was free-lancing with an ad agency.

In his early seventies and a widower for twenty years, Eldon had been a second father to Blair. He had filled in the gaps left by the demands on her father's time for as long as she could remember. Many times when he had taken his son to football games at Memorial Stadium or fishing on Lake Travis, he had invited Blair along. In Eldon's easygoing way, he had talked to her and Kenneth about such things as faith, hard work, loyalty. Blair knew that a lot of what she now believed, a lot of who she was, she owed to Eldon.

Eldon reported that Maryruth had enjoyed the best day in weeks. "Funny how she does. She woke up this morning and offered to make coffee. Course I wouldn't have let her do it even if I hadn't made it already. We went to the store together and bought groceries. Then Miss Wilson from next door came by and spent the afternoon with her."

"I hope you used that opportunity to steal a little time for yourself."

"Oh, yes." Eldon coughed loudly. "Brought in some firewood. Got a haircut. I must have been gone two hours. How are things at work, Blair? Any funerals today?"

"Just one. A graveside service."

"Miserable day for it. Did you direct it?"

"Yes. I've waited on the family twice now. First when the mother died. Now the father. Wonderful people. There's a real tenderness, a real closeness among the children."

"Your dad used to say that death either pulls a family together or tears it apart."

Blair drew her knees up tight and covered her feet with an afghan. "Sure seems to. Take this family today. The children seem even closer than when I met them two years ago."

"Too bad it doesn't always happen that way," Eldon mused. "Last year, a friend of mine lost his wife. This woman was the glue that kept the family together. Lunch after church. Birthday parties. Holidays. You name it; she got them together for it. Sad thing is, I don't think that family's gotten together since her funeral."

Blair was silent for a moment. "Eldon, I know I'm not always the best at keeping in touch with Mom. I get so wrapped up in work that I let things slide. I don't want to let my family slip through the cracks."

"Don't you worry, honey. I'm as good as family now. And I'm not about to let that happen."

"Thanks, Eldon. I love you. Sleep well. I'll call tomorrow."

In her bedroom, Blair smiled to herself as she folded back the covers. Talking to Eldon had lightened her mood.

After a brief, very hot shower, Blair returned to the bedroom to find a dog-shaped lump in the folds of her comforter. Celtic, her Boston terrier, had claimed his spot on the foot of the bed and anchored the covers beneath his twenty pounds.

Celtic was almost four now. He had been around to mourn with Blair when Sandy, their cocker spaniel, died. Had she lived, Sandy would be twelve now—the same age as Brandi.

Blair crawled to the foot of the bed and stroked Celtic's back. "Woman's best friend indeed." She pulled the covers toward the foot of the bed and drifted off with Celtic's head resting on her shoulder.

The phone jarred Blair awake. Her first thought was that Wayne was calling from the funeral home. She rolled onto her side and felt for the nightstand, only to realize she was still at the foot of the bed. The ringing continued. "Hold on. I'm coming." Her voice was thick with sleep. She kicked free of the covers and groped toward the head of the bed. Before she got there, the phone stopped ringing.

She flicked on the lamp and yawned widely. The corned beef had left her as thirsty as a sponge. She would grab a quick drink of water before calling Wayne back. He was probably on the phone again anyway, dispatching Kent to pick up the body. She swung her legs off the side of the bed and wiggled her feet into slippers.

Grumbling to Celtic about being a cover hog, Blair padded down the hall, through the entry and into the kitchen. The refrigerator light nearly blinded her when she opened the door and removed a bottle of water. Single living didn't come without its perks, she reminded herself, tipping the bottle and taking a long swallow. For a moment she stood there trying to recapture whatever it was that had cheered her earlier that evening, an exercise she had perfected for when she was feeling out-of-sorts. "My talk with Eldon. And Elizabeth William, my soon-to-be godchild." While savoring these thoughts, Blair noticed the red light blinking on her answering machine. "Oops. I forgot that thing was on." Another quick swig and she returned the bottle to the shelf. Letting the door close on its own, she hurried in its narrowing light to the breakfast room.

She turned on a small brass desk lamp and played the message. The caller had waited several seconds before mumbling something indistinguishable and hanging up. Blair frowned and replayed the tape, this time with the volume on high. Leaning forward, she listened closely. A voice, a man's voice, crackled through. The end of his sentence trailed off, as if he had moved the receiver away from his mouth. But Blair caught part of what he said.

"Your old lady must really like her night life."

Then the line went dead.

5

The old Buick sputtered along the freeway, inching forward in congested Dallas traffic. April grew increasingly nervous as she watched both the car and Lenny overheat. His face was red. A vein pulsing in his temple looked like a worm crawling beneath his skin. April flinched when a string of curse words spewed from his mouth.

"I heard one time that an ol' boy jerked out his rifle and shot some fool for cutting him off on one of these damn freeways." Lenny slapped the steering wheel. "Makes some sort of sense right about now."

When the Toyota ahead of him lurched into the lane to the right, Lenny floored the accelerator and followed. April gripped the armrest with white-knuckled fingers. A quarter mile ahead, the reason for the bottleneck became apparent.

"All this hassle because that joker lost his stupid Christmas tree out of his truck." Lenny rolled down the window and yelled as he passed the red-faced man. "Buy a fake one next year, sucker."

In the parking lot of a McDonald's in south Dallas, Lenny shoved a few crumpled bills at April and said, "I'm gonna find a mailbox. I'll be back when you see me."

The car engine stalled before Lenny was halfway across

the parking lot. April heard him cursing loudly even after the engine started and the car groaned off the lot. He got that way—loud, hot-tempered, nervous—if too many hours lapsed between "pit stops." That was what he had started calling his trips to a rest room, duffel bag in hand. Did he think she was too stupid to know what he kept in it? The way Lenny changed in those few minutes amazed and frightened April. Afterwards his thin lips wore an empty smile. His eyes were vacant, his pupils large and black. And his hands were steady—as if all the tension had been sucked out of him.

French fries. A fish sandwich. A Diet Coke. That sounded good to April. She ordered, feeling the weight of eyes on her back. She was the only white girl there. This part of Dallas was little like the city's television image.

April carried her tray to a small table near the door. From there she could see the Buick when it rolled past the golden arches. The table was near a youngish couple and their children. The two little girls, their black hair in neat braids clipped with balloon-shaped barrettes, both said "Hi" at exactly the same time when April walked by. Their accents made her giggle.

From her backpack, April removed two foil-wrapped towelettes. She peeled back the wrapper of one and wiped the tabletop with it. With the other she wiped her hands and wrists, sniffing the fresh lemon scent. While she ate her sandwich, April listened to the man warn one of the girls that this was her last trip to see Santa if she cried again this year. A tiny voice insisted that Santa did not scare her anymore. "Not since I got more bigger." The other child rattled off a list of Christmas wishes she would take to Santa.

A memory ruffled through April's mind. Jewell had taken her to see Santa each year until she was eight or nine. Sometimes Lenny had tagged along, pointing and laughing at the people in line. Once he had swaggered over to a teenage girl whose yellow hair was spiked and sprayed Christmas red and green on the tips. "Girl, if that ain't a hairdo from hell! I hope you sued."

33

April hated Lenny's mouth.

When she had finished her sandwich, April started on the fries. Her eating system required her to finish one item before starting another and to save her drink until last. The system had started several years ago. She didn't know what brought it on, but by now it had become a part of her life. Something she couldn't change. First bread. Then meat. Vegetables next. And last, her drink.

People sometimes asked why she did it. But they usually seemed satisfied when she said, "I don't know. It's just how I eat." She didn't tell them that she *had* to eat that way, that if she didn't, something really bad might happen.

Although she knew her eating system was strange, April had learned to accept it. But her other habit was more than strange. To her it was . . .well, a real mystery. And at times, it made her feel crazy.

Just before noon, the black family left. April watched them walk out the door, laughing and joking together. Seeing them made her wonder what her life would have been like if her real mother had raised her. But imagining a life with her mother was difficult, since April knew almost nothing about her, other than her first name. It was Blair.

Of course, Lenny knew her full name. "I found the adoption papers," he had told April last night after they checked into the motel. "They were in a box I threw in the trunk with all that other junk Jewell saved. It's a wonder I didn't trash them back in Virginia Beach. Then I never would have remembered your mama's name." Lenny had seemed nervous when April asked to see the papers. He had refused, saying, "It wouldn't be right to . . .you know . . .evade her privacy that way."

April had been shocked when Lenny said he'd actually tried to call Blair. "Just to say 'hi' and let her know about Jewell," he'd explained. "But her answering machine was on, so we'll try again late tonight."

"Late tonight" had turned out to be around midnight. "Well, let's see if your mama's made it home yet," Lenny had said, flicking off the television and jerking on his denim jacket. "I need a pack of smokes, so we'll call her from the pay phone at the convenience store." April had been frantic with anxiety. What if Blair was sleeping? What would she say to Lenny after all this time? And what would April do if Blair asked to speak to her?

The pay phone was outside the convenience store. Lenny had told her to wait near the door while he spoke to Blair. "I'll let you know if she . . . you know . . . wants to talk to you."

"But, Lenny, I don't know what . . ."

"Don't worry," he had interrupted, "I'll tell you what you're supposed to say." Then he had turned his back to her and placed the call. Just a few seconds later, he had mumbled a few curse words, said something about her "old lady's night life" and slammed down the phone.

Something Lenny had said after getting in the car still troubled her—something about seeing where Blair stood on things. What had he meant by that? Was he planning to see if Blair wanted to meet her, maybe even take her back?

Frowning, April picked a French fry from the sack. She wasn't sure just how she felt about meeting Blair. What kind of mother would give away her kid just because she couldn't afford her? "Jewell didn't," April whispered. "And we were always broke."

Worrying that Lenny might come into the restaurant and make a scene, April folded the papers on her tray into neat squares and cautiously slid them into the trash. Careful that her fingers did not touch the hinged lid, she tossed in the empty Coke cup and walked outside. Minutes later, the old car appeared, its tires squealing around the corner. Lenny was going too fast when he hit a speed bump in the middle of the parking lot. He was still cursing when April opened the car door and climbed inside.

In Room 6 of the Oak Cliff Inn, Lenny popped the top on a Lone Star beer and threw back a long gulp. "Man, it's good to be back in Texas. Gun racks in the rear windows of trucks.

Bumper stickers telling Yankees, 'Welcome to Texas. Now go home.' A steak so big it hangs off the edge of your platter. What a place."

Sheer adrenalin shot Lenny's spirits sky-high. His plan was firming up. The package to Blair—it was Emerson now, according to the new Mrs. Lakeman—was on its way. What a stroke of luck that Jewell the pack-rat had saved those things all these years.

Lenny stretched out on the bed and looked across the room at April. She was sitting on a ratty old sofa by the window reading a paperback book. Who'da thought it? The kid had turned out to be the answer, not the problem. He sighed so loudly that she looked up for a second. He had told her on the way from McDonald's that he'd tried to contact Blair again but that she wasn't at home. She acted like she didn't give a rat's eyelash, but Lenny knew better. Any kid would be a little curious about a thing like that.

Of course, he hadn't actually tried to call Blair. That was for later. He would drop his little bomb tonight, maybe even make April grunt a word or two into the phone. Then tomorrow Blair would get the package. She'd read his note. She'd study the things he mailed her. He'd give her a little time to remember and maybe cry. Then he would place his next call.

The plan was perfect, brilliant. But he had to be patient and keep his cool. He had called his buddy in El Paso and told him he would be delayed getting there. "I'm raising that investment capital we talked about. I want in on this deal on a big scale."

After it was all over and he had the money and Blair had the kid, Lenny Bond was going to have something in common with Jimmy Hoffa: dropping off the face of the earth. Then some old boy named Lee Pickens was going to take El Paso by storm.

"Lee Pickens." The name tasted good to Lenny. He had borrowed it from two of his favorite Americans: Lee Iacocca and T. Boone Pickens. Lenny opened another beer and said,

"Here's to you gentlemen." Just to annoy her, he offered a beer to April. If looks could kill, he decided, he wouldn't have a pulse any minute now. "You're just a party looking for a place to happen, ain't you, girl?" Lenny's laughter bounced off the plaster walls and came back to him. He rolled onto his side, cuddling his beer can to his cheek.

Life's a hoot, Lenny thought to himself as he settled into a vague half-sleep. All his life when he thought he was seeing the light at the end of the tunnel, it had turned out to be a gorilla with a flashlight. "But I'm ready for ya this time, you big hairy sucker." Words slurred between Lenny's teeth. "You're dead meat."

April stopped reading and slipped a hairpin onto page thirty-two of her book. Silently she tiptoed across the threadbare carpet while slipping on gloves she had removed from her backpack. Lenny's jeans were crumpled at the foot of the bed. He had dropped them there and crawled into bed while she was in the bathroom. With two fingers she removed his wallet from the back pocket, then counted the bills quickly. Three hundred forty- eight dollars. Great. Lots of ones. She took four and returned the wallet, certain to put it back exactly as she had found it.

She picked up her backpack on the way to the bathroom. There she spread the bills on the tile floor and sprayed them on both sides with Lysol disinfectant. Then from her back-pack she dug out a roll of bills and removed the rubber band securing them. Forty- two dollars. Tomorrow, when Lenny gave her money for lunch she would ask for a couple of extra dollars for video games. Lenny would probably ridicule her—"That's it, April. Live on the edge. Walk on the wild side."—but she didn't care. She really hated video games. The extra money would be stashed here with the rest.

Confident now that the germs on the ones were dead, she layered the bills on the outside of the roll and secured it again with the rubber band. Forty-six dollars. It had taken her months to get her hands on all that money. Until now, she had planned to buy something from a J.C. Penney catalogue. It was a foot bath that cost almost forty dollars. The catalogue said it "provided relief for tired, aching feet." But when April had read further, she found that the appliance was also excellent for soaking hands and wrists. Filled with water and a strong disinfectant, it was certain to kill the germs on her hands. She regretted that she wouldn't be able to buy it, but she needed the money for something more important now.

In water as hot as she could stand, April soaped her gloves thoroughly, then returned them to a plastic bag in her backpack. Then she removed a pint of Top Job household cleaner and poured some on her hands and forearms. The fumes irritated her eyes. The smell was terrible. The chemicals burned her cracked, peeling hands. But she had to do it.

Her obsession with germs had started last year, when she was in fifth grade. But her need to wash her hands had started long before—when she was about four years old. They had moved into a house in Virginia Beach. On the day of the move, she had been really nervous or scared. She had no idea why. Anyway, she had pulled a chair up to the sink and turned on the faucet. The feel of water running on her hands had soothed her, made her less anxious. For a long time after that, whenever she felt scared or worried, she had taken a shower or washed her hands.

When she started school, the need to wash had more or less faded away. But then in the fifth grade, it had returned. One day, after a school assembly on AIDS, she began to wonder— just wonder—if Lenny had AIDS. Then wondering had turned into worrying that he did. And worrying had caused her to think about germs and contamination. So she had started wearing rubber gloves when she did his and Jewell's laundry and spraying with Lysol things that he might have touched. She sprayed when no one was watching, but then there had been the smell. When Lenny and Jewell had complained, she had bought unscented spray. But then she had worried that the spray might not be killing the germs since she couldn't smell the chemicals.

Somehow April had managed. But things had gotten worse since Jewell's accident and death. Now April had begun to *feel* the germs on her hands. Not crawling or biting. It was nothing like that. It was their secretions. Sticky, gummy secretions that, left unwashed, became unbearable. No longer was it enough to hold her hands under running water—nor was ten or fifteen minutes washing with hot soapy water. Now she scrubbed her hands and arms and, at times—just to be safe—her entire body for twenty or thirty minutes. Always with hot water. And most of the time with a strong disinfectant, like Top Job or Mr. Clean.

Watching. Spraying. Washing. And trying to hide it all. It was becoming almost unmanageable. She had never told Jewell about her habit. It was embarrassing to tell someone that you washed a dozen times a day. Furthermore, Jewell might have told Lenny. He would have called April a mental case and said, "So, dammit, just stop it." And April knew she couldn't do that, couldn't stop—no matter how hard she tried.

Becky was the only person in the world who knew about April's problem. When Becky had told her to talk to the school counselor, April refused. "She'd tell Jewell and then Lenny would find out. No. I'm not telling anyone, and neither are you." Now she didn't even have Becky to talk to.

Lenny was sound asleep when she walked past the end of his bed. A thin line of saliva hung from the corner of his lower lip to the beer can. April grimaced and turned away quickly.

A phone book was on the bedside table. She carried it to the sofa and located the number of the bus station. Later she would use one of her quarters to find out exactly how much the fare was from Dallas to Virginia Beach. She had located El Paso on the map at the service station on the corner. The city was across the border from a town in Mexico called Juarez. She had overheard Lenny on the phone telling some man that

39

he was staying in Dallas for a while. He had been talking real softly, but she had heard him say something about Mexico and parrots. A person didn't have to be a genius to figure out that parrots was some idiotic code name for drugs. Anyway, she didn't care if Lenny was moving to El Paso to play in one of those mariachi bands; she had no intention of living there. When she had saved up enough money, she would buy a bus ticket, leave Lenny a note and go to Becky's house. He would never go to the trouble of driving halfway across the country to get her back.

Of course, her plans could change. April thumbed through the yellow pages, thinking that she might just tough it out long enough to see what happened with Blair. Of course, Lenny was probably right. Blair might just tell her to bug off. After all, she had done it once before.

6

Blair left the house just after six-thirty Tuesday morning and was at the spa before seven. Celtic had balked at the prospect of starting his day while it was still dark and had returned to bed after a quick trip outdoors. "I'm showing self-discipline," Blair had bragged, pulling sweatpants over her tank suit and zipping her corduroy coat.

When the weather was nice, she jogged on the trail skirting the banks of Town Lake, but on cold days she preferred swimming laps. Until recently, Liz had met her here. Even before she had ballooned around the middle, Liz had not been as good a swimmer as Blair and usually had quit well before her.

At the side of the pool, Blair dropped her robe, looked into the still blue water and dived in. The water was cool and invigorating. She began her regimen of slow easy strokes. She missed Liz more than usual this morning. In a few short days, Elizabeth William would make his or her debut at St. Mary's. Blair would parade around telling everyone she was the fairy godmother, empowered to make the child's every wish come true. She would be so convincing that no one would detect she was more than a little envious of Liz.

Thirty minutes later, Blair lifted herself onto the edge of

the pool. Breathing heavily, she nodded to a Jane Fonda look-alike doing stretching exercises on the other side. Unlike Blair, she had a swimmer's body. Lean, with broad shoulders, trim waist and hips. And legs that went on forever. Blair, on the other hand, had to exercise thirty minutes a day just to keep her weight at a hundred and thirty, and had yet to intimidate another woman with her looks.

"It's all yours," she called, instinctively tightening her stomach muscles. "Enjoy."

"Thanks. Have a good day." Jane's double sliced the water's surface without a splash.

Blair squeezed water from her shoulder-length hair, then just sat on the edge of the pool watching the woman's controlled movements, her graceful strokes. At the north end of the pool, she flipped over and began to backstroke. Blair made a quick comparison of their styles and chuckled. "I must have looked about as graceful as Roseanne Barr."

Dispensing with her stretching exercises, Blair hurried off to the locker room to change. She wanted to get home, down a bagel and some juice, and be at the funeral home a little early. A man named Tony Antonelli was coming in to make prearrangements for his teenage daughter's burial. Leukemia. Life wasn't fair.

Traffic was heavy by the time she reached Zilker Park. The park was lively with runners and joggers and walkers. Some chatted in fast-moving pairs. Many wore headsets.

At Robert E. Lee Boulevard, she made a right turn and headed toward her home in Barton Hills. Almost twenty-five years old, the antique-brick house was in excellent condition. Trimmed in off-white paint with chocolate-brown accents. A lovely bay window in the living room. And a yard that, in a few months, would smell of wisteria.

Inside, Blair lifted Celtic into her arms and cuddled him on the way to the bedroom. An hour later, dressed in a royal blue suit, a silk blouse the color of strawberry yogurt and black leather shoes, she was sitting in her office at the funeral home.

A two-story brick building located on the edge of the

University of Texas campus, the Austin location was the larger of the two Emerson funeral homes. But their combined volume of four hundred funerals a year didn't compare to that of Forest Lawn Mortuary where Blair had worked in Los Angeles. The Forest Lawn experience had been invaluable, particularly the expertise she acquired in restorative art. But the firm's enormous number of cases had required a sort of assembly-line approach, something she never had gotten used to.

Her intercom sounded. "Yes, Jane."

"Mr. Antonelli called to cancel his appointment. He said his wife simply wasn't up to coming. He'll call again in the next few days."

"In that case, you can bring me that stack of letters I saw on your desk. And from the looks of them, you'd better bring me an extra pen."

Simply because it was in her line of sight, Blair found herself staring at the phone. Her mind drifted back to the odd telephone call her machine had picked up late last night. What had the man said? "Your old lady likes her nightlife." Who would say such an offensive thing? No one she knew. And to whom? *Your old lady*. It sounded like a crude reference to someone's girlfriend or wife. The term certainly didn't apply to her, since she was neither to anyone. But one thing was certain. He had not reached a wrong number. Blair's taped message gave both her first and last names. Another thought occurred quickly. Could he have been the man who called Myles wanting her number? She sure hoped not. This guy was definitely not someone she wanted to talk over old times with.

A tap on the door snapped Blair back into focus. Jane entered, looking more handsome than usual in a perfectly tailored black and moss-green tweed suit. Dark hair flecked with gray lay in gentle waves and curls around her face. She laid stacks of letters, death certificates and checks on Blair's desk and said, "I'm afraid this autograph session will have to wait. The medical examiner's office is on line one. There's a

43

body to be picked up at the morgue."

For a few seconds, Blair made small talk with Norm, the medical examiner's assistant, a chatty guy with a quick wit. Norm was exposed to the gruesome details of every accidental or intentional death that occurred in Travis County. His manner and tone often signaled the nature of the death. Casual and conversational meant a routine stabbing or shooting. A single-vehicle wreck involving alcohol triggered a sort of "the-fool-was-asking-for-it" attitude. A crisp, controlled tone was reserved for an especially vicious death, like random murder or child abuse.

"This unfortunate gentleman's name is Alvin Platte." Norm slipped easily into a passable imitation of W.C. Fields. "Found last evening by another connoisseur of cheap wines. Platte's brother was contacted by yours truly. Discriminating man that he is, Joe Platte requested the services of the lovely Blair Emerson."

On a form designed for the purpose, Blair recorded the names of both men and the place of death, then asked for Joe Platte's phone number.

Norm supplied it and then said, "Hey, Blair, do yourself a favor. Let Kent or Greg make this call. And be sure he brings a body bag. This man's been dead for days."

"Thanks for the warning." When Blair hung up the phone, Kent was standing in the doorway. "Talk about being in the wrong place at the wrong time." She gave Kent a sympathetic smile, then quickly explained about the body at the morgue. "I guess you're elected. Take a body bag."

She dialed Joe Platte's number. He spoke gruffly when he described his brother as an alcoholic who had lived at the Salvation Army or on the streets. "I've been expecting this for twelve months. Frankly, I'm glad he's dead. Now I can quit dreading it."

Blair avoided saying it, but she understood what he meant. Not knowing what happened to Brandi had at times seemed far more agonizing than hearing the truth, no matter how brutal.

Platte told her he would be at the funeral home in twenty minutes to "wrap this mess up."

The arrangement conference was brief. "Just cremate him," Platte said flatly. "No service. No urn. No nothing. I'm going take his ashes down to the river and scatter them under the bridge where he used to sleep."

With a minimum of words, Blair explained costs, secured information for the death certificate and requested Platte's signature on the required forms. He seemed to make a production of not reading them. "I wouldn't have your job if it paid a hundred thousand a year," he said while writing out a check. Without another word, he left.

"Well, that was rewarding." She closed the file, walked down the hall and gave it to Jane. "I'll be in my office."

The stacks of paper on her desk had neither disappeared nor diminished. She picked up a pen and attacked them vigorously.

Just before two, her intercom sounded again. "Blair, there's a nurse from St. Mary's Hospital on line one. It's a death call."

The nurse was calling on behalf of a family named Brubaker. "They requested your funeral home," she explained. "The doctor's already been here, so you can come for Mrs. Brubaker now."

On the way to the garage, Blair opened the door to the dressing room, a spacious area used for cosmeticizing, dressing and casketing. The door to the adjoining preparation room was closed. Blair heard the roar of the exhaust fan and opened the door.

Kent and Greg, dressed in protective gowns, gloves, shoe covers and masks were treating with preservative powder the man they had removed from the morgue. His body, partially concealed by the black vinyl bag, was in an advanced stage of decomposition. Deep green discoloration on the abdomen. A frothy purge from the mouth. And a repulsive odor that now mingled with the strong scent of paraformaldehyde.

Kent looked Blair's way, then spoke through his mask.

"Makes a powerful statement about the joys of alcohol abuse, huh?"

In the garage, Blair opened the rear door of the funeral coach. Next to a casket storage rack were two first-call cots draped with blue velvet covers. *Emerson Funeral Home* was stitched on the side. She wheeled one cot to the rear of the coach and slid it into place on the polished wood floor. Minutes later she was taking it out again and wheeling it up a loading ramp at St. Mary's Hospital.

She entered through a back door, then rolled the cot down a service hallway and into a rear elevator. The doors were almost shut when a hand popped between them, opening them again. The woman smiled at Blair, then noticed the cot. She hesitated, as if riding an elevator with a funeral director was some sort of bad luck. But seconds later, she overcame her reservations and stepped into the car.

Cardiac Intensive Care was on the fourth floor. A short stocky nurse named Simms, whom Blair saw frequently at a local restaurant, spotted her when she entered the unit. He leaned toward a blonde colleague seated next to him at the nurses' station. "See that lovely creature walking toward us? That's Blair Emerson." Simms leered in Blair's direction. "Now that's a woman I would *die* to be alone with."

Blair smiled indulgently at Simms and spoke to the blonde. "I'm counting on someone here to let me know when that happens."

A chart labeled "Brubaker" was lying on the desk. Blair located and signed the appropriate form, then tore out a copy of the admissions record. By now, Simms was caught up in a crisis of some sort. He nodded to the left and said absently, "The body's in bed four."

The body. The term sounded so cold, inhuman. Instantly Blair recalled something her father had said to her on her first day of work. "The man in this casket is dead but he still has a name. Remember to use it when you refer to him."

Elsie Brubaker's bloodless lids rested like sheer silk over her sunken eyes. Eighty years of living and a month of suffering had carved lines in her face. Blair removed a sheet from beneath the cot cover and wrapped it around the frail body. Seconds later, she was buckling safety straps and covering the tiny form on the cot with a velvet cover.

Maneuvering the cot down the hallway and into the elevator, Blair was amused at how people tried not to stare. The car stopped at each floor on its way down, but only staff consented to ride with her. When the doors opened on ground level, Blair waited until the car emptied before easing the cot into the hallway. Rounding a corner, she jerked the cot to a stop so suddenly that the rubber wheels squeaked on the floor. "Myles."

"Blair. I didn't expect to see you here." Myles paused an awkward moment and said, "I guess you've never met my father-in- law. Dr. Lauzon, this is Bl—"

"I recognize her. And I have nothing whatsoever to say to her." With that Roland Lauzon disappeared around the corner.

Myles pushed his glasses upward with one finger and nervously looked at his shoes. "I didn't expect to see you here."

"So you said." Blair fiddled with the sleeves of her jacket. "Is Dr. Lauzon being admitted again?"

"No. Uh—it's Charmaine. The baby came early."

"Oh. How are they?"

"Fine. They're fine. Charmaine should be released in a couple of days. We don't know when the baby will come home."

"What did she have?" Blair finally managed to look at Myles's face, but he didn't look at her. He seemed to swallow over a tightness in his throat.

"A girl. We named her Tiffany."

Blair nodded her head—several quick little bobs—and pressed her lips between her teeth. The divorce had been final for over a year. She had known about Charmaine for even longer. Until that moment, she thought she had waded through the process of letting go. But the pain in the pit of her stomach told her otherwise. "You're going to be a busy man. I read in the paper that you're involved in a murder trial. Court appointed?"

"Yes and the case couldn't have gone to trial at a worse possible time, especially with Tiffany's premature birth. Charmaine needs me, and there just aren't enough hours in the day. If I can't be with her, Roland steps in." Myles sighed. "Even for Charmaine, too much of her father is . . . well, too much."

"How's Dr. Lauzon's health?"

"Not good, Blair. If he doesn't get his medication, his behavior can become really bizarre." Myles looked incredibly tense. "When he was healthy, he was such a gentle man. Now he's impatient and suspicious. And when he's angry, so vindictive."

A moment of awkward silence, then Blair said, "Well, I'm sure you're in a hurry to get upstairs. I hope the baby—Tiffany—can go home soon."

"Thanks, Blair." Myles touched the sleeve of her jacket. "I never called you when your father died. I should have."

As luck would have it, Myles arrived at the nurses' station just in time to see Roland having some poor, befuddled nurse for an afternoon snack. By the look on his face, Roland had already chewed her up and was getting ready to spit her out.

"I specifically asked to speak to my daughter's doctor when he made his rounds." Eyes blazing, Roland broadcast fury like a beam. "And had I not caught him with his finger on the elevator button, he would have been gone. And God only knows when I would have been able to speak to him again."

Stepping between them, Myles lay a restraining hand on Roland's shoulder. "What did the doctor say? Charmaine's just fine, right?" Sensing the nurse retreat behind him, Myles inched backward. Roland's eyes darted back and forth like a frightened bird's. A vein at his temple throbbed. Myles pictured this distinguished, well-meaning man's heart working overtime to force blood through badly clogged arteries. "Now how about walking with me to see your

48

granddaughter?"

"Incompetence is rampant here." Roland fell into stride with Myles. "With what they must be charging you, Charmaine should not have to wait fifteen minutes for assistance from her bed. It's inexcusable."

The quiver in Roland's voice, the weaving motion when he walked, the outbursts. They were all too frequent now. As soon as Tiffany and Charmaine were released, Myles would insist that Roland see his physician again. Minnie, his housekeeper, was as dependable as sunrise about seeing to his medication. But perhaps it was time for a change of drugs.

Outside the neonatal unit, they paused before glass panels. "Look at her, Myles. My granddaughter." Roland's voice softened and his eyes grew tender. He lay long, tapered fingers against the glass, spreading them slowly as if stroking the velvet skin of Tiffany's back. *"C'est un si beau bébé."*

Tears swam in Myles's eyes, blurring the infinitely tiny bundle sleeping soundly, breathing on her own, recovering lost ounces. He longed to hold Tiffany, to stroke the wisps of hair on her perfectly shaped head, to touch her lips just to watch them pucker, to look into blue-violet eyes. *Soon, sweetheart. Soon.*

In a large circular motion with an open palm, Myles rubbed Roland's back, felt the ridge of his spine and the rise of his shoulder blades. He recalled their first meeting. Roland had come to Myles about an unwise investment in a condominium complex. A sagging Texas economy had sent the value of the project plummeting. Roland had asked Myles to, in his words, quickly and painlessly extricate him from the partnership.

Charmaine had begun accompanying Roland to consultations after his first minor stroke. Her tenderness and concern for her father had blended perfectly with her respect for his intelligence and need for independence. Myles's attraction to her had been instantaneous and deeply unsettling.

Myles left Roland at the nursery and walked quickly to Charmaine's room. He had to be back in court in an hour.

49

There were flowers everywhere. Fresh flowers in vases and baskets. Silk flowers and house plants in ceramic pots. A vase of Tiffany roses stood on a table by Charmaine's bed. Myles had found them at a florist and bought all they had.

A volunteer was taking Charmaine's lunch order, so Myles waited by the window. Three years had passed since he had first met Charmaine, since his first look into those blue eyes that missed nothing. At that point, his marriage to Blair had been deteriorating for years, each of them spending inordinate amounts of time on their careers, trying to fill in the crater left by Brandi's disappearance.

During the early months of the search, he and Blair had clung to each other with fierceness, combining their strength and determination to hold on to sanity until Brandi was found. Myles hadn't felt numb, but he must have seemed that way. Anger. Sadness. Depression. Helplessness. He had hidden them all. "You have to be strong," he told himself. "Do it for Blair."

But when alone, he had unleashed his emotions—shouting, cursing, mourning. Brandi's disappearance had excised an essential, irreplaceable part of him. It had left a hole that swallowed up everything but was never filled.

Then something had happened. He had not understood it then, and he did not fully understand it now. He had started pulling away from Blair—gently at first, but not so gently as to go undetected. Blair had accused him of blaming her for Brandi's disappearance and, God forgive him, in his darkest moments he had.

Then one night he had stopped at a bar on Sixth Street, something he rarely did. In a corner booth, sitting in the yellow glow of a Miller Lite sign, he had buried all hope of ever holding his child again. No more meetings with other victimized parents. No more following leads that only led him back to pain. No more fliers or phone calls or prayers.

Then the tears came, tears of bitter reality and resignation.

He had not told Blair about that night in the bar. He had allowed her to think of him as heartless and cold-blooded

50

rather than say, "The despair is devouring me. If I keep mourning for Brandi, there's going to be nothing left of me."

Myles snapped back to the present when he heard Charmaine clear her throat. Her tone was sarcastic when she said, "I'll bet I know who you're thinking about."

"What?"

"Dad stepped in before you got here." Charmaine picked up a greeting card and opened it. "He said you ran into your charming ex-wife downstairs."

7

Minnie Erskin was stirring a pot of vegetable soup when Professor Lauzon entered the house through the kitchen door Tuesday evening. Frosty air entered behind him. "How are Charmaine and the baby?"

"Fine as long as I'm there to make sure the nurses do their jobs." He hung his hat and coat on a hook by the door and walked stiffly to the table. "You should be gone by now, Minnie. It's after six o'clock. I told you not to wait."

"I promised Charmaine, Professor. Now sit down. Your soup's ready." Minnie limped toward the table. The cold, wet weather aggravated her arthritis. With twisted fingers, she set a bowl of soup and a basket of crackers on the round maple table. "I'm anxious to see Tiffany. She could be nothing but beautiful with Charmaine as her mother."

"It's true, Minnie. She's exquisite."

Minnie pulled back a chair, but Professor Lauzon touched her wrist. "Please, Minnie. Go home, dear. You're exhausted. I promise I'll eat."

"Well, if you promise." She pointed to a tiny paper cup on the place mat. "Your pills. Don't forget to take all three."

Minnie tied a wool scarf around her tightly curled hair and pulled on the London Fog coat Charmaine had given her as

52

an early Christmas gift. Icy wind shoved at the door when she opened it. "Don't be worrying about Charmaine and the baby. They'll be fine."

The streets were clear as Minnie drove across town. She found herself worrying about Dr. Lauzon. He had become so unpredictable lately. How in the world would he adjust to a live-in housekeeper when Minnie retired at the end of the month? Charmaine had planned to start interviewing in a couple of weeks. She guessed Myles would have to do that now that the baby had come early.

Myles had his work cut out for him being married to Charmaine. But Minnie guessed it was worth it to him. He would have a family again. A second chance. Lord knows he deserves it, she thought, after the torment he went through—he and his first wife both. Their baby's disappearance had destroyed a good marriage, that was what Myles had told her.

There'd be hell to pay if Charmaine ever heard him say that.

Wind tugged at Minnie's scarf and whipped her coat around her legs when she got out of her car. The lamp in her neighbor's backyard showed Minnie the round stones that led from the driveway to the back porch. The white frame house with its black trim and gray shingles had once looked clean and inviting. Now it just looked old.

In one month, she would be out of this neighborhood. She didn't like it anymore, didn't feel at home around the people here. Who wanted to be neighborly with a man who wore camouflage fatigues and army boots? Who wanted to befriend a ditsy red-haired woman who talked about the divine mind and spirit guides? Other equally peculiar people came and went at odd hours. Minnie didn't want to guess what they did for a living.

Inside, she flicked on a light and hung her coat by the door. The kitchen was smaller than most modern bathrooms. Most of the countertop tiles were chipped or cracked and the grout was stained. The linoleum floor looked dirty even if she mopped it every day. But it had been all she could afford after her husband died.

She had eaten a bowl of soup at Dr. Lauzon's before he got home. Now her sweet tooth was aching. She took a banana cream pie from the refrigerator and cut a narrow slice. She was setting her plate on the table near the kitchen window when someone knocked on the back door.

"Who could that be?" she grumbled. "It's almost seven o'clock. I'm too tired to talk." She inched aside the curtain. It was her neighbor, Roseanne Brenner. Thick strands of unruly red hair stuck out from beneath a tattered old scarf. The trench coat she was wearing was sizes too big for her and dragged around her ankle boots. When she spotted Minnie at the window, she wiggled a greeting with her fingers.

Minnie struggled up from the table and opened the door, speaking to Roseanne through the screen. "Evening, Roseanne. What can I do for you?"

"Oh, I'm off to a gathering at the church." Roseanne's thin lips nearly disappeared when she smiled. "Thought you might want to go with me."

Not again, Minnie groaned silently. "Oh, I don't . . ."

"You'd really enjoy it, Minnie. The people there are so full of love."

"I'm sure they are . . ."

"So full of the spirit. Won't you come Minnie?"

"What church is it?" Minnie asked. She was as likely to go there as she was to volunteer for a hip replacement, but her curiosity had taken over. Or maybe it was her need to allow Roseanne to prove once and for all that she was a religious lunatic.

"It's the Fellowship of the Guiding Light."

Half church, half soap opera, Minnie thought sarcastically. She drew her sweater together in front and said, "Where do you meet?"

"Up at the shopping center. The building on the east end."

"Where the liquor store used to be?" First one kind of spirits, then the next. "I don't want to be rude, Roseanne, but you couldn't pay me to go there. And I'd really appreciate it if you'd quit bringing it up." Actually Minnie did want to be rude, rude enough to shut Roseanne's mouth until she moved.

"Well, all right, Minnie." Roseanne spoke in a tone reserved for gravely serious matters. "But I'm going to pray for you tonight. And for that family you work for."

"And just what makes you think we need..." Minnie stopped there. It was a waste of breath. Roseanne was halfway across the porch, humming to herself.

Minnie locked the door and returned to the table shaking her head. "I saw her standing there, and I opened the door anyway. Guess I was asking for it."

A warm bath soothed Minnie's aching joints. When the water cooled, she toweled herself dry, then held her flannel nightgown in front of the space heater in the bathroom. When it was nice and warm, she pulled it over her head and groaned. "Lord, how I ache."

Minnie's faded brown eyes adjusted to the dark bedroom. Rusted bed springs squeaked when she rolled onto her side and looked out the window. The ivy on the chain-link fence at the edge of the drive had given up for the winter. She wouldn't be around to see it leaf out in the spring. Its absence gave her a clear view of the familiar bluish-white glow through the curtains in Roseanne's bedroom. Minnie swore the woman had her television on twenty-four hours a day. Even when Roseanne was working in her backyard garden, she left it blaring.

Roseanne Brenner was an odd bird, all right. The old potting shed she was obsessed with painting would fall to the ground before she ever finished. Minnie would have painted the darn thing herself if she thought it would keep Roseanne inside her house. It seemed like every time Minnie pulled into the driveway, Roseanne was smiling at her from across the fence. Then Minnie couldn't get in the house without listening to some cockeyed story—usually one about that so-called church of hers.

Minnie couldn't help but laugh when she recalled the last story Roseanne had told her. Standing next to the potting shed with barn-red paint dripping from her brush, she had launched the story by declaring that Abraham Lincoln had been a spiritualist. "Bet you didn't know that, did you?" Minnie had mumbled that it was something she had long suspected about Lincoln and kept walking. Then Roseanne had gone on and on about seances in the White House and a dream Lincoln had had six weeks before his assassination. A little curious, Minnie had stopped walking away. Roseanne's eyes had widened. "It's true, Minnie. He dreamed about his own death. Saw himself lying on the catafalque in the East Room of the White House." With that, she had turned around, walked back to the potting shed and resumed slopping on the paint.

Minnie wasn't accustomed to being rude to people, but she didn't want to hear any more of Roseanne's stories. Especially that one about Blair Emerson. And if Roseanne asked one more question about Charmaine and Myles, Minnie thought she would give her a smack and say what the young people said these days. "Get a life, Roseanne."

8

Blair stopped by the supermarket on her way home from work Tuesday. She made the mistake of shopping during an attack of the munchies and left with three full bags and a cash register tape ten inches long.

At home, Celtic greeted her at the kitchen door. Happy yaps. An agile dance on his hind legs. It was a greeting that sometimes proved hazardous to hosiery and other delicate fabrics. "Hi, guy." With her arms locked around the grocery bags, she peeked at him over a stalk of celery. "Were you a good boy today?" She set the bags on the counter, then reached down to scratch Celtic's chin. "I'm glad to see you. How about a quick trot in the back yard." The question made his eyes grow round and his ears stiffen. He spun away and bounded out the door.

With groceries put away and Celtic back and fed, Blair changed to jeans and a sweater and returned to the kitchen. Since cooking a meal for one was rumored to be boring, she routinely avoided it. Assembling a sandwich, heating soup or tossing a salad required no planning, no thought and no more than a minute or two in the kitchen. On those few occasions when she had attempted a dish that her mother could have prepared blindfolded, the results had ranged

57

from disappointing to disastrous.

Tonight she opted for a pimiento cheese sandwich and chips. She ate in the breakfast room while watching the evening news and opening mail. One piece went directly into the trash. *Mr. Blair Emerson.* Mass mailings. She detested getting them.

She called Liz after supper to get her daily report. "How's my godchild?"

"Active. William Elizabeth just—"

"Elizabeth William," Blair corrected.

"Whatever. I think the kid wants out of here. Either that or the little rascal's angry because I had Mexican food for lunch."

"Mexican food?"

"I know. I know. You and my doctor. You're like broken records. No salt. No spicy foods. In other words, if it makes your mouth water, Liz, then don't eat it. It's not fair," Liz whined. "You don't know what it's like to—ouch," she squealed.

"What happened?"

"The little rascal must have heard me." Liz laughed. "Blair, this kid's kicking like a soccer player . . . But enough on the joys of motherhood. Did you have a busy day?"

"As a matter of fact, I did." Blair sipped hot tea. "I made a death call at St. Mary's and ran into Myles. He and Dr. Lauzon were there to see Charmaine. She had her baby yesterday, Liz. A little girl."

"They must be thrilled." A moment of silence, then, "Seeing Myles must have been hard for you, especially under the circumstances."

"It was a little awkward. Not so bad, really. Life goes on." She set her cup on the table, knowing she hadn't fooled Liz. "All right. It was like someone reached down my throat and twisted my insides into a knot. Is that what you wanted to hear?"

"Maybe a shade less graphically but, yes, I tend to prefer the truth."

"Picky, picky." Blair rested her head on the chair back and stared at the ceiling. "I want to be happy for Myles. Really I do, Liz."

"And some day you will be, but I don't think you should expect that of yourself just yet. You *were* married to Myles. Happily married, for the most part. That's what makes it so hard. And remember, it's only been a year since the divorce. You're still grieving over the death of your marriage. It takes time."

"I suppose."

"Listen to me, Blair. If it's all right for other grieving people to feel scared, sad, cheated—even angry, then it's all right for you." In a teasing tone, Liz added, "Contrary to what some people may believe, morticians have feelings too."

"How kind of you to notice." Blair was smiling when she said, "Gosh. We've been talking for five minutes. Isn't it about time for you to hop up and run to the bathroom?"

"Hop? Run? You don't know much about the laws of physics, do you?"

Blair's laughter was instantaneous and genuine. "Apparently not." She was still laughing when she told Liz goodnight and said, "You're the best. Talk to you tomorrow."

Stretching her arms and legs, Blair yawned widely. She was preparing to call her mother when the phone rang. It was Kent calling from the funeral home. He explained that he was getting ready to embalm a woman they had removed from a nursing home.

"But I ran into a bit of a problem when I was changing the blade in the scalpel. I sliced open my thumb, and it's going to need stitches."

"Ouch." Blair frowned and shook her head. "Go to South Austin Hospital, Kent. Get it taken care of, then go home. I'll be there in a minute to finish up for you."

Dressed in jeans, a flannel shirt and sneakers, Blair was at the funeral home and donning protective clothing in less than fifteen minutes. The mask was a nuisance but the entire ensemble was the law.

Blair gave the preparation room a quick visual inspection. Both Kent and Greg were meticulous about its cleanliness and maintenance. As she had expected, the room was all set up. It smelled of bleach, their preferred disinfecting agent. White walls. Blue vinyl flooring. Cupboards of all sizes. Some stored items found in any home: sheets, towels, shampoo, nail file and clippers, shaving cream and disposable razors. But behind other doors were items most people had never seen and probably would not care to. Drums of embalming powder and autopsy compound. Cases of dye, cavity fluid, arterial fluid and disinfectant soaps and sprays. Boxes of mouth formers to substitute for missing dentures. Small plastic caps which, when placed over the eyeball, kept lids from opening. Another box held grooved steel needles. When inserted into the upper and lower gums and joined by a silver wire, the needles kept the mouth closed during the embalming process.

A countertop ran the twelve-foot length of one wall. On both sides of a sink were two embalming machines, engineered like oversized blenders with large glass tanks. A white porcelain table was positioned by each of them. Next to one of these, Kent had rolled a tiered cart containing the instruments needed in the embalming process.

On the table lay the nude body of a woman in her mid-sixties. Strips of disposable toweling lay across her breasts and pubic area, a gesture of respect that both Kent and Greg followed faithfully. She had been bathed and her hair shampooed.

The tank of the embalming machine was filled with just over three gallons of water. Blair selected a medium-strength embalming fluid and poured in two bottles and a touch of flesh-colored dye. A flip of a switch and the whir of the machine began.

Before beginning the procedure, Blair turned over a tag attached to the woman's toe. It was automatic after twenty years—a ritual she practiced to keep from becoming calloused. *This woman is dead but she still has a name.* "Mae

Smithers."

Blair looked at the clock. In an hour, an employee of a Houston funeral home would arrive to transfer Mrs. Smithers back to Houston for burial. Barring complications, Blair should be finished by then.

With a scalpel, she made a short incision at the root of the neck. Then with an aneurysm needle in each hand, she located the common carotid artery, cautiously scraped away its fibrous covering, passed a heavy thread beneath the artery and secured it. With near certainty, she knew that the internal jugular vein would lie just lateral to the artery. And so it did. At least from a design standpoint, Blair reflected, God made us virtually identical on the inside. It was the outward packaging that seemed to cause problems.

Engorged with blood, the vein was more difficult to raise. Blair managed, then made a tiny incision in it. Working around moderate blood flow, she inserted a vein tube. Through a similar incision in the artery, she inserted a smaller tube, this one connected to the embalming machine. She secured it inside the artery with locking forceps, then turned on the machine.

Straw-colored fluid flowed through the tubing and into the carotid artery. The machine's steady pressure gently propelled the fluid throughout the arterial system. Simultaneously, thick, black-red blood streamed from the vein tube onto the table, where a steady flow of water washed it down a drain.

As fluid reached the woman's hands, the bluish discoloration of stagnant blood receded. Blair observed the same results in the feet and legs. With each second that passed, embalming fluid was displacing blood in the vascular system.

With her gloved fingers, Blair gently massaged the woman's bluish lips and lids and earlobes. Gradually, the discoloration vanished and the fluid's dye imparted a natural fleshy tone to the skin. The woman's face, slightly dehydrated from age and illness, took on a youthful firmness and healthy color.

61

For thirty minutes, the procedure continued. By the time the tank on the embalming machine neared empty, the flow through the vein tube had changed from rich red to pale pink. Finally Blair aspirated the internal organs and injected them with cavity fluid. After suturing the incisions she had made, Blair bathed the woman again, dried her and covered her with a sheet. She was tossing her protective garb in the trash when Wayne knocked on the door.

"Blair, the man from Houston is here."

"Tell him she's ready."

Blair helped the short, stocky man transfer Mrs. Smithers to his cot. "She looks good," he observed.

"Do you know her?" Blair asked while buckling safety straps.

"Yes. That's why I volunteered to be on an icy interstate highway for eight hours." He adjusted the cot cover and turned to Blair. "She's my mother-in-law and the finest woman you'd ever want to meet. I appreciate your taking care of her."

Blair left the funeral home thoroughly tired but reminded of why she had chosen to follow in her father's footsteps. Few other professions addressed Blair's scientific curiosity and provided an opportunity to help people in crisis at the same time.

At home, Blair set the timer on the coffee maker and turned to Celtic. "Ready to hit the hay, boy?" He cocked his head, looking as if he didn't understand the question. Blair chuckled. "You funny dog." She scooped him up and carried him to the bedroom. "What would I do without you?"

After a long, hot shower, she crawled into bed with damp hair. Celtic cuddled in the bend of her knees. Blair drifted off to sleep with a deep feeling of satisfaction. Despite her somewhat uncomfortable meeting with poor Mr. Platte, this had been a good day. It was from this gentle, dreamless sleep that the phone jarred her awake.

"Emerson Funeral Home," she mumbled into the receiver.

"What'd you say?"

On the edge of wakefulness now, Blair said, "I'm sorry. This is Blair Emerson. Is that you, Wayne?"

"No, this ain't Wayne."

Rubbing her eyes with the heel of her hand, Blair yawned and shook her head. "Who is this?"

"You can call me Lenny."

"Who?" she asked, flicking on the lamp.

"Hold on a second. I got somebody here wants to talk to you."

Two voices seeped through the receiver. One was high-pitched and strained. "I don't want to, Lenny. You tell her . . . Okay. Okay. I'll do it."

Blair pushed herself to a sitting position. "Hello. Are you still there?" Her heart beat rapidly. "Who is this?" Annoyed now at being awakened at midnight, she started to hang up, but something stopped her. "Are you still there? Who is this?"

A child's voice finally said, "Hello. This is April."

Blair pressed the receiver to her ear. "I can hardly hear you. Can you speak louder?" Her body tightened. She held her breath. "Tell me your name again."

"It's April. Lenny says I'm your daughter."

Blood slid through Blair's veins like ice water. "What? What did you say?" She was suddenly wide awake, shivering despite the bedcovers. "You can't be. My daughter . . ."

A thick voice cut her off. "She's your kid all right, Blair. I can give you all the proof you need."

Blair sat frozen in her bed. Her arms and legs were numb, her voice a croak. "You're lying. I know you're lying." The man spoke again, but his words were drowned by the rumble of a truck engine. "Wait," Blair said, "I can't hear you."

"I said we got a deal to strike up. Hell, I can't hear myself think. There's a rig pulling onto the freeway. You just listen and listen good. When we first got your kid, she called our dog

'Sandy.' Did you hear me? 'Sandy.' And that ain't all the proof I got. I'll call you tomorrow afternoon at five. Be at home. And don't say nothing to nobody about this if you want the kid back."

The dial tone whined in Blair's ear. She threw her head back and collapsed onto her pillow.

Oh, God, could it be? Could that tiny little voice be Brandi's?

Blair crushed both fists to her mouth. She squeezed her eyes tightly shut.

My name's April. I'm your daughter.

Through a roaring in her ears, she heard the words over and over again.

My name's April. I'm your daughter.

April. Your daughter.

Daughter.

Blair stared beyond her own wide-eyed reflection in the window into the yawning blackness of the backyard.

Sandy. The baby had called Lenny's dog Sandy.

9

The faded blue box in Blair's hand contained yellowed newspaper articles and police reports and hope that had died years ago. After recovering enough from Lenny's call to make it to the attic, she had dug the box out of a trunk packed with ruffled dresses, a christening gown and toddler toys. Now she sat cross-legged in front of a cold fireplace, struggling to get up the nerve to remove the lid and pore over the documents describing in detail the abduction of a two-year-old child from her sandbox one April afternoon.

"April. She said her name was April."

Hope took shallow breaths when the first of the newspaper articles did not mention Sandy. Of course there could be countless other explanations for how this man who called himself Lenny might know the name of their cocker spaniel. If her mind was not moving in uncertain spurts she might be able to think of some.

She skimmed a second article, this one with a picture of Brandi. Oval face. Delicate features. Wisps of fine, brown hair like Blair's. And chocolate brown eyes, round and trusting.

"I can't do this." Blair thrust the papers back into the box and fumbled with the lid. "I *won't* do this. It's crazy. It's all a lie. A con. Or this Lenny is some kind of lunatic." *Lunatic. Has Brandi been raised by a madman?* Blair slapped away the thought.

For a long moment, she sat there, staring at the box and shivering. "He could be telling the truth." The words hung in the still air, waiting for her to seize them. But fear paralyzed her, warning her that if she accepted for a moment the possibility that Brandi was alive, then there was no turning back. Then when the cruel hoax was exposed, she would be trapped in hopelessness once again—and forever.

Celtic nosed the inside of Blair's elbow and slid beneath her arm. His brown eyes begged for attention. Blair scratched loose skin on his neck and whispered weakly, "If it's all a lie, then why? After all these years, why would he admit to taking my baby?" *Baby*. The word constricted Blair's throat. "Brandi will be thirteen this month."

It was almost three in the morning when Blair struggled from the floor, clutching the blue box to her chest. She forced herself to go to bed, but sleep was beyond her. When the first light of dawn filtered through the curtains in her bedroom, she threw back the covers. Her legs trembled when she walked across the room. The call. The voices. The entire night. They were spectral dreams in the light of day.

But this had not been a dream. A man named Lenny had called. A girl named April had claimed to be her daughter.

Blair kept her shower short, put her phone on call forwarding to her private number at the funeral home and was behind her desk before eight. Unless she pulled herself together, she would be useless there today, and she had a funeral to direct. She considered calling Liz and telling her what happened.

Don't say nothing to nobody about this.

"Forget it, Lenny." Blair dialed Liz's number and asked if she could drop by her house at lunch. She had brought the box of articles and police reports and fliers to the office. She hated asking Liz to expose herself to all that again, but she had to know if Sandy had been mentioned or had appeared in any

66

pictures. And Blair simply could not handle that by herself.

At eight, Blair stepped down the hall to Jane's office and offered a shaky good morning. Then she joined Kent and Greg in the rear of the building. After reviewing the details of the two services set for that morning, Blair returned to her office and shut the door.

She found herself staring at the phone. Would Lenny call again as he said? Or was his cruel practical joke over? If he did call, what other proof would he offer that April is Brandi? A confusing rush of anticipation and dread knotted her stomach. She buried her face in her hands and prayed. "Oh, God, can this child be Brandi? After all these years? Oh, let it be Brandi." All her inner warning systems went off at once. "But what if it's a hoax? What if she's not Brandi? Dear God, I don't think I can take it again."

Minutes collected into half an hour and finally an hour. At nine she walked across the foyer and into the chapel. Taped music floated through overhead speakers. Thirty minutes from now, the organist would begin the prelude. Kent and two part-time employees were arranging flowers. The deceased was a man of fifty-three named Ray Hunt who had died of heart disease. "He's too young to be dead," his wife had said sadly.

By ten o'clock, the chapel was full. Blair seated the pallbearers on the left, the family on the right and the minister by the podium. Normally she returned to her office during the service and left an employee in the chapel to seat late comers. But today, Blair needed the distraction.

When the organ music stopped, the minister, a man in his sixties, stepped behind the podium and began the eulogy. He knew Mr. Hunt well—a dedicated Christian, a loving father, a devoted husband, and a gifted guitarist who'd played for many church functions. Blair's mind drifted as the eulogy droned on.

The girl on the phone last night. Her voice. It could have been the voice of a twelve-year-old. High-pitched. Childlike. Anxious. Blair dug her nails into her palms. Was it possible?

Had she actually spoken to Brandi last night?

Stop it, she scolded herself. You'll go crazy.

The minister had concluded his eulogy. Now he was beginning to tread on ground that always made Blair anxious.

"We wonder why God took from this earth a man still in his prime. Was it that Ray had accomplished his purpose here on earth? Was God ready to reward him for a job well done?" Then he looked directly at the family and smiled. "Or maybe God just wanted Ray in heaven so he could hear him strum his guitar in songs of praise."

Blair flinched. Oh, *please*. What was Mr. Hunt's family thinking, especially the small children? That God was frivolous and selfish and robbed families of a loved one so that he could be entertained and praised? If the minister felt he had to explain the man's death, why not blame it on heredity or smoking or poor diet? After all, the man had died of heart disease. Or did God get the blame for that too? What the family needed was comfort and hope, not speculations and platitudes.

It had been the same way for Blair after Brandi disappeared. One well-meaning man had told her that although Blair did not understand why this dreadful tragedy had struck, that she simply had to trust God. "Remember, Blair, this is God's world and everything is in his hands." The words had cut through Blair like a scalpel. If everything was in his hands, why had this happened? To punish Blair? Myles? Certainly not Brandi. What had they done that was deserving of punishment? The whole idea ran contrary to what Blair believed about a loving God.

Another woman had told Blair just to have faith and pray—that if she kept on praying, Brandi would be all right. As if prayer were some kind of charm to ward off evil or tragedy. This was little comfort when only weeks before, Blair had buried a little boy who had been shaken to death by his stepfather while his young mother was at work. If God was in charge of protecting defenseless children, what had gone wrong? Had the young mother failed to pray?

And what about Brandi? Certainly Blair had prayed for Brandi's safety and well-being, but that didn't keep her safe. She was gone just the same. Was there a required frequency of prayer? Daily? Monthly? It was a preposterous notion and a tremendous burden for a parent, one that Blair finally had rejected.

Fortunately most people, including Blair's minister, had offered no explanations and no easy remedies. They simply had reminded her that they cared deeply about her loss. Her parents and Liz had supported her in every conceivable way, mainly by just being there.

Something Eldon said once had helped so much. "Blair, I can't find any place in the Bible where it says that if we just have enough faith and pray hard enough, nothing bad will ever happen to people we love. But there is the promise that God won't let us struggle on our own when those tragedies happen. And, sweetheart, with everything in me, I believe that God is grieving for you and mourning the awful fact that Brandi is not here in your arms."

It was a belief that would get Blair through times when grief threatened to devour her. When everyone else had gone on with their lives—including Myles, so it seemed—Blair had felt totally alone in her misery. But she had managed to wade through, drawing on a mysterious inner strength, believing that God was with her, grieving and mourning her loss.

By the time Mr. Hunt's funeral service and interment were over, Blair's nerves were strung so tightly she could hardly hold a thought.

In Liz's driveway, she sat in the car, staring at the elegant two-story house. Her focus slowly shifted to the blue box on the seat next to her and to the headline of a front-page article inside it: "TODDLER VANISHES WITHOUT A TRACE." *I should be talking to the police, not Liz. What if this whole thing is just a lie—a con? Oh, God. What do I do? Should I call the police?*

Liz had prepared lunch. Cheese soup and spinach salad. Blair's hand shook visibly when she picked up her spoon. It did not go unnoticed. "Something's wrong, Blair. Tell me."

Blair closed her eyes and nervously ran the fingers of one hand through her hair. "I got a phone call last night from a man named Lenny." She spoke slowly, disciplining her voice. "He claims to have Brandi." When she spoke again, she was whimpering like a child. "And I spoke to—" Her voice failed. "—to a young girl on the phone. She said she's my daughter."

10

A recording played jazz piano in April's ear. It was interrupted periodically by a taped assurance that a Greyhound Bus Lines representative would be right with her. A grisly man in a tattered overcoat and muddy black boots came out of the convenience store and walked toward her. When he was a few steps away, he mumbled something under his breath and dug a coin from his pants pocket. April turned her back when he picked up the receiver of the pay phone next to her. The putrid smell of sweat and liquor fouled the cold air.

Across the parking lot at the gasoline pumps, a punk-haired guy dressed in black leather slammed the nozzle into the gas tank of his shabby old car. While the pump ticked away, he smeared dirt and grime across his windshield with swipes of a long-handled squeegee. When his eyes drifted her way, April faced the pay phone, wishing Lenny had chosen some other neighborhood, some other motel.

Finally, a ticket agent came on the line. Careful to keep the contaminated receiver inches away from her lips, April asked, "How much is a ticket from Dallas to Virginia Beach, Virginia?"

"One moment, please."

April hunched down inside her denim jacket. Wind roared

in her ears. She nearly gagged when it carried with it an awful stench from a nearby dumpster. She hated this place.

When the woman came on the line again, April pressed the receiver to one ear and covered the other ear with her hand.

"The fare is one hundred thirty-nine dollars one way. Two hundred sixty-four dollars round trip. When will you be traveling?"

"I don't know. Thank you." April hung up and stared at the phone. "A hundred and thirty-nine dollars." She pressed her lower lip between her teeth and frowned. Swiping the rest of the money wasn't going to be easy. It was a lot. She would have to be careful or Lenny might catch on.

It was almost noon. Her stomach growled a reminder that she had not eaten today. Inside the convenience store, she bought a Diet Coke and a bag of chips.

Walking down the street, she passed the Oak Cliff Inn. Lenny was in their room making a phone call. He had told her to get lost for an hour or so, that he had a business call to make. He either hadn't noticed or hadn't cared that it was freezing outside.

The motel was a pitiful looking place. The parking lot was full of pot holes. The building needed paint. The beer-bellied manager needed a shave and a bath. And April was almost sure that the bony blonde in the room next to the office was a hooker. Didn't Lenny have any sense at all? Why had he picked that filthy place? He deserved to have money stolen from his wallet and pockets for being so stupid.

To calm herself, April took a deep breath. She had awakened this morning in a bad mood. She was mad at Lenny for dragging her here. She was mad at Jewell for dying. And she was mad at herself for wasting so much time thinking about her real mother and how weird Lenny had acted when they called her last night.

For some reason, he had insisted on driving to the convenience store and using the pay phone rather than the phone in their room. On the way, he had said that Blair was living in Dallas now—not Austin—and that he had decided to ask her if she wanted April back now that Jewell was dead. It was what April had suspected, so she hadn't been all that surprised. But what he said next had surprised and confused her. "When I hand you the phone, say that your name is April and that I said you're her daughter. Not another word. Do you understand?" Then he had said he would snatch her baldheaded if she messed up.

He made her stand to the side while he dialed the number. When Blair answered, he had said a few words, then motioned to April. By then she was so nervous, she couldn't move. Lenny had jerked her by the arm, then held the phone to her ear. She had said exactly what he told her. Then Lenny had snatched the phone away and told her to get in the car.

The whole thing had been so strange. Even for Lenny. And she had never seen him so nervous. His body was rigid. His hands clenched. Why would talking to Blair affect him like that?

In a way, she hoped Blair did want her back. If she did, then April's problems would be solved. She wouldn't have to go to El Paso with Lenny. And if she didn't like living with Blair, she could always run away later.

April zipped her denim coat and turned up the collar. She couldn't waste any more time thinking about the call or Blair. She had to plan ahead. Swiping the remainder of the bus fare before Lenny was ready to leave for El Paso would be impossible.

Walking along the uneven sidewalk, April stepped aside each time someone approached. She didn't want any of these people brushing against her.

At the bus stop, she sat down on a graffiti-covered bench and cleaned the top of the Coke can with a fresh towelette. Then she popped the top and took a drink. Wind swirled litter around her feet and blew dirt in her face, making her eyes water. She set the can on the bench beside her and stuck her cold hands in the shallow pockets of her jacket. Her thoughts returned to Blair— her mother. There was one thing that worried April about living with Blair. Her washing routine.

Would she be able to hide it from Blair? What if Blair found out and decided April was nuts or something? Would she put her away somewhere?

April tossed the empty can in a smelly trash can and started walking again. Cars whizzed past, whipping her hair across her face. She turned right, down a street with less traffic. When she was halfway down the block, she heard footsteps behind her. Close behind her. The thud of thick soles told her it was a man. Instinctively she quickened her pace, stealing a glance over her shoulder. Dark face staring. Brown overcoat flapping in the wind. Muddy black books picking up speed. It was him—the bum she'd seen at the pay phone.

April held a steady pace, but the beat of her heart quickened. *A church up ahead.* He wouldn't dare follow her in there. She trotted toward the first of what looked like a hundred concrete steps, fast closing the gap between her and safety. When she reached the railing, she grabbed it with her right hand. Another quick glance over her shoulder and she saw him. Stained teeth. Lips twisted into a repulsive smile. Grimy black boots picking up speed.

April lunged up the steep concrete steps, taking them two, three at a time. On the landing, she grabbed for the brass door handle. With all her strength, she squeezed the latch and pulled. The door flew open, throwing April off balance. A scream that was wedged in her throat tore loose when a man appeared in front of her. He grabbed her by both arms as she tumbled backward. "Careful, child." He yanked her away from the edge of the landing. "I've got you. I've got you. You're okay."

The sound of footsteps from behind her died. Still April trembled and panted. The hands gripping her arms slipped to her wrists.

"Are you okay?" the man asked.

She pulled away and stared at him. Except for a patch of white cloth on the front of his collar, he was dressed entirely in black, this man who had just rescued her.

"You're shivering, child." He stepped aside. "Go inside

where it's warm. I'll be there in a minute."

April nodded and stumbled into the dimly lit entry. From there she heard the preacher—no, the priest; that's what he was called—scold the man outside. "Buck, how could you do such a thing? Scaring an innocent child. It's a terrible thing to do. Now go on your way."

April collapsed onto one of the folding chairs near what looked like a little marble birdbath filled with water. Nervously she ran her hands up and down her arms. She had never set foot in a church before.

The dark-skinned priest stepped back inside and gently eased the door shut. "He's gone now. I don't think Buck intended to harm you. He was just teasing. But it wasn't at all funny, was it?" The priest extended his hand. "I'm Father Ochoa. What's your name?"

"April." She ignored his offer to shake hands.

"April. That's a lovely name." He lowered his right hand, then clasped both hands behind him. "Well, you're safe now, April." He tilted his head and studied her in a friendly way. "I don't think I've seen you in the neighborhood."

"Oh, I don't live here."

"Visiting friends? Family?"

"Sort of." April's knees were feeling steadier now and her heart had stopped pounding. But she dreaded walking back to the motel alone.

"Why aren't you in school today, April?" Father Ochoa spoke gently, without accusation. "Don't tell me Christmas holidays are here already?"

"Lenny—my father—" April paused. "It's a long story."

"There's a cafe across the street that's perfect for sharing long stories. Would you care to join me?"

"No thanks. I have to go." April stood. She took one step, but her knees started to buckle and she sat back down. The priest noticed but didn't say anything.

"I wish you'd join me." His smile was gentle. His brown eyes soft. "Hot chocolate sure tastes good on a cold day."

April considered the offer. Lenny had told her to stay gone

75

an hour. And she could use something hot to drink—if the cafe looked clean enough. "Well, I guess I could go. But just for a few minutes."

"A few minutes it is." Father Ochoa excused himself to get his coat. April watched him walk up the carpeted center aisle, saw him bow when he reached the front and look up at a statue of a very beautiful and very sad Jesus. It wasn't exactly a bow. Kneeling quickly was more like it. A woman with a square of white lace draped over jet black hair stepped out from a pew and did the same before turning around and walking toward April. Then the woman dug in her pocket, found a bill and stuck it in a slot cut in the top of a box attached to the wall near the front door. The box was about the size of a tissue box. Its lid was secured with a delicate lock. April wondered what Father Ochoa did with the money people poked through the slot. Did he buy candles to replace those burning over there? She would ask him when he got back.

She was still sitting in the folding chair when Father Ochoa returned wearing a black trench coat. Still studying the little wooden box, April remembered once picking a lock like that one with a nail file so she wouldn't have to tell Lenny she had lost her locker key again.

Blair opened the door to the backyard to let Celtic out and shivered in the doorway until he came back in again. Warming her hands on a mug of coffee, she paced the living room like a caged animal. It was three-thirty. Lenny would call at five. Dear God, what would he say? What kind of proof could he possibly have that April was Brandi? She forced herself to sit down when her legs started to tremble.

Confiding in Liz had helped. Of course Liz hadn't known what to make of the call either. By now she had probably finished the grim task of reading the newspaper articles and police reports and studying all the fliers. Blair looked at her watch. She had plenty of time to call Liz before Lenny called again. She dialed the number. Liz answered after the first ring.

"It's me. He hasn't called yet. I just wanted to know if you turned up anything."

"Not a thing, Blair. I don't know how this man learned that you had a dog named Sandy, but he didn't find out from any of these clippings."

"Well, I guess that's . . ." Blair stopped. "Good news? Bad news? I don't know."

"Call me later. Whether you hear from him or not."

"I will."

"And think about what I said about calling the police."

"I have been. All afternoon. I just think I should wait until . . ." The doorbell rang. Blair groaned. "Someone's at the door, Liz. Call you later."

Celtic's stubby tail wiggled a welcome to the familiar sound on the porch. The peephole framed the back of the postman's head in a tiny oval as he walked away.

A package shaped like a shoe box was wedged behind a planter of freeze-damaged aloe vera. Blair retrieved it and a handful of mail. The scratchy handwriting on the package was unfamiliar. The letters were cramped and irregular, and there was no return address. The postmark was Dallas.

Blair tore off the brown paper—a supermarket shopping bag turned inside out. She tossed it into the fireplace. Flames licked at the thick paper while Blair tore away masking tape holding the lid on a Kinney shoe box.

Wads of tissue paper shaped like the toe of a woman's shoe were wedged on both sides of the handle of a red plastic shovel. A note was attached to the scoop. Blair sank to her knees and closed her eyes. Celtic sniffed the box when she set it on the floor.

"It's her little shovel." Blair peeled off the note but left the toy in the box, resting on a piece of faded pink cloth. If she touched the shovel, if she put her fingers on the handle where Brandi's fingers had been, Blair thought her heart would burst inside her chest.

"'Well, here's your proof,'" she read aloud. "'The kid was

77

holding this when my wife took her. Now my wife's dead and you've got the chance to get your kid back. By the way, I hear you're divorced. I hope you got your share from the old man. You'll need it if you want April back. Remember, this is our little secret. Not a word to nobody. Your friend, Lenny.'"

Over and over she read the note, finally laying it on the floor beside the open box. The red shovel looked worn. The edge of the scoop was notched and rough. Lenny and his wife must have had a sandbox too, or they spent lots of time at the beach.

As cautious as if she were handling explosives, Blair plucked the wads of tissue from around the shovel. She palmed the scoop in one hand and watched helplessly as the fingers of her other hand closed around the handle. She drew the shovel to her chest and hugged it against her. The intensity of burning tears surprised her. She thought she had cried them all years ago.

"Oh, Brandi, honey," she sobbed. "I want you back."

Blair's upper body swayed back and forth in rhythm with her sobs. Tears streaked down her cheeks.

Finally her crying subsided. She stared at the shovel, then at the box. Celtic was nuzzling something at the bottom. She eased his head aside. It was a piece of fabric. Pink. Knit.

The instant Blair's fingers touched the folds of soft knit fabric, the instant she felt the rows of ruffles on its underside, tears welled up in her eyes again. When she held it up, the faded little swimsuit blurred.

Once hot pink trimmed in black, it now had a drab tie-dyed look. The rows of ruffles on the back were frayed and dotted with hard little knots of thread. She had bought the suit at the ABC Shop only a few days before Brandi had disappeared.

Blair gently placed the swimsuit on the floor, crossing the frayed black straps into an X in the back. She touched a pea-sized hole where a button had torn through and was missing. She was staring at the sad little suit, rubbing her fingers along the tucks and gathers, when the phone rang.

It was Lenny. The sound of his voice made Blair quiver inside.

"Didya get my little package?"

"Yes," she whispered.

"Well, praise the post office." An oily tone crept into his voice. "Well, Blair, my girl, I'm gettin' ready to make you an offer you can't refuse."

11

The winter sky framed by Minnie Erskin's kitchen window was slate gray streaked with white. Cold air whistled in around the sill. Needle-sharp pains shot through Minnie's hands as she scrubbed sticky lumps of oatmeal from a bowl and wiped it dry.

With brittle fingers, she folded the pink blanket she had crocheted for little Tiffany and wrapped it in tissue. The ready- made bow and matching paper had been expensive, but making a bow herself would have been impossible.

When she finished wrapping the gift, Minnie was pleased with the results and looked forward to taking it to Charmaine. She was being released from the hospital today. There was still no definite word on when the baby could go home, but Tiffany had already gained four ounces. That was a good sign.

Minnie pulled on her coat and tied a scarf around her head. She was halfway to the car when Roseanne Brenner stepped out of her back door. Dressed in navy blue knit pants that sagged at the knees and a cable-knit sweater that was several sizes too large, she looked like a bag lady. Her red hair, the color of rust, stuck out wildly in all directions. Hooked over one thin forearm was a large straw bag, the kind sold by the hundreds in Mexico. Over the other forearm hung an old corduroy jacket, its dingy yellow lining hanging loose at the bottom. What a sight, Minnie thought to herself.

"Where are you off to this morning, Minnie?" Roseanne called from her porch.

"Same place I'm off to every Thursday morning," Minnie mumbled.

"What'd you say, Minnie? Couldn't hear you." Roseanne stepped over a garden hose coiled like a cold-stiffened snake and trotted across the yard. Brown grass crunched beneath her tennis shoes. "You don't mind giving me a ride to the bus stop, do you? I'm running a little late, and I don't dare miss the bus." Before Minnie could answer, Roseanne was in the car. "Those little darlings at the day-care center pitch an awful fit when I'm not there to meet them at the door." She pulled the safety belt across her thin middle and said, "They used to call these things seat belts. Wonder why they changed. Just to emphasize safety, don't you guess?" Roseanne picked up the package from the seat. "Who's this pretty thing for?"

Minnie backed onto the street. "Dr. Lauzon's new granddaughter."

"Oh, Charmaine had her baby? You didn't tell me." Roseanne shook the box. "What is it?"

"Just a little blanket I crocheted." Minnie always felt like a patient undergoing exploratory surgery when Roseanne was around. Her endless stream of questions probed inside Minnie until Roseanne knew far more than she needed to know.

"What'd they name her?"

"Tiffany."

"Spell it."

"T-i-f-f-a-n-y."

"Well, I'll be."

You'll be what? Minnie waited for Roseanne's next question. When none came, she glanced to her right and found Roseanne staring out the car window. Her pale blue eyes

81

darted searchingly from side to side. Her purplish lips moved as if she were talking, but no words came out.

The bus stop was just ahead. A teenage girl huddled with her toddler inside the Plexiglass shelter. Her cheeks were chapped and she was wiping her child's nose with a tissue.

"Poor little angel," Roseanne said, shaking her head slowly from side to side. "That child doesn't stand a chance, does she, Minnie?"

"She's probably off to a rough start," Minnie agreed.

Roseanne struggled into her jacket. She was silent for a moment, then said, "Like the Lakeman baby."

Minnie pulled to a stop and turned down the heater. "Tiffany had a rough start, being premature, but she's got everything else in the world going for her."

"Oh, I wasn't talking about Tiffany. I meant Myles Lakeman's first baby. His and Blair Emerson's. The one you told me was stolen."

Roseanne twisted in the seat as much as the safety belt would allow. "I told you how I met Blair, didn't I?"

"Oh, yes." At least ten times, Minnie figured. "It was when you were working at the mental hospital." The thought had occurred to her that Roseanne might actually have been a patient there. Out of curiosity, as well as a desire to avoid hearing the story again, Minnie inquired casually. "What kind of work did you do at the hospital?"

"Oh, this and that." Roseanne waggled her head. "Whatever I was told."

"Did you cook or clean or . . ."

"Yeah. That's right." Roseanne tugged at the safety belt, squirming like a child. "Anyway, about the day I met Blair. I was walking around on the grounds when up came this long blue hearse. Blair—of course I didn't know her name then—got out. She looked so pretty. I knew even from a distance that she was a nice person. I mean, you'd have to be a nice person to want to take care of dead people, wouldn't you, Minnie?"

"I suppose." Minnie looked at her watch, but Roseanne did not take the hint.

"So I just walked right up to the hearse and asked Blair who died. I don't remember who it was but it seems like his name was . . ."

"Then you noticed her pin," Minnie interrupted, trying to keep Roseanne from running headlong down a rabbit trail about some dead patient.

"Right, I noticed her pin. Shining against her black suit." Roseanne's thin fingers gently stroked her corduroy lapel. "Oh, Minnie. It was so beautiful."

Minnie checked her watch again, and again Roseanne didn't notice. She had drifted into a sort of reverie. After a few seconds, Minnie said, "The pin was silver, right?"

"Oh . . . uh . . . yes. Silver." With her index finger, Roseanne traced a shape in the air. "It was a single rose, Minnie. On a stem with two tiny leaves. I thought it was the most . . ."

"So you told Blair how pretty it was," Minnie prodded.

"Yes. I told her it was the prettiest thing I'd ever seen." Roseanne's voice became wistful. "When I told her my name was Roseanne, she took off the pin and gave it to me. Can you imagine such a thing, Minnie?"

"It was very generous."

"And you know what she said?"

Minnie knew exactly what Blair had said, but she didn't get a chance to repeat it.

"She said the name Roseanne suited me because of my pretty red hair." One hand sprung to her forehead. Gently she touched her wiry bangs. "It was the nicest thing anyone ever said to me." Roseanne smiled with remembered delight. "And the prettiest Christmas gift I ever got."

"That's a lovely story," Minnie said, reminded again of how much Blair's kindness had touched Roseanne. Unfortunately, though, Blair's kind gesture had led to an obsession of sorts. Roseanne talked about Blair as if they were close personal friends when, according to Roseanne herself, she had spoken with her only that one time more than a year ago. Minnie was shocked to discover recently that Roseanne read the obituary notices without fail—not with the usual interest, but for the sole purpose of seeing how business was at Blair's two funeral homes.

Roseanne hooked the handles of her straw bag over her arm and thanked Minnie for the lift. As Minnie pulled away from the curb, she caught Roseanne's image in her rearview mirror. She was taking off her corduroy jacket and putting it around a stranger's shivering shoulders.

12

On Thursday morning, Blair sat at her desk at the funeral home signing papers without really reading them. Her thoughts returned to the shameful lie she had told Liz yesterday evening. "Lenny didn't call, Lizzie. I guess the game is over." Liz had been outraged, asking again and again who could have done such a wretched thing and why. Blair had said things about the world being full of crazies, had rambled on about pranks played on funeral homes and funeral directors. She had ended the conversation after half an hour by offering a final explanation. "I guess there's some whacko out there who gets his jollies out of tormenting people with missing children."

She hated lying to Liz, but she kept hearing Lenny's warning. *Don't tell nobody nothing about this if you want to see your kid again.* So she had obeyed. For now at least, Lenny was calling the shots.

"April has to be Brandi," Blair whispered. Lenny's story had a ring of truth about it. His wife had kidnapped Brandi. Now eleven years later, his wife was dead. And Lenny saw an opportunity to make some quick cash and get rid of a teenage girl at the same time. "My baby," Blair moaned.

Her thoughts started down a seemingly harmless path. Brandi would be thirteen this month. Had she ever had birthday parties with Lenny and his wife? Did she know how old she actually was? How had Lenny's wife enrolled her in school without a birth certificate? Did Brandi know they kidnapped her, stole her from safety like an innocent fawn from her mother?

The path had become rocky. Tears burned Blair's eyes. She blinked them away and stared at the phone. She had called her stock broker, Hal Bishop, the minute she got to work this morning, telling him to sell all her bonds. He said he would call back to let her know how much money she could anticipate.

Lenny had made his deal and set the price. One hundred and fifty- thousand dollars. So that was Brandi's value to him. At least he had been reasonable about the time needed to raise that much cash. "Just to show you what a good guy I am," he had joked on the phone, "you can give me twenty-five grand a few days from now, then the rest real soon afterwards."

The sale of the bonds and the money she had in savings should come close to sixty-five thousand. Where in the world would she get anther eighty-five thousand? Blair rested her elbows on her desk and buried her face in her palms. The equity in her house fell far short of that even if she could borrow against it or sell the house quickly. For a moment last night she had considered turning to Myles. Then she had asked herself if she could trust him not to call the police. Her gut and his past actions shouted *No*. All the crank calls they had received, offers to sell information about Brandi's abduction, had been reported immediately to the police. Right or wrong, the attorney in Myles had responded that way. Eleven years later, why would he react differently?

Blair found herself longing for her father. He would help her, no questions asked, even if it meant... "The funeral home. My stock." Blair slapped the desk with her open palm. "Yes. I can get a loan against my stock. Why didn't I think of that last night?" She pushed back in her chair and breathed deeply. "It's going to be all right. Everything is going to work out."

In case Lenny called over the weekend, she would go to the bank tomorrow and withdraw twenty-five thousand. "Then I'll be ready for him," she whispered. "And after I raise the rest of the money and get it to him, Brandi will be home."

The intercom sounded. Jane reported that Hal Bishop was on the phone. He told Blair that the sale of her bonds would generate just over forty-five thousand dollars. "When do you need the money?"

"Yesterday."

"Gotcha."

Jane was standing in the doorway when Blair hung up the phone. "Mr. and Mrs. Antonelli are here. They came without an appointment. Do you want to see them or shall I ask Kent or Greg?"

"I'll see them. Just give me a couple of minutes first." Blair used that time to put on lipstick and to calm herself with a few deep breaths.

Tony and Norma Antonelli were from Amalfi, Italy. Tony, dark-skinned and handsome, was a graduate student at the University of Texas. His wife, Norma, was a petite woman. Reed thin and trembling, she only glanced up at Blair when Tony introduced them and was silent while her husband provided statistical information about their daughter Maria, who was dying of leukemia.

"We would like to have Maria's funeral service at the Church of the Good Shepherd. We have spoken with Reverend Denny."

"Yes, he called me," Blair said. "He also mentioned that you would like a wake service here the night before the funeral." Blair turned slightly in her chair, trying to include Norma, but the grieving mother was unable to contribute so much as a nod. Sad, brown eyes hid behind lightly tinted glasses. Thin fingers crumpled and then smoothed a tissue against the hem of her skirt. "And where will Maria be buried?"

"My wife wants to bury our daughter here in Austin." Tony stopped to clear his throat. "Then when we move back to Amalfi in June, you will have to . . ."

"Disinter the casket." Blair completed his sentence, something she routinely avoided. It had seemed needed at that moment. "I sympathize with your need to be near your daughter even after her death, Norma."

Blair swallowed hard and fought to control her voice. These people have their daughter now and are losing her, she thought. I lost mine and now I'm getting her back.

"Let me assure you, the procedure six months from now will not be nearly as complex as you might think." Blair stood and smoothed the front of her skirt. "You indicated on the phone that you want to look at caskets while you're here. Our selection room is across the hall. This may be the most difficult thing you'll ever do your life, but I think you're wise to get the decision behind you now."

Blair half expected that Tony would go alone, but Norma accompanied him without being asked. She opened the door to the selection room and led them past caskets appropriate for a teenage girl. Norma seemed to be holding her breath. Her eyes scanned the room quickly, so quickly that the open caskets had to appear as mere blurs of color.

Suddenly, Norma released her husband's hand and walked purposefully toward a sky-blue casket with the words *Going Home* stitched in the crepe-lined head panel. With a shaking finger she pointed at doves appliqued above the words. "Look, Anthony. The birds in flight. They are doves." It was the first time Norma had spoken. Her voice was velvet smooth. But it was the look in her eyes that moved her husband to say, "We choose this one. It says what we believe, that our Maria goes home to Christ." Tony embraced Norma tenderly. She sobbed softly, burying her face in his chest.

Blair moved toward the door. "I'll wait for you in the hall."

Outside, she leaned against the wall and closed her eyes. Pressure swelled inside her chest. Finally she released a long sigh. "Oh, Brandi."

The afternoon passed mercifully fast. A steady stream of calls—inquiries about price information, death notification procedures, laws regarding cremation—focused Blair's thoughts on the present, on safe ground. She realized she was beginning to relax a little.

Just before five o'clock, Jane stuck her head in Blair's office, looking as uncomfortable as a student called to the principal's office. "I just did something I've never done before," she said.

She looked so guilty that Blair couldn't help but laugh. "Well, was it criminal?"

Jane stepped forward. Hands folded. Head bowed. "Not criminal. It was . . . presumptuous."

Blair snatched up the phone and pretended to press the intercom. "Kent. My office. Now. Bring a rope."

Snickering, Jane said, "Hanging may be a little drastic. I'll let you decide."

Blair put down the receiver, still chuckling. "Call me crazy, but I get the impression this has something to do with me."

Jane nodded. "While you were on the phone, Matt Byerly called. He said he was waiting for you at the . . ."

"Matt." Blair slapped her forehead with her palm. "The Austin Club. I forgot all about it."

"I assumed that." Jane hunched her shoulders and cringed. "So I told him you left a few minutes ago. I hope you intended to meet him."

Blair bolted out of her chair and stomped to the closet. "Darn you, Liz Elrod." She grabbed her coat and purse. "You just couldn't stay out of my social life, could you?"

"What?"

"Never mind." Blair struggled into her coat while she headed for the door. "See you tomorrow."

Jane called to her as Blair rushed down the hall. "Does this mean I still have a job?"

Blair was home by six-thirty, certain that she wouldn't be hearing from Matt Byerly again. She had met him at a dinner party at her sister's home months ago. It was one of those rare evenings when Blair had allowed herself to be cornered by a single male. Since then, they had met at the Austin Club a couple of times and had dinner once. Matt was pleasant company, had a sharp wit and a self-deprecating humor that amused Blair. But tonight, even Matt hadn't been able to hold her attention. Had Jane not intervened when Matt called, Blair would have come up with some excuse and asked for a rain check. As it was, she had spent an hour with him and could remember almost nothing of what they had talked about. When they were leaving, Matt had told her to stop by the spa on the way home and take a swim. "You seem really tense."

Tense. Frenzied was more like it. Even Celtic seemed to sense her mood. He followed her outside when she brought in firewood, watched while she arranged logs and kindling and lit the fire. Hoping the warmth, the glow, the crackle would soothe her, Blair dropped into her chair. Celtic curled in her lap and licked the back of her hand. She stroked the fine hair on his back and massaged the loose skin under his chin. "I wonder if Brandi still likes dogs. She loved Sandy." Blair let her head drop backward and closed her eyes. "Please, God. Help me get her back."

It was Thursday already and she hadn't checked on her mother since Monday. She dialed the number and Eldon answered. When he heard Blair's voice, he said, "I was just about to call you. How's my girl?"

"Real good." Blair pressed sincerity into her voice. "Is Mom nearby?"

"Sitting right over there in her recliner with a bowl of popcorn. Hold on. I'll get her."

How will she sound tonight? Blair wondered. Alert? On

guard? Confused? What will Brandi's sudden return do to her?

From the table near her chair, Blair picked up a brass framed picture of her parents. Millard Emerson. Round, gentle face. A soft sag beneath his chin. Wisps of salt and pepper hair, thin on top, thicker above the ears. And an easy smile crinkling the corners of his eyes. Maryruth Emerson. Ash-blonde hair fluffed around her oval face. Green eyes softened by full, untouched eyelashes. Enough of her mother's features had combined with her father's for Blair to be described as pretty by some people, wholesome-looking by most. Charlotte, on the other hand, was an identical remake of her mother, but with each feature a degree closer to perfection. If Charlotte weren't so genuinely oblivious to her striking beauty, Blair would have grown up feeling like a Shetland pony at the Kentucky Derby.

"Blair? Is that you, dear?"

Blair smiled. "It's me, Mom. You sound terrific."

"Couldn't be better. How's my daughter?"

"Fine. How was your day?"

"Busy. Busy." Maryruth explained that Eldon had taken her to San Marcos to see her doctor. "Just a check up. I'll probably live to be a hundred, he said." She talked about the barbecue lunch she and Eldon had enjoyed afterward. "I had a brisket plate. Eldon had chicken. It was delicious."

"Sounds like it." Blair asked if she had talked to Charlotte this week. Seconds of silence alarmed Blair. "Mom, are you there? Mom?"

"I'm here." Maryruth's tone had changed. She was uncertain, doubtful. "I think I talked to your sister today. But . . . I'm not sure. It could have been yesterday or . . ."

"It doesn't matter." Blair tried to sound unconcerned but she wasn't. She was baffled by her mother's disease.

Blair ended the conversation quickly and hung up the phone with a familiar sense of ambiguity. On the one hand, she loved talking to her mother, loved the sound of her voice. But talking to her or being with her hurt, too, and always left

Blair sad.

As the evening dragged on, anxiety about Brandi became almost unmanageable. Blair tried to elude it. She mopped the kitchen floor, put in a load of laundry, then cleaned out the refrigerator. She dragged out the vacuum, then put it away again. Her nerves couldn't take the noise. Besides, what if the phone rang? She might not hear it. Lenny wasn't supposed to call, but what if he did? Still, she had to keep moving, to do something constructive.

"Her room. If Brandi comes home, it has to be ready."

With a sense of urgency, Blair took her spring and summer clothes from the guest room closet and put them in boxes. "This is Brandi's room," she told Celtic. "We're going to have everything ready for her. I wonder if she likes blue?"

Next she emptied a white wicker chest and nightstand, then pulled down blue print curtains and washed them. While they dried, she dusted furniture and cleaned windows.

By the time she had the curtains up again, Blair was fighting back tears. Dear God, how would she make it through this with no one to talk to, no one to tell her she was doing the right thing by complying with Lenny's demands. Was she crazy for not going to the police, or even to Myles? No. She would do what Lenny said, exactly what he said.

"And you might as well be done with the worst part," she told herself.

On the phone, Lenny had told her to write two letters. One to Brandi. "I don't have to tell you what to say to her," he had laughed. "But be sure to give her your full name and say how to get in touch with you." The second letter was for April. Lenny had called it an "insurance policy" and then told her what to write.

Blair turned out the light in Brandi's room and walked across the hall to her own. At her desk, she picked up a pen, slid a note pad in front of her and steadied her hand. "My precious daughter. Your call home was a miracle. It gave me a reason to live that I lost the day you disappeared. I am certain you are my daughter. I recognized your shovel and your swimsuit. And I can hardly wait to hold you in my arms again. My name is Blair Emerson." She printed her address and phone numbers in large letters in the middle of the page. "I'm doing everything exactly as Lenny tells me to. I love you, Brandi, and I'm praying for us both." Battling back tears, she folded the note, put it inside an envelope and penned Brandi's name on the front.

Then she picked up the pen again and stared at the note pad, recalling the kind of lies Lenny had told her to write. She scribbled out words. "April, this is very difficult to say, but I think you need to know the truth. Eleven years is a long time. A lot has happened to both of us. I have a life of my own now, a life that doesn't include you. I think we would both be better off if you stayed with Lenny. Good luck."

Quickly she folded the paper and stuffed it in an envelope. She scrawled *April* on the outside and tucked both envelopes under a box of checks in her desk. Lenny had told her not to seal them. "I'll be needing to check them for accuracy," he had said with a grating laugh.

Soon she would give both letters and the first payment to Lenny. She shivered when she recalled his final warning. "If you try to double-cross me, you can guess which letter your kid's gonna end up reading."

13

Minnie returned from the market in the middle of the afternoon on Thursday. She found Roseanne Brenner working furiously in her garden. The cuffs of Roseanne's bell-bottom trousers flapped in the wind like navy blue flags. Her tattered and faded corduroy coat was fastened in the front with little wooden toggles. The one at the neck was missing and had been replaced by a diaper pin capped in pink plastic. Next to her was a stack of evergreen branches almost as tall as Roseanne. It threatened to topple onto a pile of burlap bags next to the chain-link fence. Minnie waved to her with her free hand while clutching a bag of groceries with the other. She hoped Roseanne would keep working and not stop to chat. Hope was wasted.

"Hey, there, Minnie. I see you've been to the store. Didn't you work this afternoon?"

"Just this morning." Minnie kept walking. But when Roseanne struggled to her feet and tromped over to lean against the fence, Minnie felt compelled to visit.

"Why just half a day?"

"Professor Lauzon's spending the afternoon with Myles and Charmaine."

"How's little Tiffany?"

"Up to five pounds ten ounces now. She'll be home the middle of next week if everything goes right." Minnie shifted the bag of groceries to her other hip and glanced toward the corner of her neighbor's yard. Her curiosity was stronger than her need to avoid Roseanne. "What's all that stuff?"

"What?"

"That," she answered in an annoyed tone, pointing at the stack of branches.

"Oh, that's for my rose bushes." Roseanne wiped a dirty palm on a bright pink bandanna and the strip of her forehead just beneath it. "Got a late start protecting my tea roses from the cold this winter. Cut the last blooms yesterday. Now I have to wrap those bushes. I wouldn't have to mess with all that except that nutty old man who planted the garden put it here in the corner where the north wind blows right across it."

She was right, not that Mr. Tipton had been nutty—not compared to Roseanne anyway, but about the placement of the rosebushes. "Next to the house would have been better, huh?"

To accentuate her words, Roseanne tapped the shears she had in her hand against the fence. "By all means. Now I have to go to all this trouble because he didn't know diddly about hybrid teas."

Minnie watched her trot across the yard, then return with a sprayer filled with liquid. The woman loved to talk. About her garden or her church. About the children at the day-care center where she worked. And she was forever asking questions about Myles and Charmaine, particularly after Minnie told her that Myles had been married to Blair Emerson. Had Minnie known earlier about Roseanne's obsession with Blair, she would have kept her mouth shut.

Roseanne held the sprayer near her face and smiled, as if she were doing a television commercial. "First I spray each plant with this. It's an anti-desiccant spray. Know what that does?"

"No idea."

"It seals in moisture to fight off the drying effects of the wind," Roseanne answered proudly. "Wish I had some for my face, don't you, Minnie?"

Roseanne's laugh was harsh, continuing far longer than her stab at humor warranted. "Then what do you do?" Minnie asked, more to stop Roseanne's laughter than out of interest.

"Well, then I truss the plant with these branches and wrap them in burlap." She made a broad circular motion with her hand. Then she scooped imaginary soil with both hands, waving the shears carelessly in the process. "Finally I mound the dirt about eight inches deep around the base. Whew! It's a lot of work, Minnie."

"Sounds like it, " Minnie said. "Just talking about it has you out of breath."

"But you know, Minnie." Roseanne's voice took on a remorseful tone. "I've got nothing else to care for but my roses. I'm not lucky like you. You've got the professor to look after. He has his family. And Charmaine has it all: you and her father and Blair's husband, and now she even has a baby."

"Myles is not Blair's husband, Roseanne." Minnie spoke the words sharply, but Roseanne didn't seem to notice.

"Some people have everything." Her tone was grave. "More than they ought to, maybe. And they don't care who knows how they got it."

Was she referring to Charmaine? Minnie wondered. The thought stirred protective instincts. Roseanne's eyes were drifting eerily. Minnie was preparing to slip away when Roseanne sucked in a quick breath, like someone about to plunge into ice water. "Did you hear that, Minnie?"

"I didn't hear anything."

"No? Well, I guess you wouldn't." Roseanne's voice became secretive. "It was a spirit, Minnie."

"A what?"

"A spirit. It spoke to me."

Minnie shifted uneasily, not sure what to say. "What did it say to you?"

96

Roseanne paused, as if a bit hesitant to say any more. But then she plunged on. "It said that I should pray for Charmaine."

"Pray for Charmaine? All right, Roseanne," Minnie snapped. "Enough. This is not the first time you've suggested that Charmaine was somehow in need of your prayers." Minnie's angry words spewed across the fence. "And I'm sick and tired of hearing about that church of yours, and the . . .the divine mind, or whatever you call it. And you can talk to your spirit friend until you're blue in the face. I don't care. But you listen to me. Don't you be talking to it about Charmaine or Myles or any of us."

"But, Minnie, Charmaine took Blair's husband."

"Hush. Just you hush now." Minnie was surprised by the anger in her voice, but she couldn't stop herself. "Furthermore if you want to talk to someone divine, why don't you try talking to the Lord Jesus? And you're not likely to find him at that oddball place you like to call a church. Fellowship of the Guiding Light, indeed!" Heart pounding, she spun around and stomped back toward her house. "A bunch of screwballs if ever there was one." Gravel crunched beneath the soles of Minnie's sturdy shoes. Frustration forced her to hurl one last thought over her shoulder. "If I were you, Roseanne, I'd find out what kind of mind those crazy people are teaching you to speak to."

Roseanne's lips, chapped from the wind and cracking in the corners, parted to say something, but her words seemed to tangle on their way out.

"The woman is nuts. Nuts." Minnie mumbled, stomping across the driveway and up the back steps. "And it must be contagious. I'm acting as crazy as her."

At her rose bushes, Roseanne snatched and peeled and jerked at the remaining foliage. A north wind shoved at her back, threatening to snatch the evergreen branches from her.

When she finally managed to get the branches in place, she grabbed the nearest burlap sack and struggled to wrap it around the protective trussing. A greedy gust of wind grabbed it from her hand and sailed it over the fence into Minnie's backyard. Roseanne watched it tumble and roll across the dry brown grass. Finally the wind dropped it onto a rusty brown glider on Minnie's porch. Roseanne watched it ride there for a moment, then grabbed another bag, careful this time to keep a tight grip on it as she wrapped it around the bush and tied it securely with twine.

The wind had died down considerably by the time Roseanne finished wrapping the last of the bushes. She mounded soil around them all, then struggled up from her knees. Slapping dirt off her trousers, she walked across the yard toward Minnie's house.

The round stones that made a walkway across Minnie's yard were so far apart that Roseanne had to stretch her short legs to reach from one to the next. She climbed the sagging wooden porch steps, hoping Minnie didn't see her. At the glider, she snatched the sack, rolled it up and stuck it under her arm. She was just starting down the porch steps when Roseanne heard Minnie's voice. She was on the phone in the kitchen. The windows were down, making it hard for Roseanne to hear the words, so she stepped closer. Then Minnie's voice rose a little.

"But, Professor, it's not Myles's fault that he ran into Blair at the hospital, now is it? I wish you and Charmaine wouldn't get so upset."

Blair. They were talking about Blair. Hunching down inside her coat, Roseanne inched her way across the porch until she was near the kitchen window. That nasty old Professor Lauzon and his selfish daughter were always complaining to Minnie about something. It seemed like this time Charmaine was upset because Myles had seen his real wife, Blair.

"I agree, Professor. But remember, Charmaine's still unsure of herself when it comes to Blair. Give her time. Remind her that Myles is her husband now. He loves her. She and Tiffany are his life. All right. Yes. I'll be over to help her just as soon as I can. Goodbye."

Flattening her body against the wall, Roseanne waited until Minnie left the kitchen, until her footsteps had faded. Then she tightened her grip on her sack and inched her way across the creaking wooden planks. "That dreadful Charmaine, wallowing in jealousy like a pig in slop."

When Roseanne reached her yard, she stopped suddenly and held her breath. "There it is again," she whispered. An afternoon haze was settling over the neighborhood. She shivered at the sight of it. It looked like a whisper-thin veil, but Roseanne knew that it was actually an energy field. It settled on the charcoal gray shingles, drifted down around the windows, finally blurring her freeze-damaged shrubs. She had seen this hazy veil several times in the last few weeks, but until this very moment had not realized what it meant. The spirits were back.

Thursday afternoon, April walked into Jesse's cafe. Jesse, a tall, heavy man with a thick mustache, recognized her. "Ah. It's Father Ochoa's new friend. What will it be? Hot chocolate with no marshmallows?"

April nodded, surprised that he remembered. "Yes, thank you."

Jesse's cafe was a small place, with marred wooden tables in varying sizes scattered around the room. Each had a little vase of crepe-paper flowers in the center. The plaster walls were decorated with Mexican hats that Father Ochoa said were called *sombreros* and colorful blankets called *serapes*. Yesterday, when she had gone to the rest room to wash her hands, April had been confused by the door signs. She knew now that the one marked *Damas* was for women. A tiny little Mexican woman wearing a cook's apron had told her so.

Father Ochoa had suggested they get together again today for hot chocolate. At first, April had said no, that she and Lenny would be gone by then. It wasn't true, and she didn't really know why she had said it. So she said later that she'd see.

The fact was that April wanted to see Father Ochoa again. She enjoyed listening to him. He told wonderful stories about growing up in a large family. "Two parents, four brothers and one sister. All in a house no larger than Jesse's cafe. Lots of people. Lots of love." Part of his family still lived in south Texas in a town called Kingsville. There his father was one of hundreds of cowboys on a huge ranch, one of the largest in the world. It was called the King Ranch and was spread over thousands of acres. Father Ochoa had been gone from there a long time, but he still knew a lot about horses and cattle roundups and barbecues.

There was something else that Father Ochoa knew a lot about: children. Although he had none of his own, he seemed to know how kids felt inside. When she asked him why he didn't have children, he had smiled and kind of chuckled. Then he said something about promises he made to God a long time ago. April didn't understand what he meant by that, but it seemed a shame that nice men like Father Ochoa made that promise and men like Lenny didn't.

April looked up when Jesse set a mug of hot chocolate on the table. "Thanks."

"Are you meeting Father Ochoa again today?" he asked.

"Yes."

"The padre comes here every day at four o'clock for coffee." Jesse's mustache moved up and down when he talked and broadened when he smiled. "But for you, he orders hot chocolate. He's a good man. A good friend."

April nodded and watched Jesse walk away. Then she sneaked a towelette from her purse, wiped the tabletop, the rim of her cup and her hands. She had done the same thing yesterday. Father Ochoa had watched her, but he had acted as if it were no big deal. That was another thing she liked about him. He didn't ask lots of questions like most grown-ups did. If he had been nosy yesterday, she wouldn't have come today.

There was something different about Father Ochoa, something she couldn't quite put her finger on. But whatever it was made April feel almost at ease around him.

Because of that, and because she wouldn't see him again after a few days from now, she had told him a little about herself. "Lenny and Jewell adopted me when I was two. About a week ago, Jewell died," she had explained, surprised and embarrassed when her voice cracked. "Now Lenny and I are moving to El Paso. Do you know where that is?"

He nodded his head. "Such a long way from your friends. Did you leave a special friend behind in Virginia?"

She had told him about Becky and how much she missed her. She hadn't told him anything about Blair, though. It would have been humiliating to say, "Lenny told my real mother that we're here in Dallas and that she can have me back if she wants. But she hasn't made up her mind yet."

She hadn't told him about her plan to take the bus back to Virginia Beach, either. He might decide that was something Lenny should know about and warn him.

Father Ochoa had insisted on walking her back to the Oak Cliff Inn yesterday. In the parking lot, he had asked to meet Lenny. "He's not in there," she had lied. "I'm sure." The old Buick was parked in front of their room. If Father Ochoa noticed the Virginia license plates, he hadn't let on.

When the little bell on the door jingled, April looked up. It was Father Ochoa. He was rubbing his hands briskly up and down the sleeves of his trench coat and stamping his feet. When he spotted April, he smiled and started toward her. He was a small man, much shorter than his friend Jesse, and much younger. His hair was jet black and cut short. His dark skin made his teeth look sparkling white.

"April. You're here." He slipped out of his coat and pulled back a chair. "I was afraid you and Lenny might have left for El Paso."

"Not yet."

Jesse came to the table. "Hot chocolate again, Father?"

"Think I'll have coffee today."

"*Y pan dulce?*"

"*Gracias.*" He turned to April and smiled. "*Pan dulce.* It's a delicious sweet bread. You can try it." Then he reached into the pocket of his trench coat. "I brought you something." It was a box about the size of a paperback book, wrapped in midnight blue paper with snowflakes. The ribbon and bow were red. "Merry Christmas, April."

April hesitated, then took the gift. She stared at it a moment. "Thank you."

"Would you open it now?"

April could feel her face getting warm and red. She slipped off the ribbon and carefully removed the paper. The box was white. She removed the lid and folded back a piece of tissue. Her eyes widened. "Oh. A diary." She took it out of the box and ran her fingers over the pink cover. The border was embossed with pink and blue and yellow flowers connected by vines of ivy. Imprinted inside the border was an image of a girl's thin face. She was wearing a straw hat with a yellow ribbon flowing over the brim. She had long straight hair, large round eyes and a slight smile. Under her ruffled collars were printed the words, *My Secret Thoughts*.

"If you already have a diary you can . . ."

"I don't." April had wanted one for a long time. She had looked at several, but this one . . . It was perfect. April couldn't stop staring at the image on the cover. It looked so much like—almost exactly like her.

Jesse came with Father Ochoa's coffee and the sweet breads. They were the size of hamburger buns but were the color of sugar cookies. One had pink icing, the other light green. Father Ochoa picked up one and took a big bite. "Ummm. Care to try one, April?"

"I'm not hungry." She was still studying the drawing on the diary cover, running her fingertip along the gold embossed trim.

"The girl is pretty, isn't she?" Father Ochoa leaned forward. "Does she remind you of anyone?"

April nodded but said nothing. She was afraid to say that the girl looked like her. If Father Ochoa hadn't noticed, she would be humiliated.

"Who does she look like?" he asked.

April kept her eyes down. She considered her answer for several seconds. Finally she said, "Me?"

"Yes. You." Father Ochoa sounded relieved and excited. "I was hoping you'd say that. When I went to get you a gift, I hadn't intended to buy a diary. But when I saw the cover, the girl looked so much like you...well, I could hardly wait to give it to you." He sighed. "I was afraid to mention the resemblance. I would have been embarrassed if you didn't agree."

"Embarrassed? Really?"

"Open the cover. It's unlocked."

April pressed a little button. The flap popped open. Carefully she opened the cover. Father Ochoa had written something there. *Friends are a mirror of God's love. Merry Christmas. Father Ochoa.*

Her eyes began to mist. She closed the cover and put the diary back in the box. When she looked up, Father Ochoa was sipping his coffee. He was too nice to stare at her as if he were waiting for her to say something.

Maybe talking to Father Ochoa about Blair wouldn't be too bad. She needed to talk to someone.

14

Blair returned to the funeral home from the bank just after three o'clock Friday afternoon. There was now a satchel stacked neatly with twenty-five thousand dollars in assorted denominations in the trunk of her car. This morning she had telephoned the bank and arranged to withdraw the cash. This afternoon she had been escorted to an office by a teller who had requested identification, Blair's account number and her signature on a withdrawal form. Blair's patience had snapped when the man had asked for her social security number and said something about a C.T.R.

"What's that?" she had growled.

"A Currency Transaction Report. It's required of the bank by the I.R.S. on all large cash transactions."

While there, she had also spoken to an officer about pledging her stock certificates as collateral on a loan. The stock was worth far more than a hundred thousand. But, he had said, the loan would have to go before committee and that might mean ten days before she could have the money. She completed the application anyway. By the time the loan was approved, she certainly would have the money from the bonds sale. Would Lenny wait that long? He would have to. He had to give her time.

With no funerals and no families to see, Blair told Jane she would be in her office, wrapping up some paperwork before the weekend.

"Blair, are you feeling all right?" Jane's expression reflected concern. "You haven't been yourself the last few days."

"It's been a long week. I just need a quiet weekend."

Blair pulled a tax form from one of the folders on her desk, took one look at it and immediately put it away. Concentrating on business was impossible. She gave in and turned full attention to thoughts of Brandi. She tried to fantasize about their reunion, but instead remembered the aftermath of her kidnapping, the agony of grief that had set in after the shock wore off.

The phone rang gently. It was her private line. She sucked in a quick breath and put the receiver to her ear. "Hello." She felt herself start to tremble.

"Is that you, Blair?"

"Yes." Was it Lenny? He sounded different. Excited. Eager. "Who is this?"

"It's Bill Elrod."

"Oh. It's you, Bill." Her tone registered her disappointment. Her hands clammy, her lips still trembling, she said, "I was expecting...someone..." She let her words trail off. "So what's up?"

"What's up?" He sounded incredulous. "What kind of question is that for an expectant godmother?"

"I'm sorry, Bill." She attempted to mask her disappointment. "How's Liz?"

"Terrific. And so is your godchild."

"What?"

"You're a godmother, kid."

"Oh, Bill. This is wonderful. Wait. Let me guess." The excitement she forced into her voice couldn't quite disguise her regret that it wasn't Lenny calling. "I have a god-daughter."

"Wrong. William Clayton Elrod. Clay. What do you think?"

"Ummm. Let me try it: Governor Clay Elrod. Senator Clay Elrod. Doctor Clay Elrod." Bill's throaty laughter eased the knot in her stomach. "Why didn't you call me earlier? I wanted to be there."

"No time. But Liz is fine. Says for you to get yourself over here tonight. She's sort of wiped out right now."

"Nothing could keep me away. Give them both a kiss, Bill. Bye."

Sleet pelting against the glass drew Blair to the window. "Thank you, God, for their healthy baby boy." She touched the cold pane with her fingertips. "And for the chance to have my baby back."

Trees beyond the funeral parking lot were stark, bare shapes. This spring their leaves would shimmer and whisper in gentle breezes, but for now they were silent. Grass the lawn service had nursed through a dreadfully dry summer was crusted with ice. Ivy on the portecochere was leafless. Flower beds were empty. Despite it all, Blair liked Texas winters. Winter weather. Winter sports. Winter clothes. And now, with Brandi coming home, the holiday season would be a time of joy again, a celebration of miracles.

Blair hugged her arms around herself and inhaled deeply. She could almost smell the scent of the pine tree she and Brandi would decorate, the sweet smell of Christmas cookies, the spicy aroma of potpourri simmering on the stove in a small copper kettle. Blair's lips relaxed into a smile. "Miracles do happen. Brandi's coming home."

The gentle jangle of the phone sent her thoughts fluttering like startled birds. It was her private line. She hurried to her desk, but had to force herself to pick up the receiver. "Hello."

"Hello to you. It's your friend Lenny."

Weakened by his voice, Blair lowered herself unsteadily into her chair. Through quivering lips she managed to say, "I've been waiting to hear from you."

"Well, ain't that special."

Lenny's "good old boy" accent was warped with alcohol

or some other drug. That worried her. A man could get dangerous when he was drunk or high. Did he have a hair-trigger temper? Was he capable of harming Brandi? How had he treated her all these years?

When she spoke, Blair heard an edge of desperation in her voice. "I have the money. Twenty-five thousand."

"You know, I kinda thought you would. How does a trip to Dallas grab you?"

"Dallas? Is that where you are?"

"For now, yeah. But I'm running a little low on cash. How about bringing the twenty-five grand on up here."

"Just tell me when and where." Blair made her voice smooth, conciliatory.

"There's a pay phone at a Texaco station at the corner of I-35 and Kiest. Be there tomorrow night at nine sharp. I'll call you there. Got that?"

"Interstate Thirty-five and Kiest. Texaco. Nine o'clock Saturday night."

"And just a friendly little reminder. All you better bring is the money and them letters. You got them written?" A tone of menace had crept into Lenny's voice.

"I have the letters and the money. I haven't said a word to anyone, Lenny. I promise. I have no reason to. I'm just grateful for the chance to get my daughter back. Is she there? Could I speak to her?"

"She ain't here."

"Could I talk to her or at least get a glimpse of her tomorrow night?"

There was silence on the other end of the line. Suddenly worried that she might have pushed too much, Blair quickly added, "It's not that I don't trust you."

In the midst of a burst of ear-splitting laughter, Lenny said, "What's not to trust? I've got something you want. You've got something I want. No need for things to get messy."

"You're right." Blair's nails dug into her palm. "And it won't. I promise."

"Well, I got to go. It's a pleasure doin' business with ya, Blair."

"I'll be waiting for your call at the pay phone."

"Oh, there's one more thing."

"Yes."

"I don't take checks." Another burst of laughter, then Lenny was gone.

When April walked through the door to their motel room on Friday afternoon, her cheeks were red and her eyes watered. Snowflakes clung to her hair. She tossed a sack of pork rinds and Lenny's change onto the sofa without speaking and surveyed the filthy room. Empty beer cans on the coffee table. A half-eaten cheeseburger and soggy fries on the nightstand. She went straight to the bathroom to wash her hands after being in the convenience store. She came out spraying Lysol around the room. It wasn't germs she was concerned about, it was the stench of stale cigarette smoke.

"Enough with that," Lenny barked, waving his hands in front of his face.

"It's Lysol, Lenny," April quipped. "Not tear gas. Besides, it stinks in here."

"Can't you just crack a window?"

April returned to the bathroom and came out this time with a towel and trash can. Covering one hand and forearm with the towel, she knelt beside the coffee table and with a swoop shoved the empty beer cans into the trash. Then she dumped the ash tray, careful not to breathe in the ashes when they rose in a little puff. Lenny was such a pig. She glanced at him over her shoulder. He was standing at the window, separating the blinds with his fingers. He was wearing one of his plaid flannel shirts, the cuffs folded halfway up his forearms. His thin, unshaven face looked dirty. His dingy blonde hair curled over his collar in the back, but he kept it short on the sides, as if he couldn't decide between styles.

"I hate winter," he grumbled. "Damn cold wind slicing

through you like a switchblade. Cars ramming each other on icy freeways. And here I am with nothing but this lousy thing." He slapped at a denim jacket on the chair next to him, then was silent for a moment. "A guy over at the pool hall told me that church up the street has one of them clothes closets. You know anything about that?"

"Why would I?" April stuffed the dirty towel in the trash can and put the can back in the bathroom. Then she lay down on her bed, picked up her book and pretended to read.

"Jesse up at the cafe told me you been in his place a couple of times with that preacher from the church."

"He's a *priest*. And so what if I have?"

"It just ain't like you to take up with a stranger that way. Not even if he is a *priest*."

"You don't know anything about what I'm like," April snapped. "And I haven't taken up with him."

Lenny threw up his hands. "Hell's bells, April. You don't have to get in a snit. I just thought maybe you could talk to him about getting me a coat."

April stole another glance at Lenny over the top of her book.

"Well, will you do it?"

"Maybe."

"How about going down there this afternoon? I got some business tomorrow night, and I'm gonna have to be out in the cold."

"I guess I could." Lenny rarely asked her to do anything for him, not anything like this anyway. If there really was a clothes closet at the church, she was sure Father Ochoa would give Lenny a coat. But how would she let Father Ochoa know he needed one without sounding like she was begging?

"I'm gonna see your mother tomorrow night." Lenny slid onto the couch and covered himself with the bedspread he had dragged from the bed. "She talks like she might want you back."

The words stirred flutters in April's stomach. Blair might want her back again. She might not have to move to El Paso after all. Stop it, she told herself. Lenny could be lying or teasing. Any minute, he could burst out laughing and say, "I'm just fooling with you. I ain't heard another word from your mother."

Lenny pulled the bedspread over his shoulders and rolled onto his side. "She's gonna tell me for sure when I see her tomorrow night. That's what you want, ain't it? To live with your mother instead of me?"

April didn't say anything, but Lenny was right. She did want to live with her real mother, and it wasn't just because of Lenny and El Paso. That was what she had decided after talking to Father Ochoa yesterday. He'd said that her mother had probably done what she thought was best at the time. "Raising a child alone is very difficult. She may have thought you would have a better life with Lenny and Jewell. But that doesn't necessarily mean that she didn't want you."

The clock on the nightstand read four o'clock. Lenny had fallen asleep. His breathing was raspy. He coughed frequently, but even that didn't wake him.

April slipped out of the room. If she hurried, she might catch Father Ochoa at the cafe. If she could get a coat for Lenny, then maybe he would have something nice to say about her when he talked to her mother.

The few cars that traveled the street moved slowly, making April nervous when they came up behind her. She hated Dallas, couldn't imagine having to live here. But maybe Blair lived in a better part of town. She sure hoped so.

She found Father Ochoa in the cafe eating sweet bread and drinking coffee. When April saw he wasn't alone, she started to leave. But Father Ochoa called to her. "Ben was just leaving, April. Come and sit down."

April smiled shyly at the man who offered her his seat. "The snow is really beginning to fall," she said. "I wrote about it in my diary today."

"I've kept a diary for years," Father Ochoa remarked. "Only I call it a journal. It's like having a close friend to confide in even when you're alone."

April declined Jesse's offer of hot chocolate. "Nothing today. Thank you." She put her hands in her lap. They were shaking from the cold and nerves.

"What brings you to the cafe if not for hot chocolate?" Father Ochoa's expression became serious. "I hope it's not to say goodbye."

"No. I just wanted to get out of our room for a while." She shivered and said, "It's freezing out there. I'm glad I have warm gloves and a scarf. I passed a boy on the way down here wearing only a skimpy windbreaker."

"Really? That's too bad. We have a clothes closet at the church. We would gladly give him a coat."

Hands still under the table, April rubbed the knuckles of one hand with the palm of the other. "You give coats away?"

"Oh, yes. Lots of them. To poor people. Every winter."

"That's nice." April clenched both hands into fists and said, "Lenny's coat is awfully skimpy."

Father Ochoa picked up his coffee cup. "Then send him up to the church. We'll gladly . . ."

"No. Uh . . . I mean . . . he's real busy getting ready to leave for El Paso."

"Then you could select one and take it to him."

"I suppose I could do that." April relaxed her hands.

"There's probably one in there that's your size, too." Father Ochoa nodded to her jacket. "If that one's not quite warm enough."

The question put April on guard again. "Oh, it's a lot warmer than it looks." The fact was that her jacket was far too lightweight, but there was no way she would put on a coat someone else had worn. No way. She would freeze first.

"Are you sure you couldn't use a coat, April?" he asked gently. "I would like to give you one. Would it be okay?"

A number of excuses for not trying on a used coat clicked off in her mind. None made more sense than the truth. "I can't do it, Father."

"But why not?"

She leaned toward him and whispered. "There's no telling

who in the world wore those clothes."

"But, April, the clothing is cleaned before it goes into the closet," he argued softly.

"Yes, but just think how many people may have tried them on since then."

Father Ochoa nodded his head and thought for a moment. "I get the feeling that you're worried about picking up someone else's germs. So how do you go about shopping? I mean, many new clothes have been tried on."

"Right." April relaxed a little. Father Ochoa didn't act as if he thought her thing about germs was weird, so what would it hurt to tell him about how she handled shopping. "I have an almost foolproof system for finding out if clothes have been tried on before." When Father Ochoa indicated interest, she continued. "New clothes have these little plastic clips on them. They look like hairpins but they're thicker and made out of clear plastic. Anyway, they poke them through a button hole and hang tags off of them." April paused when Father Ochoa slowly nodded his head. "You know what I'm talking about?"

"I am getting the picture."

April spoke confidently now, proud of her own cleverness. "So, if those little clips are still on a coat or a blouse or whatever, I can pretty well know it hasn't been tried on. Know how?" Father Ochoa looked fully interested so she explained. "In the dressing room, you'll find those little plastic things all over the floor. See what I mean? So if something I want to try on has the clips still on it, I figure it's safe."

"That's very observant." Father Ochoa sounded impressed. "I have an idea. I will get Lenny a coat at the church. Then we can go to a new clothing store and you can show me what you mean about the clips. If we find a coat that hasn't been tried on, would you let me buy it for you? Then every time you put it on, you will remember me."

April nodded but didn't look at Father Ochoa. His eyes seemed to look deep into her, almost as if he could read her mind. And if he could see what she was thinking right now, he sure wouldn't want to buy her a new coat. Not if he knew she had taken seven dollars and ninety-three cents from the little wooden box at the church.

15

It was two o'clock Saturday afternoon. For over an hour now, the wipers on Blair's car had slapped sleet off the windshield, clearing her view of the heavy northbound traffic on Interstate Thirty-five. The drive to Dallas would take four hours. She had allowed herself eight. The money and the letters were in a satchel in the trunk.

Though she tried to concentrate on her driving, Blair's mind drifted to its recurrent preoccupation of the last four days. She wondered what Brandi was like now, how she looked. For years after Brandi's disappearance, Blair had seen her child everywhere. In strangers' arms. In strollers wheeled down shaded sidewalks. On playgrounds all over town. Sometimes Blair's heart had leaped to her throat, sure that she had seen her. Brandi's name would form on her lips. Then Blair would turn away quickly, before anyone could see the agony in her eyes.

And now—soon—she would open a door or step into a room or turn a corner, and Brandi really would be there. What would she look like now? As a toddler, Brandi had been pudgy—not chubby, but plump and cuddly. She'd been a cheerful, undemanding child who had laughed at the slightest provocation. Because of that, Blair had loved taking her places. Brandi had smiled and waved her little hands at strangers, even reached for those who had stopped to comment on her smile or her dimples or her big, brown eyes. Was she still like that? Happy? Friendly? Trusting?

Blair relaxed her grip on the steering wheel and twisted her head from side to side. The muscles in her neck were stiff, and her shoulders ached. She had slept only a couple of hours last night, and those had been dream-filled and fitful. Before leaving Austin, she had gone to St. Mary's to see Liz again. She had found her sound asleep, her pretty face framed by a fluff of thick hair and the lace collar of the Christian Dior nightgown Blair had given her last night after Bill's call.

Blair had been more than a little relieved to find her sleeping. Liz's antennae managed to pick up the slightest change in Blair's emotional signals. Today, even in the midst of her excitement about the baby, only a general anesthetic would have kept Liz from noticing that Blair's nerves were strung to the breaking point.

Blair had gone alone to the nursery to get another peek at Clay. "My godson," she had whispered. Olive skin the color of Bill's. Swatches of dark brown hair sticking up like a rooster's comb. Nine pounds, eight ounces. "That one's half grown," a grandfatherly type had joked. "He's twice as big as the little- bitty ones next door."

Last night, Blair had been tempted to slip around the corner to the neonatal unit for a glimpse of Tiffany. But she had been afraid that she might run into Myles or Charmaine or, worse yet, Dr. Lauzon. It was more than just curiosity that had made her risk it today. It was the realization that Tiffany was Brandi's half-sister.

There were four infants in the neonatal unit. Blair had scanned the names. One child was blocked from Blair's view by a wide- bodied nurse who was jotting notes on a chart. When the woman had finally stepped aside, Blair's eyes widened. Wispy blonde hair. Flawless fair skin. Perfectly shaped lips puckered around a tiny thumb. Tiffany Lakeman.

Then a doctor, whom Blair recognized as the hospital's top pediatrician, had entered the unit and walked straight to Tiffany Lakeman. He had studied her for a moment, read the chart and given instructions to the nurse. After much smiling and head nodding, the nurse opened the incubator, lifted Tiffany into her arms and showed her proudly to the doctor.

"No more tubes for you, Tiffany," Blair had whispered. "You get to join the big kids now."

A voice from down the hallway had sent Blair hurrying to the stairwell exit. Charmaine.

On the way downstairs, Blair had pounded past a security guard chatting in the stairwell with one of the housekeeping crew. On the fourth floor she had found the elevator and rode it down to the lobby, disgusted with herself for acting like such a coward.

Traffic on the interstate slowed to forty miles an hour north of Temple. The winter storm was moving to the southwest, from Dallas toward Austin. Sandwiched between a gravel truck and a van whose driver insisted on tailgating despite the icy roads, Blair clenched the steering wheel, her left foot poised over the brake, prepared for a sudden stop.

Waco was twenty-three miles ahead, a road sign informed her. She was almost halfway to Dallas. Kiest Boulevard was a major street in the Oak Cliff area of south Dallas—not exactly where she would like to be pacing outside a pay phone at nine o'clock at night. Where would Lenny send her from there? Blair worried. She knew Dallas reasonably well, but she had brought a street map, just in case.

Would he let her see Brandi? The possibility overwhelmed Blair, set her heart pounding, her mind racing ahead. Trance-like she stared through the windshield into a frightening fantasy.

In a vacant parking lot in south Dallas, shivering in the car, her breath clouds the windows. Headlights of a slow-moving car appear. It rolls to a stop. Headlights die. A door swings open. For seconds, the dome light floods the car with bright yellow. With frantic swipes, Blair clears away moisture on her window, hoping to catch a glimpse of Brandi. Too late. The light goes out. Lenny grinds out a cigarette on the pavement. Tall. Powerfully built. His parka zipped up to a broad chest. He covers the distance between the cars in seconds and raps her car window. Blair lowers it cautiously and studies his features as he speaks.

Brown eyes, cruel and pitiless.

"There's going to be hell to pay if anyone followed you."

A broad, carelessly clipped mustache.

"You'll never see April again."

Thin lips set in a sneer.

"Where's the money?"

In a flicker of fantasy time, she is opening the trunk, reaching for the satchel. A black leather-gloved hand jerks it away.

"If anyone follows me, April is history."

April pushed aside the limp beige curtain on the window overlooking the motel parking lot. At seven o'clock it was like midnight. The forecast had warned that the sleet would turn to snow by early evening, and so it had. The parking lot looked almost clean now with its thickening layer of white. It glowed in the light from street lamps and the occasional headlights of cars braving the treacherous streets.

White was April's favorite color. Clean. Sanitary. When a girl wore white, she never had trouble deciding if her clothes were dirty. Of course, there were people like Lenny who wore the same tee-shirt for days without washing it. "What sweat stains? What ashes?" For the most part, the smidgen of concern he showed about his appearance was the result of Jewell's mothering.

This morning, because she was tired of seeing them piled in the corner of the room, April had volunteered to take Lenny's dirty clothes to a coin-operated laundry and wash them. She had asked for five dollars. "You're out of razor blades and stuff, too." Lenny had given her the money

117

without argument.

She had washed two loads of clothes, and, to save money, had put them all in one dryer. Then she had stepped next door to the convenience store and picked up the other things for Lenny. She had scraped off the price stickers so Lenny wouldn't know how much she spent, then pocketed the change.

Friday afternoon, after getting Lenny a coat from the clothes closet at the church, Father Ochoa had taken April to a discount store. He had asked her to demonstrate her safe shopping system in the coat department, so she had. Unlike Lenny, who would have been a total embarrassment—loud and impatient—Father Ochoa had watched quietly as she studied the coats, found one she liked and located her size.

"Now tell me about the clips again," he had said softly, so that no one else could hear.

April had pointed to the floor beneath the coats. "Look. See all the tags and safety pins and little plastic clips. That means that these coats have been tried on a lot."

"I see. What about the one you picked out?"

April had taken the coat off the rack and held it out in front of her. It was a beautiful bright blue with red and white knit bands on the bottom, the cuffs and the collar. It zipped up the front and had a detachable drawstring hood. It was the nicest coat she had ever seen. "This one is okay. The brand name tags are here. So is the price tag. The pockets are snapped shut. And it's zipped all the way to the top. I'm sure no one has tried it on."

"Do you like it?"

"Well . . . yeah . . . sure."

"It looks so warm." Father Ochoa had glanced around to see that no one was listening. "It would make me happy if you'd let me buy it for you."

Father Ochoa wouldn't be at all happy—in fact, he might even be mad—if he knew that today she had taken the bus back to the store and returned the coat. She hated doing it. She loved the coat. And it was special: Father Ochoa had

118

given it to her. *I hope you'll think of me now and then, April, when you wear it.*

But what choice did she have? As much as she wanted the coat, she needed the money worse. Thirty-nine dollars and eighty-seven cents. All that money would go a long way toward her bus fare. And she needed every penny she could get her hands on in case tonight Blair said, "Tell April I just can't take her back."

The rest of the day had been awful.

Shivering, April moved from the window to her bed. Again she checked her watch. Seven-fifteen. In less than two hours, Lenny would be talking to Blair—unless something went wrong, of course. And with Lenny, there was always a chance that it would.

April often wondered why Jewell had tolerated Lenny and his problems. Spending grocery and rent money on drugs. Getting thrown off one job after another for being high or being late or not showing up at all. If he held a job for three months, Jewell had bragged on him as if he had graduated from Harvard.

Jewell and April had not discussed Lenny's problem, not one time. When Lenny had come home high, Jewell had sent April to Becky's. "April, honey, Lenny's picked up a bug and I don't want you to catch it. Becky's mom said you could stay there till he's better." Or when he had not come home at all for a day or two and Jewell had to go and get him, it had been, "April, sweetie, Lenny called today. He was real sorry he worried us, but his crew got called out of town yesterday. Some kind of rush job somewhere downstate. Anyway, he'll be back today. Maybe you ought to spend the night with Becky. You know what a bear Lenny is when he's dead tired."

It had been the same way for years in Becky's family. Her father was an alcoholic, but neither her mom nor her big sister had discussed his problem with Becky. After ten years of it, the three of them left him somewhere in Pennsylvania and moved to Virginia Beach. Becky said she hated her father, but sometimes she missed him just the same.

119

April sat cross-legged on the bed to take off her sneakers. The carpet was soiled and probably crawling with germs. She wouldn't walk across it with her socks on, much less barefoot like Lenny did. She put her sneakers in a drawer in the nightstand, then slid her diary from beneath her pillow. With the pillow propped against the headboard, she leaned wearily back and closed her eyes. They popped open when she realized she had not checked her watch for a while. Only seven-thirty. Another hour and a half. Before Lenny left, she had asked him why he was meeting Blair so late in the evening.

"Uh . . .she works late," he had said.

"Where?"

"Hell, I don't know, April. Some bar over on Greenville Avenue maybe."

"Am I going with you?"

"No way, Miss Personality. You don't wanna ruin your chances, do ya?"

Before she could turn away, April's eyes had pooled with tears and her lips had begun to quiver. She hated when that happened, hated anyone seeing her cry.

"Well, hell, April," Lenny had laughed. "Can't you take a joke? I was just kidding." Then he had pulled on the pea coat Father Ochoa had found for him. "Cheer up. I'll lie for you, tell Blair what a great kid you are. Top student. Cleaner than a heart surgeon heading for the operating room. Never in trouble. Can cook that—that chicken and rice concoction better than my mama could, God rest her ol' soul."

The last thing he had said before walking out the door was, "Don't worry, kid. You're gonna be back with your mama. Lord knows, I don't want you." Then he had winked and closed the door.

April opened her diary. In small, tight letters, she wrote *Saturday* at the top of page two, then: *Tonight Blair will tell Lenny if she wants me back again. But I know better than to get my hopes up. Wherever Lenny is now, he's probably high. It wouldn't be the first time he has been a no-show at a critical meeting or, worse yet, shown up with an attitude. But maybe tonight that will work in my favor. No mother would want her daughter raised by a junky. Will write more later.*

Closing her eyes gently, April fantasized about her first meeting with Blair. She did this by pretending the insides of her lids were a movie screen. The scene opens: *She is inside the car with Lenny, parking in front of Blair's house. It is on a short crowded street with potholes and cracking sidewalks. April is so nervous she keeps hiccuping the way she had the time she recited "Trees" in front of her sixth-grade class. Then the front door opens. A short, tired looking woman walks out. Thin lips smiling. Frizzy brown hair framing her face. She wears tight jeans and a Dallas Cowboys sweatshirt. She holds a cigarette between long, red nails.*

They share an awkward embrace. "Hi, April. I'm Blair. Call me Blair or Mom, whichever." She takes April's suitcase and looks at Lenny. "Lenny, I'd invite you in, but I've got to be at work in half an hour." Before Lenny leaves, he gives April a nudge in the ribs and a quick "Take care of yourself, kid. If I ever get up this way again, I'll give you a call."

Within fifteen minutes, Blair leaves for work. "The bar closes at two. I'll be home around two-thirty. We'll do some catching up in the morning."

April roams the five-room house. Two crowded bedrooms. A tiny kitchen. Greasy dishwater stands in the sink. The bathroom is neat enough, but it smells of mildew. April gets out her gloves and Top Job and goes to work.

April sighed deeply and rolled onto her side. Drawing her knees up and wrapping her arms around them, she regretted her fantasy and willed herself not to indulge in it again.

For now, it was the worst-case scenario. That was an expression April had heard the politicians use on television, and she understood it all the way to the marrow of her bones. For years she had practiced it. Prepare for the worst and you won't be caught off guard. Expect that things will go wrong, and you won't be disappointed when they do. Don't get excited about anything that's going right because it won't last long. If things start going right, mess them up before some-body else does.

"For the next few hours," April decided, "that woman is just a waitress named Blair who works in a bar. I won't even think of her as my mother. If she doesn't want me back, that's fine. I'll take all the money I need from Lenny's wallet after he goes to sleep. Before he wakes up, I'll leave for the bus station, and I'm off to Virginia Beach. If Becky's mom won't let me stay, or if Lenny tries to make me come back to live in El Paso, I'll dye my hair, burn my clothes, change my name and run away to California. Lots of kids do that when they've got no place else to go."

16

The regulars who hung out on the vacant lot behind the convenience store had tagged him "Easy Buck" a year or so ago, and shortened it to "Buck" somewhere along the line. A nickname carried a dual significance with that homeless, hopeless huddle of men warming themselves around the flames in a trash drum. A nickname was a sort of initiation rite. It meant a man wasn't alone on the streets of south Dallas anymore. He had a family of sorts. And he had a home: this vacant lot with its wobbly aluminum chairs, its table made from a sheet of plywood balanced on stacks of bricks, and the back seat of an old Ford for a sofa.

A nickname also meant the men liked you well enough to razz you a little. "Easy Buck. He'd give a brother the last buck he had to his name. But look out, stranger. Buck will open a door for you with one hand and pick your pocket with the other."

Tonight Buck was pulling down an easy fifty bucks. The job was a referral from Sticks over at the pool hall. All Buck had to do was wander over to Kiest about nine tonight and hand over an envelope to some white woman waiting by the pay phone.

At first he had started to tell the skinny white dude in the pea coat—Lenny, he called himself—where he could stick his "five now and forty-five by midnight." But after hearing him out, Buck had decided what the hell? It sounded like easy money, and he could use some easy money.

Leaving the warmth of the oil drum for his twenty-minute trek to the Texaco station on Kiest, Buck grumbled to himself about the flesh-biting cold. His breath came out in puffy clouds from his mouth and nose. The overcoat the priest at the church had given him flapped around his boots. A dark blue stocking cap covered his head, and he had wrapped a drab wool scarf around his neck, pulled up in the back to block the wind.

Stubby black fingers poked through holes in Buck's frayed gloves. He felt inside his pocket for the envelope Lenny had given him. "She'll be there at nine waiting for my call. Don't just walk right up to her. Be cool, know what I mean?"

"Outta my face, man," Buck had growled. "I know how to do a number on a cop what might be watchin'." The poor sucker's face had faded from white to whiter.

Snow on ice-crusted streets kept everybody at home except cops and fools. The interstate was just two blocks away, but the whizzing and honking was strangely absent.

Kiest was the next block ahead. In the glow of street lamps on the snow, Buck picked his way along the icy sidewalk, hugging the row of buildings. Turning east, he spotted the Texaco star.

When he was almost there, he surveyed the area with street-wise eyes. The only souls to be seen were the young kid working inside the pay booth and a woman sitting in a sedan with the window rolled down no more than an inch. "There she is—just like Lenny said she'd be," Buck said to himself. "So far, so good."

He walked slowly alongside the red brick building. The sedan was a good twenty-five feet away. Chances were the kid in the booth would see him talking to the woman, but he would assume Buck was hitting her up for some coins. So would any cop that might be watching.

124

The car was a late model, but it was as dirty as the heap Buck sometimes slept in at the salvage yard. Slush was splashed all the way up to the windows. From a few yards away, Buck noticed that the rear tires had snow chains on them. "This car's been on the road a while," Buck decided, walking around the rear toward the pay phones.

It was then she noticed him. Slowly the ice-crusted window crawled up. The woman inside looked straight ahead. It was kind of pitiful the way she pretended not to see him there, four feet from her car.

"Hey, lady." Buck rapped the window with his gloved fist. "Spare a coupla bucks?" She looked straight ahead, her eyes fixed like a drug-dazed junky. He knocked on the window again, this time harder. "I asked you a question. Could ya help a guy out?"

The woman looked like she was paralyzed, like some invisible force was pinning her to the car seat. Lenny had said she was expecting a call at the pay phone, not a note. Her mind must be racing like a bandit, Buck figured. *What will I do if the phone rings? I don't dare open the door*. Buck laughed inside, then smiled broadly when the woman spilled the contents of her purse on the car seat and snatched a bill from her wallet. The window inched down, just far enough for her to slip the bill through it. When Buck's fingers brushed against hers, the woman flinched. Then the window crawled back up and the woman stared straight ahead again—as if she could make him leave by ignoring him.

Enjoying the game now, Buck waited, smiling. Seconds later, the desperate woman cracked the window again and spoke. "Will you please go now? I need to make a phone call." Her voice tapered off at the end of her sentence. Then she pleaded, "I gave you what you needed."

"Yeah, sister, you did," Buck said in a voice not at all menacing. This woman wanted to scream so bad she was about to blow out her teeth. "Lenny ain't gonna call you at this phone tonight. He said to give you this." Buck thumped the envelope through the crack. It fell onto the woman's lap, but she just stared at it. "You can fire up that engine and turn on the heater while you read that. That phone ain't gonna ring."

17

Blair held her breath while she watched the frightful man retreat into the shadows. Even when he was out of sight, his face loomed in her mind. Was Lenny anything like that?

For nearly a minute after he left, Blair stared numbly at the envelope that still lay in her lap where it had fallen. Then, with trembling fingers, she ripped off the end and removed a piece of notepaper. A small key was taped to the upper right corner. The writing was cramped and difficult to read in the dim light of her car. Needing to hear the sound of her own voice, she read aloud. "Hope you know how to get to Prestonwood Mall. You got till ten to get there and find the skating rink and lockers. Use this key to lock the money in locker seven. Then wait at the table closest to the big Christmas tree. Put the letters and the key on the table so I can see them. Then wait till something happens. Just a little word of warning. The man that just gave you this note knows what to do with April if things don't go just right while I'm gone. And he ain't near as nice a guy as he looks. Your friend. Lenny."

Blair shivered and groaned loudly. "Brandi. That dirty, pathetic man. How horrified you must be." She started the engine and put the car in gear. Her legs were trembling so badly that she could hardly press down the accelerator. Clenching the wheel, she drove off the parking lot and onto the slick street.

The side roads between the gas station and the interstate were sheets of glazed ice. Blair drove with intense concentration, grateful that she'd thought to have chains installed on the rear wheels before leaving Austin. After anxious minutes, she was on a well-sanded interstate highway and able to pick up speed.

Half an hour after she had left the Texaco station, Blair entered the sprawling acres of parking around Prestonwood Mall. She had no idea where the skating rink was. She would park outside Neiman-Marcus and ask directions the minute she got inside. It was fifteen minutes before ten.

Neiman's was ablaze with lights and color and swarming with shoppers despite the late hour and forbidding weather. A teenage boy, the picture of boredom as he tagged along with his parents, directed her to the skating rink.

The satchel of money slapped against her leg with each step. In minutes Blair found herself standing next to a huge twinkling Christmas tree near the skating rink. A busy attendant pointed her toward the lockers.

She walked around the end of a partition and into a narrow area walled on both sides with lockers and divided down the middle with wooden benches. A group of giggling girls stuffed skates into bags and fluffed hair in front of mirrors while their dates waited nearby.

Locker seven was mercifully close. She inserted the key, turned it and pulled back the narrow metal door. On end, the satchel fit easily in the space. Quickly she locked the door, glanced nervously around her and let out a protracted sigh of relief. Three minutes before ten.

The table nearest the tree was occupied, so she chose one next to it. From her purse, she removed the two letters and lay them on the sticky table. Not wanting to think about the lies she had written in the letter to April, she put the letter to Brandi on top, then finally the locker key.

128

Blair kept nervous eyes on the young skaters and the teenagers at nearby tables, feeling as conspicuous as a mink coat at a rodeo. The waiting was agony, especially since she didn't know what she was waiting for.

"Ma'am."

Blair jerked around to find a pimple-faced boy standing beside her, his expression as startled as hers. "You're supposed to . . .uh . . .put the . . .the key in here." He slipped her a manila envelope. "And the . . .uh . . .letters." She did as he said. "Now you're supposed to go home. Your friend will call you." The boy sprinted away like an Olympic athlete.

Blair tried to get up but her legs refused to support her. A harrowing headache came out of nowhere, just as the boy had. She was suddenly fatigued, drained of all emotion but one—the sickening fear that Lenny was more than a kidnapper and an extortionist, that he was a low-life liar with no intention of returning Brandi.

That fear walked with Blair across the parking lot and rode with her in the car like an unwelcome companion. By the time she reached the outskirts of Dallas, she was talking to it, arguing with it. "Lenny won't let anything happen to Brandi. He and his wife raised her as their child. He must care a little. Besides he wants the rest of the money, not a thirteen-year-old girl to raise." The logic of her argument calmed her, and Blair breathed more freely, felt the muscles in her chest relax just a little.

"Everything went fine tonight. Lenny has the money. He knows now that I didn't and won't tell the police. I followed his orders precisely. He knows he can trust me." And she had to believe she could trust him or she would go out of her mind between now and the time she got Brandi home again.

Two hours later, with the interstate beginning to clear, Blair pulled into a truck stop in Waco. A short, stocky man whose jacket patch read "Chubby" trotted to her car. She lowered the window and asked if he knew anything about the road conditions south of here.

"All clear. Been listening to the weather reports all

129

evening." Chubby turned up his collar and hunched down in his coat. "There might be a few icy patches on bridges and overpasses, but other than that, it's okay."

"Then could I get you to take off my tire chains?"

"You betcha." Chubby opened the car door. "Want me to put them in your trunk?"

"Please." Blair handed Chubby her car keys and said, "How's the coffee in there?" She nodded toward a cafe across the parking lot.

"Good. Real good." When Chubby grinned, his eyes almost disappeared. "Even better with a fresh doughnut. Tell Mabel I said to give you a chocolate one."

"Sounds good." And it really did. Blair remembered that she had eaten almost nothing all day.

Mabel's coffee was definitely for truckers. Too strong and tongue-scalding hot. But her doughnuts could have sold in a ritzy French bakery. Blair took Chubby's advice and ordered a chocolate doughnut with chocolate icing. She polished it off on the way across the parking lot. Chubby was finished with the tire chains. He refused payment, but Blair pressed a bill in his hand anyway and took to the interstate again.

By now Lenny had removed the money from the locker. Had he gone there himself? Probably. He wouldn't have trusted that to the boy who had taken the key and the letters. Brandi. Was she with Lenny now? Please. She couldn't still be with that awful-looking man from the gas station.

Tired of thinking and worrying and wondering, Blair turned on the radio. It was tuned to an Austin station. The reception wasn't good, but she left it there. The broadcast faded in and out at times, finally clearing when she was halfway home.

"This is KLBJ-AM, Austin," reminded the station announcer at a break in the broadcast. "Tune in at the top of the hour for a statewide weather forecast and an update from KLBJ's Donna Dillon, live at St. Mary's Hospital."

"St. Mary's." Blair leaned forward and turned up the volume. As the talk show resumed, Blair's mind clicked off possibilities of what could be happening at the hospital. A fire? A power failure? A hostage situation? More speculations whizzed through her mind. Blair had just thought about Liz and little Clay when the report began.

"Live outside St. Mary's Hospital, I'm Donna Dillon. It was a somber assistant police chief Ken Wilson who spoke with reporters outside St. Mary's Hospital just minutes ago. He confirmed rumors that a baby has disappeared from the hospital nursery. The baby, whose identity is being withheld pending notification of the parents, was reported missing shortly after eleven o'clock this evening. The hospital's director of security ordered the building sealed off. Hospital Administrator Margaret Billings was then notified. The Austin Police Department was called in at approximately eleven-thirty to assist with the search. According to Chief Wilson, the child was not found after an exhaustive search of the hospital, and an investigation is underway. Authorities fear the infant was abducted but refuse to speculate on possible motives. Again, an unidentified infant has disappeared from the nursery at Austin's St. Mary's Hospital. This is Donna Dillon, reporting live . . ."

Blair eased down the volume but left the radio on. A bitter rush of remembrance sent a chill through her. "Those poor parents." She turned up the heater and visualized her godson cradled securely in Liz's arms. She held the image there for a long moment, but then it faded and was replaced by a gathering image of tiny little Tiffany. The image lingered. "Not Tiffany. Not Clay." she whispered. "Some other poor child."

18

Frank Traxill's rugged face was set firmly in deep thought. In his long years on the force, he had investigated nearly every type of crime, but few in recent memory had received as much press as this one would. His expression tightened into a frown. In a few hours, reporters would be crawling on him like fire ants, swarming toward premature conclusions, chewing on him for information that wasn't available.

He was waiting for Margaret Billings, the administrator at St. Mary's, to return to her office. She had excused herself to confer with the hospital's head of security. Nervously, Frank picked up a globe-shaped paperweight from her desk. In the center of the fine crystal were tiny figures, a woman and her child, delicately carved and painted. Hand in hand, they stood next to a Christmas tree, decorated with bells and balls no larger than pin heads. It was a beautiful thing, and obviously expensive. Frank shook the globe lightly and set it back on the desk. He was watching the snow swirl gently around the tiny figures when he heard a voice in the hallway.

Frank turned when the door opened behind him. Margaret Billings, her face grim and white against her jet black hair, moved across her conservatively furnished office. Stiff, brittle, she seemed to be struggling desperately for control.

132

She pulled back her desk chair and sat down. "Our director of security, Howard Jackson, is waiting at the front entrance for the parents," she explained. "He will escort them to my office and then stay while we tell them what has happened." Her clear blue eyes, deeply set behind thick wire rim glasses, fixed a penetrating gaze on the paperweight. "I cannot believe this has happened. Not here." Her eyes closed. "But most certainly it has."

Knowing that reassurances would be wasted, Frank merely nodded his head, taking a seat and glancing at his watch at the same time. Eleven fifty-eight. The parents would be here any minute. He tightened the knot in his tie, and gulped the last of his coffee. It wouldn't look right for him to be drinking coffee when they got here. High on Frank's agenda was gaining the absolute confidence of the couple who, any minute now, would walk into this office and have their lives explode.

"Sergeant Traxill, it goes without saying that we will cooperate in every way. Mr. Jackson's regular duties will be reassigned so that he can devote his full attention to whatever you might..." The door opened. Margaret Billings and Frank Traxill rose in unison. "Please come in, Mr. and Mrs. Lakeman."

Frank watched Myles Lakeman press his hand against the small of his wife's back. When she didn't move, he put his arm around her waist and gently pulled her toward the chairs in front of Margaret Billings's desk. "Why did you call us here in the middle of the night? What's going on?"

Frank and Margaret Billings exchanged glances. Frank knew how she must be feeling right now—as if she had been ordered to slap these two unsuspecting people across the face. Seconds later, she took a deep breath and swung.

"This is Sergeant Traxill. He's a police detective. I called him to St. Mary's to assist us with a crisis that occurred this evening." A look, compassionate and troubled, deepened the lines in her face. "The crisis involves your child." She swallowed hard. "Just after eleven, the head nurse on the night shift reported Tiffany missing from the nursery, and we have been unable to locate her."

Color drained from Charmaine Lakeman's face. She cupped one hand over her mouth—as if to stifle the scream that had formed there. But it clawed its way out and shattered the air in Margaret Billings's office.

Frank's eyes shifted to Myles Lakeman, expecting him to throw his arms around his beautiful wife. But Lakeman sat rigid and detached in the green leather chair. Right hand on right thigh. Left hand on left thigh. Face totally blank.

The look was not unfamiliar to Frank. He had seen it many times before. A man or a woman at one moment was body and soul, whole and integrated. Then in a flicker of time, after a blow like this, it was as though the soul split off, found a solitary place above it all and stayed there until it was safe to return. Meanwhile the body was nothing more than a statue, unable to react or respond. A full minute passed before Myles Lakeman's soul fluttered from wherever it had been and breathed life back into his body.

"What's being done?" His voice was flat, emotionless.

"The hospital was sealed off immediately, inside and out," Mrs. Billings explained. "Anyone leaving is being searched. The only entrance in use is the emergency room. Every inch of the building and grounds is being searched."

"How did this happen?"

Frank studied Lakeman's eyes. They were hard, unblinking. His lips had narrowed to two slashes. Muscles in his jaws twitched.

"We simply don't know yet how it happened," Margaret Billings answered. "Sergeant Traxill and Mr. Jackson are in charge of the investigation and the search."

Charmaine Lakeman's blue eyes were fixed on a spot to the right of Margaret Billings's head. She twirled a wide gold band around her ring finger. Frank wondered if she heard anything that was being said. When she finally interrupted her husband in the middle of a question, Frank knew that Charmaine Lakeman was up to the collar of her

134

fancy coat in denial.

"This is ridiculous. Tiffany's not missing." Her voice was light and trivial. "I'm sure one of the nurses was just walking her up and down the hall. Tiffany was probably fussing. I've given strict instructions that she's not to cry for over fifteen seconds without someone comforting her." With that she stood. Folds of mink slipped from her lap. "Come on, darling. She's probably back in the nursery by now."

Margaret Billings rose and walked around her desk, trailing her fingers along the edge, pausing when they touched the paperweight. "I wish that were the case, Mrs. Lakeman."

"But that is the case," Charmaine insisted sweetly. "Right now Tiffany's in her crib, sound asleep." She turned to Myles, pleading with her eyes. "Come with me. You'll see." When she spoke again, fingers of fear had tightened around her vocal cords. Her voice was strained. "Myles, it's true. She's fine." Her final sentence was a shout. "Tiffany is not missing." Charmaine whirled around, her coat fanning out behind her. Before anyone could move, she was at the door, grabbing Howard Jackson's arm and ordering him out of her way.

"Charmaine, stop," Myles barked. The burst of energy propelled him from his chair. "She's not there. And you won't go screaming down the halls of this hospital looking for her."

The cold harshness of Myles Lakeman's voice startled Frank. He had learned to anticipate all sorts of reactions in situations like these, but Myles Lakeman surprised him. Frank had figured him to be a caring kind of fellow, a rock for his much younger and more fragile wife. So much for first impressions.

The tension in the room was almost tangible. Margaret Billings turned anxiously to Frank. "Sergeant Traxill, please."

Frank stepped to a point halfway between Myles and Charmaine Lakeman. His tone was comforting but commanding, and it drew their attention. "Mrs. Lakeman, I don't have children, so I can't even imagine the horror you're feeling right now. But I want you to know we're doing everything possible to find Tiffany." Frank extended his hand to Myles Lakeman, inviting him to stand closer to his wife. "Mr. Lakeman, I think it would be wise to walk to the nursery. Your wife needs to see that Tiffany is not there." Frank eased Charmaine away from the door. "Mr. Jackson, go clear the detectives out of the nursery, please."

What happened next was so sudden, so unexpected, that even Frank, a cop studied in quick reactions, barely had time to get out of the way. With his right hand, Myles Lakeman grabbed the paperweight on Margaret Billings's desk like a baseball. Then he raised it shoulder high and hurled the heavy object across the office. "No!" he boomed. "Not again!" A midair collision with a reading lamp hanging above a chair sent glass flying. A battered lamp shade fell like a wounded bird. Splinters of glass exploded onto the cushion. The room was silent and much too dark.

Frank rang the doorbell at the Lakeman's modest home on Exposition Boulevard. Single level. Native white stone. It was situated toward the back of a tree-covered lot, a serene, quiet setting.

Myles Lakeman opened the door and invited Frank into a family room at the back of the house. A heavy shadow of stubble darkened Lakeman's face. His lids were puffy and he wore the same brown corduroy pants and plaid sweater he had worn to the hospital. His clothes looked as if they had been slept in—maybe on the couch or in the burgundy leather recliner near the fireplace.

"Mr. Lakeman."

"Just Myles is fine."

"Myles, I wish I had more to tell you than I do, but sometimes this kind of investigation moves slowly." When Myles sat on the hearth in front of the cold fireplace, Frank lowered his tall frame into a wide armchair near him. "This is what we know: Tiffany was in the nursery at ten forty-five. A nurse gave her her medication and recorded it on her chart. We know Tiffany was not there at eleven ten. I was told by the head nurse that they were unusually busy last night. Several births. Babies in and out for feedings. Two transfers to the neonatal unit from other towns. All that activity made it real easy for someone to slip in and out without drawing attention—especially during a shift change. That occurred at eleven."

"So that means that whoever took my daughter had ten minutes—maybe more—to get out of the building and off the grounds."

"That's the way we see it." Frank leaned forward and put his forearms on his knees. "My investigators are still interviewing personnel—did they notice anyone, anything peculiar, that sort of thing. Mrs. Billings is giving us a list of parents who've lost . . . who've had children die at St. Mary's recently. Grief can make people do some bizarre things."

"I know." Myles ran the fingers of both hands through his thin hair, ending by massaging the muscles in his neck. "I spent the night in this recliner, feeling as if something crawled into my stomach and died. I keep hoping for a ransom demand."

"What will you do if you get one?"

"I'll handle it myself," Myles snapped. "If I can't trust a hospital to protect my child, why in hell would I trust a bunch of cops to help me get her back?"

His question gave Frank a perfect opening. "Myles, do you have any idea who might want to take Tiffany, assuming it wasn't a random abduction?"

Myles shook his head. "I spent half the night racking my brain, trying to think of someone who hates me that much, or has it in for me. But I came up blank. And Charmaine doesn't have any enemies."

Something was stirring in the back of Myles's mind, like a dark curtain parting on painful memories. Frank sat quietly, waiting for him to speak.

"It's just like before," Myles finally said. "One second she's there and the next second she's gone."

After Charmaine and Myles had left the hospital in the early hours of the morning, Margaret Billings had told Frank about the disappearance of Myles's child from a previous marriage. She had called it a cruel coincidence. Frank acknowledged that coincidences occurred, cruel and otherwise, but to have two children vanish into thin air was just too bizarre to be believed. Yet how could it be anything but a cruel coincidence? How could there be a connection? The events had occurred eleven years apart. The children had different mothers. One was a toddler who had disappeared from the Lakemans' back yard. The other, an infant who had disappeared from a hospital. The only similarities Frank could see were that they were both girls, no ransom demand was made—not yet anyway—and they both had the same father. "Myles, Mrs. Billings told me what happened to your first child. I know it's highly unlikely, but do you think . . . can you see any possible connection . . ."

'No. How could I? I still don't know what heartless scum took Brandi." Myles flung both hands in the air. "I'll never know. I don't know if she's dead or alive. So how could I speculate about a connection between her disappearance and Tiffany's?"

"You're right. Of course you couldn't." Frank rose, sensing that nothing more would be gained by prolonging this discussion. "I'll be in touch. Remember, it's only been eleven hours. Don't give up hope. It doesn't have to be like last time. Children are recovered, Myles."

19

April dried her body with the thickest white towel she had ever touched. It smelled of fabric softener and a hint of chlorine bleach, just like the linens on her comfortable queen- sized bed.

After his meeting with Blair Saturday night, Lenny had come storming into their room in that gross motel in Oak Cliff, grabbed his clothes and started jamming them into his bag. And he had ordered April to do the same. Was someone after him? The cops maybe?

"Get your duds together. Pronto." His voice had risen to an eager shout. "We're outta this dump, kid." April had never seen Lenny so excited. He had thrown both arms up in the air, his fists balled in a victory gesture.

"Where are we going?" April had asked, gathering the few items that weren't already neatly folded in her bag or in her backpack.

"We're gonna find out how the other half lives."

Lenny had paid cash for two adjoining rooms at the Holiday Inn. She figured he had pulled off a drug deal that night after meeting Blair. How else could he have gotten the money?

April's heart fluttered. Blair. She almost wanted to risk

139

calling her *Mother* now. Blair had told Lenny that she wanted April back, but that there was one problem in the way: her boyfriend. They were living together, and he wasn't that crazy about kids. "It might take Blair a little while to convince him," Lenny had said, standing in the door between their rooms that night. "Meanwhile we just cool our heels here in this luxury hotel. Have a little taste of the good life."

And the good life it was. April sighed with satisfaction as she dried her hair with a blow dryer built right into the wall of her own bathroom. No Lenny to clutter the room or contaminate things. No need to worry about clean linens—housekeeping came every morning to change them. No drunks lurking behind the convenience store like nightmares in broad daylight. There was only one thing she missed: Father Ochoa. She hadn't had time to say goodbye to him. She would miss his wonderful stories and their long talks. Maybe she would call him and tell him the news about Blair. She needed to talk to someone about everything that was going on.

April turned off the dryer and returned it to its gray plastic holder on the wall. With a tissue, she wiped strands of hair from the sink and the counter top. She was glad it was her own hair and not Lenny's. There was one problem, though, about having a room of her own. Going through Lenny's wallet at night would be more difficult now. But she would manage somehow. She had to. She still needed over fifty dollars for her bus fare—just in case Blair's boyfriend said, "Tell that kid of yours to take a hike."

As soon as she had a chance, she would search the pockets of Lenny's pea coat, the one Father Ochoa had given him from the clothes closet. She had seen Lenny stuff some bills in his pocket a couple of times. If he happened to remember doing it and found the money missing, he would probably think it had fallen out somewhere.

A sharp rap on the bathroom door. "April, get your skinny body out here. I need to talk to ya."

"Just a minute." April hurriedly tucked the tail of her

140

white shirt into her jeans and pulled a sweater over her head. She had to hurry. She didn't want to give Lenny time to sit on her bed or touch her things. What was left of her Diet Coke breakfast would have to be poured out. Lenny was probably drinking from it right now.

April stepped out of the bathroom and immediately looked at her bed. The mauve bedspread was perfectly smooth, just the way the maid had left it. But Lenny was standing within touching distance of the Coke can on the dresser.

He turned and caught April's stare. "Why are you always watching me with those hawk-eyes of yours?" Lenny leaned against the dresser. "You act like I'm a dog sniffing for a place to lift my leg, and you gotta be ready to shout 'No'." He lit a cigarette. "Maybe I oughta offer to pay your mama to take you off my hands. Might speed up the process."

April swallowed hard. "When is she going to make up her mind?"

"Hard to say." Lenny plucked his wallet from his back pocket. "Listen...I gotta go to El Paso this afternoon. Business trip. Be gone two, maybe three days. I don't think the Buick will make it, so I'm gonna fly. You can leave the room some, but you need to be here most of the time in case Blair calls." He tossed a bill on the dresser. "Here's twenty bucks. That oughta keep you supplied with that junk." He thumped the aluminum can and started toward the door. "See ya in a few days."

When Lenny was halfway out the door, April screwed up her courage and said, "Lenny, what does my mother look like?"

He tilted his head back and squinted his eyes, as if he were trying to spot something small on the ceiling. "Well, let me think. She looks sort of like that actress—Aww, what's her name? MacGraw. Yeah, Arlie MacGraw."

April nodded, not bothering to tell him the actress's name was *Ali*. She had seen Ali MacGraw in some late movie on television but she couldn't remember what she looked like.

"Blair's a nice old gal," Lenny said casually. "I kinda like

141

her." April thought his smile looked peculiar when he added, "She's sure been nice to me."

April left the twenty on the dresser and picked up the Diet Coke can with two fingers. "Want the rest of this?"

"Hell, no. Tastes like dirt."

When he left, Lenny closed the door between their rooms and locked it. April plucked tissues from a box on the dresser and used them to protect her fingers when she picked up the twenty dollar bill. While she sprayed the bill with Lysol, she wondered why Lenny had locked the door between their rooms. Was there something in there he didn't want her to see?

Blair woke before dawn Monday morning, conscious of a dull throb of worry. She rolled onto her side and buried her face in the warmth of her pillow. How much time did she have to raise the remaining money? *Soon after that*. What did Lenny mean by that?

The focus of her worry shifted slowly to the letters she had written and turned over to Lenny. What if Brandi stumbled onto them? What would she do? What would she think? Would she realize that her name was really Brandi and not April? That the letter to April was all lies?

"Stop it." she muttered. "He won't let her see them. The letters are leverage over me, not her." Lifting her head, Blair yawned and blinked at the daylight coming through her window. It hurt her eyes. "I thought things were supposed to look better in the light of morning," she grumbled, closing her eyes and dropping back onto the pillow.

Well, at least she knew for certain that Lenny had the money. There had been a message on her machine when she arrived home from Dallas early Sunday morning.

"Hey girl. You ain't home yet? I sure 'preciated the gift. I hope I can get yours to you before Christmas. Be talkin' to ya. Bye."

Blair had called Liz just after eight o'clock Sunday

142

morning. "How's my godson?"

"Safe and sound. Thank God." Liz's tone was almost desperate. "I guess you know what happened here last night?"

"I heard. Have they found the baby yet?"

"No." Liz had paused for a long moment. "Apparently you don't know whose baby it is."

"No. The radio report didn't mention any names."

"Blair, brace yourself. It's Tiffany."

Had she not been lying in bed at the time, Blair would have collapsed. The sheer force of the words had made her head spin. Dizzy and exhausted from the long drive and the long night, she had lain there and cried.

The remainder of the day had gone by in a blur of fear and worry. If she wasn't worrying about Brandi, she was agonizing over little Tiffany. How could it be? Why Tiffany? Poor Charmaine. She must be dying. And Myles. It seemed impossible, incomprehensible that he was going through the same hell again. What a ghastly, horrendous coincidence. How would he survive until Tiffany was found? And she would be found. She had to be.

Celtic jumped onto the bed and curled up in the bend of Blair's knees. His warmth made the prospect of getting out of bed this morning even more unappealing. She had promised Bill Elrod she would be at the house when he brought Liz and Clay home today at noon. Facing Liz today would be the endurance test of all times. How could she gush and rave over little Clay when thoughts of Brandi and Tiffany were eating away at her?

Liz had been too distracted yesterday to react to the Dallas shopping trip story Blair had offered on the phone. What she wouldn't give to tell Liz the real reason for the trip. More than anything, Blair needed to hear Liz say she had done the right thing.

If only she could pull the covers over her head, burrow deep in them and sleep until Christmas. But that was a luxury she couldn't afford. There was the funeral home to run and money to raise and questions to avoid.

She dressed and drove to work.

A death call had come in while she was on her way to the funeral home. Greg had gone to Seton Medical Center to remove the body. Since he and Kent were both scheduled to direct services that morning, Blair would have to embalm. But first she would try to reach Hal Bishop.

His secretary said he wasn't in yet. "I expect him shortly, Ms. Emerson. Can I have him call you at the—the—"

People never quite knew whether to say *the office*, *the store*, *the shop*. "At the funeral home, please."

An hour later, Blair stood over the body of a man named Willie Frye. He was eighty-seven and looked sixty. After bathing him with disinfectant soap, Blair dabbed shaving cream on his square chin and hollow cheeks. Too much coffee, too much worry and too little sleep had Blair's nerves at full stretch. The razor, the needle injector and scalpel, and finally the aneurysm needles trembled in her unsteady hands. She spent an unusually long time trying to locate the carotid artery. When she finally hooked the aneurysm needle beneath it, her hands were shaking so badly, it slipped and sank out of sight again. On the second attempt she was more careful.

After awkward efforts to raise the jugular vein, Blair inserted tubes in both vessels and turned on the embalming machine. Its peculiar whirring caught her attention. She looked over her shoulder and found the tank empty. She had forgotten to fill it.

"Get yourself together, Blair," she moaned.

If leaving the process to Kent or Greg wouldn't raise suspicions from an already concerned Jane, Blair would have conceded defeat. A process that normally took an hour required almost two. Blair's back ached, her head pounded and she was miserably nauseous. She hoped Liz didn't ask her to whip up lunch for them both.

She was draping a sheet over Mr. Frye's body when Jane's voice floated from the intercom. "Mr. Bishop is on the phone.

He asked to hold. Is it convenient to speak to him?"

"Tell him I'll be right with him." Blair peeled off her gloves and tossed them in the trash. The other protective clothing followed. She washed up quickly and hurried to her office.

By the end of the phone call, she sounded as disappointed as she felt. She had nearly forty-seven thousand dollars coming, Hal told her, but he could not say for sure when the bonds would sell. "It shouldn't take more than a few days, Blair," he promised. "Bear with me, just bear with me."

She thanked Hal, fighting back an impulse to scream that she'd already taken more than she could bear.

Clay Elrod was as beautiful as his mother. In the nursery, all blue and white, Blair leaned over his crib. "Liz, he's perfect. Look at that nose. Those lips. Can you believe he's finally here?"

"My labor was so short and easy, it is kind of hard to believe." Liz tucked the soft blue blanket around her son's feet. "I find myself needing to touch him every few minutes. I climbed the walls at the hospital, frantic to get him out of the nursery and safely home. They still haven't found Tiffany, have they?"

"No. I heard a report on the way over here. Some detective said they're following leads, for what that's worth."

"Let's let him sleep now," Liz said, stroking Clay's back. "I'm a little tired, too."

In the master bedroom, Liz crawled between fresh sheets. Blair curled up on a chaise in the corner. "Poor Myles. It's so pathetic, Liz."

"First Brandi. Now Tiffany. It makes you wonder if there's a connection. Someone who has it in for Myles. I know it sounds ridiculous. Have you talked to him?"

Blair raised a cup of tea to her lips. "What could I say?" Any number of things could be said, but none would help coming from her.

"Oh, Blair. I keep thinking that if this was just a random

145

kidnapping, it could have . . .it could have been Clay."

Blair watched Liz inch down in the bed, deep in thought. She suspected Liz was lying there condemning herself for being thankful that it had been some other child who had disappeared. Blair understood. She knew something about wishing that if tragedies had to happen, they would happen to someone else.

As Liz drifted in and out of sleep, Blair's thoughts returned to the image of the transient's face inches from hers, to the note he had slid through the window, to the key, the locker, the pimple-faced kid. Had Lenny been watching from across the skating rink, gloating while she stuffed the letters and the key into the envelope?

The late afternoon drifted by. Blair managed to avoid discussing her trip to Dallas. Still, she left Liz's house feeling even more anxious than when she had arrived.

As she so often did when she was at home these past days, Blair reached beneath her favorite chair in the den and pulled out the shoe box. The shovel. The swim suit. To her they were like the letters she had given to Lenny. They were guarantees, assurances that Lenny actually had Brandi, that he would return her as soon as he had the money.

20

Tuesday was wasted. With no funerals, no death calls, no families making arrangements, Blair worried away eight hours. Now, as she drove to the Hyatt Hotel to meet Eldon for dinner, she still fretted anxiously.

Blair turned up the radio volume to hear a news broadcast. The lead story was a live report from St. Mary's. "Sergeant Frank Traxill, heading up the investigation of the disappearance of little Tiffany Lakeman from St. Mary's Hospital, announced moments ago that new information has surfaced. According to Traxill, an orderly on duty at the hospital Saturday night recalls seeing a woman near the nursery shortly after eleven o'clock. It is known that the infant was abducted between ten forty-five and eleven-ten. The orderly recalls that the woman was carrying a multi-colored straw bag and seemed in a hurry to get to the exit. Sergeant Traxill further reports that a composite is being put together at this time. When the drawing is complete, it will be made public. Anyone recognizing the woman, or anyone having seen a woman carrying a multi-colored straw bag in or near St. Mary's Hospital in recent days, is asked to contact the Austin Police Department immediately."

Blair turned down the volume and pulled to a stop in the

hotel parking lot. She found Eldon sipping coffee and drumming thick fingers on the tabletop. Gray hair. Thin, wrinkled face, dotted with rust-colored spots. A blue-gray suit and the red Countess Mara tie Blair had given him for Father's Day. "The hostess said I'd find you here." Blair hugged Eldon firmly. "It's so good to see you."

Actually, Blair had no appetite for food and had wondered all afternoon why Eldon had called. They often met for lunch to discuss her mother's health and financial matters, but rarely for dinner. Eldon usually was at home in the evenings, well before the nurse left. Tonight his grandson Kenny was standing in for him.

The waitress appeared. Blair hid her fidgety hands in her lap while Eldon ordered hot tea for her and more coffee for himself. After the waitress left, they discussed Maryruth for several minutes. Blair was embarrassed by her inability to focus, to ask caring questions. But her mind worked only in short, uncertain spurts. Eldon would have to be comatose not to notice that something was wrong.

He chatted about the goings-on in Liveoak. "Everybody's getting ready for the holidays. Lights are going up all over town."

When the waitress returned with their drinks, Eldon ordered for them both. The mere thought of biting into a chicken fajita constricted Blair's throat, but she smiled approval nonetheless and nervously sipped her tea.

"After your mother and I finished breakfast this morning, I ran over to the funeral home to pay my respects to Laird Dobbs. Mr. Snelling sure is doing a good job running that place for you." Eldon rained sugar into his coffee and began to stir. "He said he checks in with you every day or so."

"Oh, yes. He keeps me well on top of things. I don't know what I'll do when Mr. Snelling retires."

Eldon blew gently on his coffee, then smiled. "Ran into Paul Dillard at the cafe today. He told me to ask you a question the next time I saw you."

"Oh?" Paul Dillard was a deputy sheriff, an old friend and

148

a long-time verbal sparring partner.

"He said to ask you if you'd marry him."

"Marry him, huh?" Blair smiled, beginning to relax a bit. "And what tender, heartfelt reason did he give for asking?"

"He said he figured that since you're a funeral director, you'd make a loyal, trustworthy wife."

"I know I'll regret asking, but how does he figure that?"

"He said you'd be the last woman in the world to . . ."

" . . .to *let him down*." Blair chuckled. "Tell Paul I said that line is older than dirt." Eldon's easy laughter was like a balm for her spirits. "And you can also tell him that he's wasting his time asking Marla Whetstone to go out with him. She's far too intelligent for him. She told me that she wouldn't get in a car with Paul Dillard if he showed up at her house with an arrest warrant and handcuffs."

Eldon laughed harder. "I'll pass that on to him . . .and I'll do it when there's a passel of his buddies around."

The waitress returned with a large black tray. She took a sizzling platter of fajita meat from it and set it on the table. Then followed tortillas and the other fixings. The food smelled good. Blair was surprised to find herself feeling hungry. She thought she might actually be able to eat something.

Eldon spread a thin layer of sour cream on a tortilla, piled on meat and lettuce and tomatoes, then topped it all off with a generous spoonful of *pico de gallo* and jalapenos. "Ummm. This looks good." He folded the tortilla, raised it to his mouth and took a big bite.

As Blair assembled a much smaller fajita, she wondered why Eldon had suggested they have dinner together. Chit-chat and fajitas just didn't seem a good enough reason. "Eldon, everything's okay with Mom, isn't it? I mean, did you need to tell me something this evening?"

"Your mom's fine." Eldon's expression changed. He rested both elbows on the table and leaned toward Blair. "But there is something I need to ask you about."

Blair folded her tortilla over the fixings, but she didn't pick

149

it up. "What is it?"

"I got a very surprising phone call this morning, Blair. It was from Clark Brooks at the bank."

The words hung in the air between them. Clark Brooks was the loan officer she had spoken with at the bank. Why had he called Eldon? Surely he hadn't told him about the loan request.

"To tell you the truth, I didn't know quite what to make of what he told me."

Blair swallowed hard. She could feel the color draining from her face.

"He said you intended to put up your stock in the company for collateral on a rather large loan."

Every sound in the restaurant faded into the background. The loudest sound in the room was the pounding of Blair's heart. "Why did he call you?"

"He said I should know since I'm your mother's temporary guardian."

"He had no reason to involve mother." Her voice was sharp, defensive.

"Now I'm no expert at this sort of thing, Blair. But, according to what Brooks said, your stock has a restriction on it. The way he explained it to me, it can't be pledged or sold without the permission of the person who has a right of refusal on it. And that would be your mother."

Blair expelled the air she had compressed in her lungs. He was right. Of course. She had completely forgotten about the restrictions on the stock. In a detached motion, she ran the fingers of one hand through her hair and gripped a fistful in the back, squeezing it. *God, what do I do now?* She sat like that for a long moment, her head hanging forward. Then both hands collapsed to her lap.

Eldon reached beneath the table and put a large, rough hand over Blair's. "Honey, why you need that loan is none of my business, and I wouldn't think of prying into your affairs. But is everything all right? Do you need to talk about something?"

Thoughts were spinning wildly in Blair's head now. She couldn't snatch one from the blur and define it. "I can't talk about it, Eldon."

He nodded his head and squeezed her hand. "All right. But if you change your mind, you know you can trust me."

Tears burned in Blair's eyes. She fought them back fiercely. "I do trust you, Eldon, but this is something I can't tell you about. I just can't."

"I wish you could. Obviously you need money, and, knowing you as I do, it has to be for a really important reason." Eldon squeezed Blair's hand again, harder this time. "You're not sick are you, honey?"

Blair felt numb. The stock. She couldn't use it to get a loan without involving her mother. And she couldn't do that. What was she going to do now? How was she going to raise another eighty- five thousand dollars in a matter of days?

"Blair, you know I'll do anything in my power to help you. You're like a daughter to me."

She took in Eldon's worried, sympathetic look and said, "I need eighty-five thousand dollars, and I have to have it in the next few days."

The waitress had returned to the table. She pretended not to have overheard, but her expression said she had. "Is there anything else I can bring you?" When Eldon shook his head, she walked away without a word.

Blair looked away from the food and from Eldon's long, silent scrutiny.

"I'm sorry. I don't mean to upset you," Blair apologized. "I'm not sick. And I'm not in legal trouble. I just need the money, Eldon. And I can't tell you why."

"Then you'll have it. Your mother has more than that in the bank. Is there anything to stop us from withdrawing it?"

Blair shook her head. Inside she burned with guilt and worry. "Eldon, if there was any other way . . ."

"I know, Blair. And I know something else. If your father were alive, he'd be doing everything he could to help you with whatever this is. And if your mother was thinking clearly, she would too.''

"I'll put up my stock—all of it—as collateral. The dividends...they'll go to her until the loan's paid.'' Blair spoke rapidly, urgently. "We can see my lawyer tomorrow.''

"Blair, wait.'' Eldon gripped Blair's forearm and squeezed its tense muscles. "None of that's necessary. I know you'll pay her back. But, listen, I can't possibly go to the bank tomorrow. Will Thursday be soon enough?''

Blair pressed her fingertips to her lips, closed her eyes and nodded. "Yes.'' Tears spilled down her cheeks. She dabbed at them with her napkin. "Thank you, Eldon. I promise...''

"Shhh.'' He shook his head. "You don't have to promise me anything.''

The remaining fajita meat had stopped sizzling. A thin layer of grease was congealing on the metal platter. Eldon motioned for the waitress. His smile was friendly, his tone playful, when he said, "Do you think you could toss that chicken on the grill again. We got so busy talking, we forgot to eat.''

"No trouble, sir.'' She picked up the platter. "Be back in a jiffy.''

Blair took in a deep breath and released it slowly. They would go to the bank Thursday and transfer the money to her account. Any day now the bonds would sell. Then all she had to do was wait for Lenny's call. *Brandi, honey. Everything's going to be okay.* "Eldon.'' Her voice was steadier, the tears were gone. "I love you. And I'll explain all this soon. I promise.''

21

Frank Traxill took the chair Myles offered him at a round table in a breakfast nook. The room was meant to be cheerful. Lattice print wallpaper. Well-tended violets on a brass and glass teacart. A ceramic Cheshire cat sleeping on a cushion in the corner. The setting was a stark contrast to Myles's expression.

Frank accepted coffee from a thin, nervous maid and fiddled with the mug while Myles studied the drawing Frank had removed from the inside pocket of his jacket.

"I just got that an hour ago." Frank explained. "It's an x-ray technician's sketch of a woman he passed in the hospital parking lot Saturday night. It was a little after eleven." Frank paused while Myles held the paper in front of him. This was a complete color sketch, not just a drawing of the woman's face.

"Believe it or not, the technician drew that himself. Drawing and painting are his hobbies. He said what triggered his memory of her was the orderly's mention of the straw bag."

Frank raised the coffee mug and took a drink, watching the movement of Myles's eyes over the drawing. His face was blank. He focused on the straw bag the woman clutched to her chest.

"What's that?" Myles pointed to a splash of color on the side of the bag, just above the woman's coat sleeve.

"The technician's not sure. Said it was decoration of some sort. You've seen those bags made in Mexico. Sometimes they'll have a straw bird or maybe a flower on the side." Again Myles grew silent. His eyes inched down to the white pants legs showing beneath a drab coat.

"She was wearing a white uniform beneath her coat," Frank explained, "just like the orderly said. She may work in uniform, or she may have just been using it as a disguise."

"Is that a pin?" Myles pointed to the woman's lapel.

"Yes. The glint of it in the light from a pole lamp caught the technician's eye. Again, he's not sure exactly what it was, but it was gold or silver." Footsteps from behind brought Frank to his feet. "Mrs. Lakeman."

"Sergeant Traxill. This is my father. Dr. Lauzon."

Frank nodded. Charmaine Lakeman's voice was flat. Her face was pale, almost bloodless. Long tapered fingers held her father's hand.

"I'm going to drive Dad over to his house to get a few things, Myles. Call me there if . . ."

"I will, honey." Myles stood and embraced Charmaine. "I love you," he whispered in her ear. "Roland, I noticed you're running low on your medication. I called the pharmacy. It'll be delivered here."

When they were gone, Frank asked if Dr. Lauzon had a health problem.

"Hardening of the arteries. Cerebral arteries are affected most. It worsens under stress." Myles sat down again. "About three o'clock this morning, Charmaine found him in the nursery rocking this bear he'd had sent over from Paris for the baby. She managed to get him back to bed. Then she spent the rest of the night in the nursery crying. I found her there this morning. And there wasn't a thing I could do to help her." Myles's lips quivered. "I couldn't even say, They'll find her." He rested his forehead on his fingertips. "They never found Brandi."

"I wish I could promise you it would be different this time, Myles. All I can say is that we're doing everything we can." Frank sat down again and pulled out the other drawing, the police composite, and placed it alongside the color sketch. "Myles, every staff member's seen the drawings of this woman's face now. No one but the orderly and the technician claim to actually have seen her. I'm confident she didn't work for the hospital. Since the orderly said she was wearing a hair net, we're canvassing the restaurants and other places where there are food handlers. It's slow, and it may lead nowhere, but we've got to try everything. And we have to get the public involved. Someone, somewhere knows this woman."

"You don't even know she did it," Myles snapped, pushing the papers away.

Frank stirred in his chair. "No, I don't know for sure, but . . ."

"But what? The x-ray technician heard some lunatic woman mumble something? Heard her cooing to my baby in the bottom of her straw bag?"

The words had come suddenly, furiously. Frank flinched.

"What in hell is this world coming to? What kind of maniac would walk right into a hospital and steal a baby?" Myles was shouting. He sprang up, shoving his chair backwards. It fell over, crashing against the hardwood floor. "Find this woman," he demanded. "Find her before it's too late." Myles planted both palms on the table and leaned on stiff arms. "My daughter was on medication for a minor infection. Today I find out that an infection—any infection—in a premature baby can be life-threatening if it's untreated." Myles closed his eyes and swayed. "I can't take this again. Find her, damn it!"

Frank's insides coiled like a snake. Occasionally he wished he was married, wished he had kids. But not often. He had pretty well decided he wasn't cut out to be a parent. The agony on Myles Lakeman's face put a stamp of approval on his decision.

At the front door, he turned to Myles and laid a firm hand on his shoulder. "You said if you got a ransom demand you wouldn't tell me. Does that still stand?"

Myles lowered his head a moment, then looked up. "No. I'll tell you."

"Good." Frank stepped onto the porch in the cold morning air. Then he turned back to Myles. "There's something you need to know, Myles. It's about your father-in-law."

"What about him?"

"He's called me at the station three times. Left several demands that I call him."

"What does he want?"

"He's demanding that I interview someone he considers a prime suspect."

Myles's face collapsed in disgust. "Who, for Pete's sake?"

"Your ex-wife. Blair Emerson."

Roland Lauzon's two-story, white brick home on Twenty-second Street was shielded from traffic noises by oak trees and magnolias. Iron gates swung open when Charmaine's car rolled onto the skirt of the driveway. Roland knew that the house was far too large for a socially inactive French professor, but he could not bear the thought of leaving it. It held too many memories of a life that once had been full and good.

All the downstairs rooms were spotless. Minnie kept it that way. He assumed the four bedrooms upstairs were just as clean, but he had no way of knowing. Charmaine had made him promise he wouldn't use the stairs after he tumbled down the bottom steps a few months ago.

In his study, Roland handed his checkbook to Charmaine and asked her to pay Minnie for her housekeeping duties last week. "I'll go get a change of clothes."

His bedroom was at the end of the hall. He hurriedly took a pair of trousers and a shirt from the closet and lay them on the bed. Then he stuffed underclothing and pajamas in an

156

overnight bag and snapped it shut. The telephone was on the nightstand. Roland listened for voices in the hallway. When he heard none, he picked up the receiver and dialed a number from memory. Surely Frank Traxill was back at police headquarters by now. How long could it take to explain to Myles the pitiful results of the investigation?

"Let me speak to Sergeant Traxill."

"One moment, please."

Roland looked over his shoulder, listening for Charmaine's footsteps, but still he heard nothing. In a moment, Frank Traxill answered.

Roland stiffened and said, "Sergeant Traxill, this is Roland Lauzon. Did you tell my son-in-law about the conversation I had with you?"

"As a matter of fact, I did, Dr. Lauzon."

"And what did he say?"

"He understands your concern but feels that Blair Emerson is incapable of doing such a thing as this. Nonetheless we agreed that I should talk to her. I see her first thing tomorrow morning."

"See her?" Roland's voice rose to a near-shout. He lowered it quickly. "I demand that you arrest her. She kidnapped my granddaughter." Each word was precisely enunciated. "I want her in jail."

"Dr. Lauzon, you don't . . ."

"She hates my daughter. She blames her for breaking up her marriage. She is viciously bitter toward Myles for leaving her and starting a new life." Roland hunched over the phone, speaking in a strong whisper. "Can't you see? With one single act—stealing Tiffany—that pathetic, deranged woman gets back at the two people she blames for the mess that is her life. Myles and Charmaine."

"I see what . . ."

"Has the fact eluded you that the woman is a mortician? She is expert at coming and going in hospitals without drawing attention to herself. She must know obscure ways of going in and out of every hospital in this city."

157

"But Dr. Lauzon..."

"And she was in the hospital the day or the day after Tiffany's was born. I saw her myself. She was..." Roland stopped and jerked his head toward the door. Was someone in the hallway? When he heard nothing, he continued. "Sergeant Traxill, Blair Emerson stole my granddaughter. I know it. And I'm giving you eighteen hours to arrest her."

"Dr. Lauzon, I assure you I'll..."

"Your assurances mean nothing." Roland spat the words out. "You have eighteen hours in which to arrest Blair Emerson, or I will go to the press. I am not without influence in this city, Officer Traxill."

Minnie armed the security system and left through the back door of Professor Lauzon's house. Concentrating on driving in the thickening rush hour traffic was nearly impossible. She was terribly upset by what she had overheard Professor Lauzon say on the phone. How could he make such dreadful accusations against Blair Emerson? How could he possibly believe that she could be so revengeful?

Darkness and soft yellow porch lights softened her neighborhood's generally run-down appearance. Even Roseanne Brenner's house looked as nice as her freshly-painted shed when you compared them in the dark. To Minnie's amazement, Roseanne had actually finished painting the shed last Friday, the day after Minnie had told her where she could go with that oddball church of hers.

Minnie hadn't seen Roseanne since then, not to speak to her anyway. Saturday morning, she had driven past the bus stop and seen Roseanne sitting with a bag of groceries on one side of her and some poor, unsuspecting girl on the other. Minnie could hear Roseanne now, telling the girl about her latest communique from the spirit world.

Supper consisted of a piece of fried chicken straight from the refrigerator and leftover cornbread sticky with honey. Charmaine's face haunted Minnie while she tried to eat.

158

Clear, blue eyes clouded over in despair. Full lips pressed into thin slashes. Minnie had yet to see Charmaine really cry, to let it all out. Did she think that if she held the agony and fear inside she could control them?

No one was ever prepared for this kind of tragedy. But Charmaine was especially unprepared. She had been raised in a fantasy world where people were always gentle, civilized, untouched for the most part by tragedy. Money. Education. A secure home in the right part of town. All those things had insulated her from the ugly, evil things in the world.

Minnie's flannel gown was like a hug from her grand-daughter. And, unless Tara surprised her, there would be another one under the tree for her this year. Children. So precious. Maybe too precious to risk bringing them into this vicious world.

In the solitary glow of her bedside lamp, Minnie pulled a low, padded stool from under her bed. She and Herman used to kneel on the floor, but she couldn't get down that far anymore—not if she wanted to get back up again. If he were alive tonight, though, Herman could do it. On his seventieth birthday, the day of his death, he had been as spry and agile as a fifty-year-old.

Minnie's heart ached so badly and her mind was so cluttered that she couldn't form a thought, much less put sentences together into a prayer. So she just knelt there, letting God read her heart for a long time. She rested her head on the backs of her hands as tears trickled between her knotty fingers.

When she finally struggled to her feet and nudged her prayer stool back under the bed with her foot, Minnie felt a little calmer, a little stronger. She turned off the lamp and crawled between the sheets. The room seemed unusually dark. Minnie looked out the window. The street lamp was burning. Roseanne's front porch light was on. So why was the room so dark?

Several minutes passed before Minnie realized what was different tonight. The drapes in Roseanne's living room were completely shut. Usually only the shades were lowered, and then sometimes not all the way. Minnie propped herself onto one elbow and craned her neck to see the windows in Roseanne's bedroom. They were completely black too.

"What's going on over there? She must really be mad at me for what I said to her."

Minnie lay on her back thinking that over. Finally she closed her eyes and sighed. "Maybe I should apologize to her."

After some more thought, she decided that was the right thing to do. She would do it with a loaf of banana bread. Roseanne was always poking fun at herself for being such a lousy cook and laughing about how the children at the day-care center always asked who had fixed lunch, Roseanne or the other woman.

Yes, that was the thing to do. In the morning, she would take a loaf out of the freezer and put it on Roseanne's back porch, along with a little note. Minnie wouldn't risk talking to Roseanne. She didn't know if she could control her tongue if Roseanne made some crackpot comment about this whole awful thing with Tiffany being a lesson from the divine master.

22

Frank arrived at Blair Emerson's house just before eight o'clock Thursday morning. She greeted him pleasantly then led him down a short hall to the right of the entry. It ended in a den or family room. There a Boston terrier eyed him suspiciously from his wicker bed by the hearth.

"That's Celtic. He won't bite if you don't."

When she offered him coffee, Frank accepted. He studied her as she stepped into an adjoining kitchen. He judged her to be about his age—late thirties. She had smooth, clear skin. Her cheekbones were dusted with subtle color. Her black suit was well cut and expensive looking. Small gold earrings dangled from her ears. She was a classy-looking woman who, judging from the muscular contour of her calves and her smooth, simple haircut, made keeping in shape a priority. A runner, he decided. "But not in those shoes," he whispered, smiling. Next to the couch was the saddest looking pair of Reeboks he had seen since looking in his own closet that morning.

"You wanted me to look at the drawings of your suspect," she said, returning to the room with a mug in each hand. "Why me?"

Lying never set well with Frank, especially not this early in

161

the morning. But it seemed better than telling Blair Emerson the truth—that her former husband's father-in-law was convinced that she was some kind of monster. "Hospital records show that you were at St. Mary's recently removing a body. Since you're connected in a way to the parents . . . well, it's a long shot." Frank exchanged the sketches for a coffee mug and noted that Blair Emerson had a bad case of the shakes this morning.

Watching her study the drawings, Frank found himself drawn to her eyes. They were almond-shaped and as soft and dark brown as his leather coat. There was something fragile, something searching in them as she studied the drawings.

"I've never seen this woman. Are you sure she took the baby?" Her voice cracked. She swallowed hard and blushed.

"I know this is difficult for you. Myles told me about your little girl. Brandi, right?" Something flashed in Blair's eyes and she looked away to hide it. "How long has it been?"

"Eleven years this April."

"I don't guess there's anything worse than not knowing."

"And now Myles is going through it again. It's incredible."

She was looking at him now, fully into his eyes. Frank spoke gently. "Myles says there's no connection between the two children's disappearances. What do you think?"

"Of course not."

"Someone who has it in for Myles, maybe?"

"That's out of the question. Myles has never hurt anyone."

"Not even you?" Frank watched Blair's eyes, waited for them to flare in anger or defensiveness or guilt. She looked away, but not to hide any of those reactions. Tears had pooled in the inner corners of her eyes and she was trying to blink them away.

"We hurt each other," she finally said. "The sad thing is that neither of us set out to do it. I can say now that even his affair with Charmaine probably hurt Myles as much as it did me." She cleared her throat and sat up a little straighter. "But why am I telling you this? That's not what you're here to talk about. I'm sorry I can't help you with these, Sergeant Traxill."

"Call me Frank."

"Okay." Her smile was forced. Almost as an afterthought, she said, "And, please, call me Blair." She glanced nervously at her watch and frowned.

Frank took a quick sip of his coffee then stood. He got the distinct impression that Blair Emerson was anxious for him to leave. To protect his ego, he decided it was because she was late for work.

"Good luck with your investigation," she offered when they reached the entry. "Maybe making the sketches public will be the turning point."

"I believe it will." At the front door Frank paused. "How long have you been a mortician?"

"I've been licensed since I was twenty-four. I'll let you guess how long ago that's been."

"Followed in your father's footsteps, I understand."

"Plan of action since I was a kid."

"Interesting." Frank hated to press this nice woman, but if he was going to cool Lauzon a few degrees, he needed to leave here knowing more about Blair than he did now. "I hope this doesn't offend you, but I have to ask you one more question."

"Sure."

"Would you mind telling me where you were last Saturday night?"

The question clearly startled her. Frank could see it in her eyes. She struggled to recover.

"Uh . . .gosh . . .that was almost a week ago."

"Right, but just take your time. It'll come to you." Blair's eyes were darting back and forth. She was fidgeting with a gold button on her jacket.

"Let's see. Saturday. Oh. I was out of town. In Dallas."

"I see. Do you have family up there? Friends?"

"Uh . . .no. I just went up there to . . .to shop."

Frank watched Blair grow increasingly anxious. He won-

163

dered why. His gut told him it had nothing to do with Tiffany Lakeman, but something was definitely weighing on this woman. "What time did you leave for Dallas?"

"It was around noon, I guess."

"Saturday?"

"Right."

"So you spent the night up there?"

"Actually, I drove home late Saturday night. I got home about . . . I don't know . . . two o'clock."

Frank did a quick calculation. "Seem like an awful long drive to spend such a short time in the stores."

Her silky eyebrows rose a little. "The funeral business is not exactly predictable. I grab free time when I can get it."

Frank removed his sunglasses from his pocket and put them on. Blair Emerson was hedging, and she was doing a pitiful job of it. "If asked to, I'm sure you could give us proof of that, right?" Even with his dark glasses on, Frank saw Blair's face grow pale.

23

A sleet-chilled wind shoved Eldon and Blair along a sidewalk outside Texas Commerce Bank. Both their signatures had been required to transfer funds from Maryruth Emerson's money market account into Blair's. Blair left feeling thankful for large, impersonal banks and their incurious tellers.

When they reached her car, Eldon opened his arms. Blair stepped into them and sighed when they closed around her. "I know it's not the same as taking your problems to your dad," Eldon said, "but I'm here if you need me."

"I know, Eldon." She touched the gentle folds on his cheeks. "Promise me you won't tell anyone about this. No one."

A service had just concluded when Blair reached the funeral home. A stooped little woman in a black crepe dress approached Blair and said, "That was a lovely service. Do you know the vocalist's name?"

Embarrassed, Blair said, "No. I'm sorry. I didn't have a chance to meet him."

Blair realized she was better off in her office shuffling papers when the woman snickered and said, "Obviously not. The vocalist was a woman."

Blair spent the remainder of the morning returning phone

calls, signing letters and checks and death certificates and assuring Jane that she was feeling fine. "Despite how I look, I'm not sick. I haven't been sleeping well. That's all."

Her thoughts turned to Frank Traxill's visit. She had been looking out the window when his car pulled up and he got out. He was about her age. On the tall side of six feet. Handsome in a mildly rugged way. Light brown hair tipped the back of his coat collar. There was a confident, purposeful intent to his walk, to the way he had sized up the neighborhood while approaching the house.

Blair recalled studying the sketches of the suspect. The woman's image was with her even now. Round eyes. Thick hair pressed tightly into a hair net. Who was she? Why had she done this? *And why did Frank Traxill insist on showing the sketches to me?*

At first Blair had accepted his explanation—that she might have seen the woman while making the call at St. Mary's. But the death call had been on Tuesday, and Tiffany disappeared on Saturday— four days later. When Frank had asked about her whereabouts that night, Blair had felt like a suspect. Surely this was just routine questioning, though. What else could it be? No one in their right mind would think she was involved in Tiffany's disappearance.

Frank's questions had made her so nervous she could barely think straight. "Shopping trip." Blair shook her head. "I should have come up with a better reason than that—for Liz *and* Frank Traxill."

The phone rang just before noon, her private line. Blair answered it expectantly. It was Liz. Her voice was apologetic. "Blair, I hate to bother you at work, and I know this is going to make you crazy, but there's something going on that you need to know about."

"What now?"

"It's Dr. Lauzon. A friend of Bill's who works at the *Statesman* called a few minutes ago. He said that lunatic Lauzon is at the newspaper this morning making all sorts of insane accusations."

"About what?"

"About Tiffany's disappearance." Liz paused. "And about you."

"Me? What about me?"

"He's accusing you of kidnapping Tiffany."

"Me?" Blair's voice rose an octave. "You can't be serious."

"I am, Blair, and so is he. He's claiming that you disguised yourself as that woman they're looking for, sneaked into the hospital and stole his granddaughter."

"What?" Blair bolted from her chair, banging it against the credenza behind her. "But, Liz, why me? Why?"

"Lauzon is nuts. That's why." Liz's voice had bite. "He says you hate Charmaine and—get this—you are viciously bitter, to quote him, about Myles getting a second chance at happiness with a wife and a child."

Blair collapsed into her chair. Thoughts began to come together. This morning Lauzon had been spreading his lies at the newspaper office, but at some point, he had been at the police station. Frank Traxill lied. He questioned her because of Dr. Lauzon's pressure. It had nothing to do with the fact that she had made a death call at St. Mary's recently. Had Dr. Lauzon actually convinced Frank Traxill that she was capable of stealing a child? Could he do the same at the newspaper? "Liz, what does he want the paper to do?"

"He wants them to put pressure on the cops to act."

"They don't need more pressure. I've already been questioned."

"By the police?" Liz's voice was disbelieving.

"Frank Traxill. The detective who's heading up the investigation. He came by the house early this morning."

"What did he say?"

"That he wanted me to look at the drawings of their suspect. He said it was because I'd been at St. Mary's the other day and because of my 'connection'—he called it—with Myles and Charmaine." Anger flashed in Blair's voice. "But he was lying through his straight, white teeth. He questioned me because of that insane old man's accusations."

"What did you tell him?"

"The truth. That I was in Dallas the night Tiffany disappeared."

"Right. Well, that should be good enough. I'm sure you have proof."

"You sound just like him." Blair banged her fist on the desk blotter. "Thanks for the vote of confidence."

"I'm sorry, Blair. I just meant . . ."

"I know." Blair relaxed her fist, threw back her head and stared at the ceiling. "I didn't mean to bite off your head. I just can't believe this, Liz. What if this gets in the papers? What if someone believes him? And some people will. People who don't know me—maybe even some who do. If this gets out, I'm ruined. Think what it could do to the business, to my family." She silenced her next anxious thought: did men like Lenny read the newspaper? "The paper wouldn't run a story like that, would they?"

"I don't know. That man may be bonkers, but he's still got a lot of clout in this town. Isn't this slander or something?"

"This can't get in the papers, Liz. But what can I do? How do I stop it? Talk to Dr. Lauzon, maybe?"

"No way. You stay away from him. He's deranged— maybe dangerous. Just tell that cop you talked to the truth, and everything will be all right. But Blair, you're going to have to come up with something better than this shopping trip story."

"It's *not* a story, Liz," she snapped.

"Right." Liz's voice was edged with sarcasm. Seconds passed before she said, "You're a terrible liar, Blair. Now how about the truth?"

Blair kicked her brain into fast forward, searching for a plausible explanation. But Liz didn't give her time.

"What's going on with you, Blair? When you first told me where you went Saturday, it hurt my feelings that you would leave town the day after Clay was born. I should have known better. Only an absolute emergency would have made you go off and leave me like that. Blair, does this have anything to do with the call you got about Brandi?"

"What?"

"That man Lenny called again, didn't he?"

"No...no...of course not," she stammered. "Don't you think I would have told you?"

"Maybe not—if he threatened you."

"You're way off base here." Blair's pulse was racing. Her hands felt clammy against the phone's hard plastic. "Furthermore, Lenny told me to keep quiet the first time he called and I didn't do it, so why..."

"The first time? So he *has* called again."

"No, Liz. You know what I mean."

"All right. If you didn't drive to Dallas to see him, then why *did* you go?"

"Liz, please," Blair sighed.

"And don't tell me you drove four hundred miles to Christmas shop. That's absurd, Blair Emerson, and you know it."

Blair was trapped. The walls of the hole she had dug for herself were steep, and there was no climbing out. "Okay. I didn't go to shop, but, please, just drop it, Liz."

Long seconds of silence, then: "Blair, in all those years that you searched for Brandi—when you followed every lead, when you talked to every well-meaning citizen and every whacko and psychic that contacted you—did I ever once discourage you or call your efforts a waste of time? Did I ever once say you were crazy?" Liz paused. "No. And I wouldn't do that to you now."

"I know, Liz. But please...I can't handle this right now."

"All right," Liz said softly. "Just call me when you're ready to talk. Whatever it is, I'll do my best to understand. I love you."

A dial tone droned in Blair's ear. She listened to it for several seconds, then hung up the phone. Her head was pounding. She rested it on the chair back. Would she open tomorrow's paper and find Lauzon's accusations in print?

Would Lenny see them and decide the deal was too risky and keep the twenty-five thousand and Brandi too?

"What if the police arrest me and I can't get to Brandi?"

24

Unless the phone had rung while April was out of her room at the Holiday Inn, Lenny was the only person who had called in four days. "About to get things wrapped up here in El Paso. Be back some time tomorrow. You're staying in your room most of the time, ain't ya?"

"Yes, but she hasn't called."

"Who?"

"Blair," April had snapped.

"Oh. Right. I'll give her a buzz when I get back," Lenny had promised. "See how much headway she's made with her old man."

How could women be like that? April cleaned the top of a can of Diet Coke with a towelette and pulled back the tab. She removed plastic wrap from a tumbler and filled it. She would never let a man run her life like Jewell and Blair did. It was disgusting and unfair. Jewell's whole life had revolved around Lenny. *Lenny'll be home in a little bit. Lenny's not feeling well. Lenny's been on the same job for nearly a month now; isn't that great?* And now it looked as if Blair did the same thing with her boyfriend.

April sipped her Coke, then pulled back the drape on a sliding glass door that opened onto a little balcony. In the distance, the downtown skyline blended into the gray winter sky. She hated Dallas. She wished she was back in Virginia Beach with Becky. "I've been stuck in this room for four days waiting for Blair to call. I'm sick of it." She kicked a chair leg with the toe of her sneaker and turned away from the window. Blair had had plenty of time to persuade her boyfriend to let April live with them. If he hadn't agreed by now, she decided, feeling a heaviness in her chest, then he probably wasn't going to. "And I know exactly where that leaves me." She picked up her room key and headed for the door. "This whole thing was a big mistake."

The elevator was empty when April rode it to the lobby. She walked across thick beige carpet to the front desk. "Excuse me. I locked my key in my room and my dad's out for a while. Can you give me another one?" April was proud of the way her voice sounded. Confident. Mature. It was easier to be that way when Lenny wasn't around.

"What is the name, please?"

"My dad's name is Lenny Bond. We're in room . . ."

"Please," he interrupted politely. "For security reasons, we don't announce room numbers." He clicked computer keys. "I'll be happy to have someone open the room for you."

Five minutes later, the door to Lenny's room closed behind her. He had hung the *Do Not Disturb* sign on the knob the morning he left. "Those maids will steal you blind if you don't stay in the room while they're cleaning. I've told 'em heads are gonna roll if they set foot in my room while I'm gone. And when they're in your room, I want you watching them like a hawk. Understand?"

Lenny was paranoid. Or maybe not, April reconsidered. Maybe there was something in here he didn't want anyone to see. Drugs? Money? Probably both. She hadn't bothered to ask him how he could afford two expensive rooms and airfare to El Paso. He would have probably said, "Paid for it with my good looks."

The day before he left, he had bought new jeans, a really nice white shirt and a kind of tacky-looking pullover sweater.

Fortunately he had covered the sweater with a brown corduroy coat trimmed in soft leather. It had looked like something J.R. Ewing used to wear on the "Dallas" TV show. So did his new boots. April thought the idea of wearing ostrich skin on your feet was repulsive.

Standing at the closet door, she removed her rubber gloves, one from each back pocket of her jeans. She would start her search here.

The pea coat was pushed to the back of the long, narrow closet. With gloved fingers, she slid the other clothes to the left, clearing room for her to step into the closet. The coat reeked of smoke. She tried not to breathe while she felt inside the pockets. In one she found a crushed cigarette pack. Surprisingly, Lenny hadn't tossed it on the ground somewhere. Something crumpled when she stuck her fingers inside the second pocket.

Needing to breathe, April stepped out of the closet. In her hand were three bills. A twenty and two ones. Did she dare take them all? Yes. He might never wear that coat again.

She returned to the closet to check for inside pockets but found none. A quick check of his jeans and shirts, and she came up empty. But twenty-two dollars wasn't bad at all. Remembering to slide the clothes back into place, April then checked dresser drawers. All were empty except for one. Underwear. Socks. Handkerchiefs. She wasn't about to touch any of those—gloves or not.

In her room now, she sprayed the bills with Lysol, then soaped and rinsed her gloves so they would be sanitary when she touched her backpack.

Her backpack was on the closet shelf next to her suitcase. Lenny had acted like he wanted to take her suitcase to El Paso, saying it was the only decent one between them. But minutes after taking it into his room, he had returned it to the shelf, saying it looked too much like a girl's bag. Lenny was too weird for words sometimes.

She took her backpack to the table by the sliding glass door, removed the roll of bills and counted them. One hundred and seven dollars. Thirty-two dollars more and she had her bus fare. But it was a long trip from Dallas to Virginia Beach. She would need spending money. At least twenty dollars.

The roll of bills was really thick now. Too thick. If Lenny happened to poke his nose in her backpack, he couldn't help but see it. So she sorted the bills and flattened them, then slid them into four small plastic bags. She would hide them in the zipper compartment of her suitcase, now that she knew Lenny wouldn't consider using it.

After washing her gloves again and returning them to their bag, she went to the closet again. Steadying herself against the door frame, she reached for her suitcase. As she began to ease it off the shelf, it slipped from her grip and tumbled down, banging against the mirrored door and landing on top of her foot.

The suitcase was heavy when April lifted it and limped across her room. "Lenny must have put something in there." She set the suitcase on a luggage rack next to her bed and felt along the zipper for the brass lock that held both zipper tabs together. "He locked it. Why did he lock my suitcase?" Of course that was no problem to her. Even if she didn't have a duplicate key, she could pick that lock in ten seconds.

April quickly located the second key, which she kept in her backpack. She inserted it in the bottom of the lock, turned it and felt the snap. Her curiosity growing, April opened the suitcase.

A satchel lay inside, one she hadn't seen before. It was sturdy leather, about eighteen inches long with a flap locked in front.

"Drugs or drug money...one or the other." April removed the satchel and studied it. "Why did Lenny put this in my suitcase?" She thought a moment, then said, "I guess he was afraid the maids might swipe it. And he knew I wouldn't be using my suitcase." She carried the satchel to the table and laid it beside her backpack. She found a paper clip, straightened it out and picked the lock on the satchel in seconds.

The satchel smelled of leather and—just what she had

expected—money. Lots and lots of it. She spread the top of the satchel to get a better look. There were thousands and thousands of dollars in there. Stacks with paper bands around them. Torn, empty bands lay in the bottom, probably ripped from the piles of bills that Lenny was spending.

April stared at the money. Lenny would be back tomorrow. Then he would call Blair. If Blair's answer was *no*, April would buy a bus ticket and leave before Lenny took off for El Paso. But what if Blair said *yes*?

April pushed aside the thought. The chances that Blair would say yes were probably about as good as the chances that this money was from Jewell's will.

"Worst case scenario," she reminded herself and slid a fifty from inside one of the banded stacks. She had enough now for her bus fare, but less than ten dollars for spending money. Would that be enough? "No way." She took a twenty from another banded stack. The bills were crisp and clean and unwrinkled. "Lenny will kill me if he finds out."

When she spread the top of the satchel to return the stacks, April spotted the corner of a white envelope. Curious, she grasped it with her fingertips and pulled it out.

A single name was penned across the front. "April." The handwriting was unfamiliar. It wasn't Jewell's. Hers slanted the other way. It definitely wasn't Lenny's. Far too neat.

On her knees now, she held the letter up to the lamp. The paper inside had been folded so it was impossible to read. She was burning to open it, but she didn't dare. The first thing Lenny would do when he got back would be to make sure the money was still in her suitcase. If the letter was important enough to be kept hidden with the money, he would look for it too.

She returned it to the satchel—at least until she could figure out a way to read it without Lenny finding out.

Later, April did a quick mental check. The satchel was locked in her suitcase. The suitcase was locked and on the shelf. But what should she do with her money? She couldn't risk simply sticking it in her backpack again. Lenny might see it there. No. She would do what Becky's father did one time to hide a whiskey bottle. She would hollow out a book and hide the money inside it.

Using fingernail scissors, April cut away bill-sized holes in the pages of a paperback book. It was a tedious process, but when she was finished, she was able to fit the bags of money neatly inside the book. Then she wrapped a rubber band around the book and slipped it into a zippered compartment in her backpack.

She spent the next quarter hour scrubbing her hands with Top Job until they were blood red, and thinking about the letter in the satchel.

Frank turned in early Thursday night. Rain tapped at the windows and cascaded down the panes. He usually slept soundly in winter rainstorms, but not tonight.

The investigation was moving at glacier pace. The chief was putting pressure on him because Dr. Lauzon had been doing his irate dance on the chief's desk. Tomorrow morning he might wake up and find in the paper Lauzon's accusations about the "rampant incompetence and stubborn territorial attitudes of the police detectives," along with his argument that Blair Emerson had abducted her ex-husband's child.

If Lauzon knew what Frank had found out at the bank late this afternoon, he would spit fire. And Blair Emerson would be covered with third-degree burns.

Frank tossed and turned for several hours. Finally at two in the morning he gave up and turned the stereo on low. Willie Nelson sang "Blue Eyes Crying in the Rain." Charmaine Lakeman's face flashed before his eyes.

The chair beside his bed embraced him like an old friend when he sat down. The yellow legal pad he had been thinking on before going to bed lay on a nearby table. He picked it up and stared at Blair Emerson's name. The evidence against her was all circumstantial, but it kept growing.

Frank focused on the image of Blair that hovered in his

mind. Soft brown eyes moist with tears when she talked about Myles and Charmaine and herself. The sadness in them at the mention of Brandi. The tightness in her pretty face when talking about the shopping trip to Dallas.

"Why did you really drive to Dallas in an ice storm, Blair? And why did you go to Texas Commerce Bank last Friday and withdraw twenty-five thousand dollars in cash?"

25

Blair thrashed through the morning paper. Six days had passed, and the continuing search for Tiffany had slipped farther from the front page. Coverage of the investigation had shrunk accordingly. Frank was quoted in snatches. Blair's name was mercifully absent from all reports.

Today was Friday. Tomorrow it would be a week since she had turned the money over to Lenny. Had he told Brandi about the money? Had he explained that the only thing keeping them apart now was one final payment? Probably not. Surely he hadn't told Brandi that he was *selling* her back to her mother. How was he explaining the days away? What must Brandi think?

That I don't want her back. The thought was almost too much for Blair. *My baby. Where are you? What are you thinking?*

Blair dragged herself to work. There Jane and the other employees greeted her with worried looks and questions about her health. Even if she had not left early yesterday, they would have good reason for their concern. She moved and spoke—and probably looked—like a zombie.

For an hour or so, she shuffled papers in and out of her "Do It Today" folder. Things that seemed so important before,

178

now paled to nothingness.

Eldon called at nine. "How are you feeling, Sweetheart?"

"Much better," she lied.

"Remember, Blair, if you want to talk, I'm here."

Minutes later, Frank Traxill called. He tried to sound casual, even friendly. His request was anything but. He tagged it with, "You can bring your attorney if you like, Blair."

"My attorney? Why would I need an attorney?" Blair dug her nails into sweaty palms. "Furthermore, why do you want to talk to me again? I don't know anything more than I did before."

Frank was evasive but insistent, and an hour later Blair was sitting in front of his desk.

It was an unimpressive cubicle, not an office. The sounds of muffled voices and ringing phones came from every direction. Blair assured him again that she had no reason to call her attorney. "Now. I want to know why I'm here, why you want to talk to me again." She knew darned well why she was there, but she wanted to hear Frank Traxill admit that Roland Lauzon was behind it.

"It's like I explained the other day at your house."

"No, Frank," she said sharply. "You said you were there to show me the sketches of your suspect." Blair struggled to contain her anger. "But somehow we ended up talking about where I was Saturday night. Why is that?"

"Why are you being so uncooperative?" Frank snatched up a folder and opened it. "I'm trying to investigate a crime, Blair."

"Then do it," Blair snapped. "And quit letting Roland Lauzon jerk you around by your badge." Frank's eyes found hers. "Yes. I know about Lauzon. And I can't believe you would listen to him. The man is sick, Frank. Sick."

Frank sighed deeply and nodded his head. "Then help me shut him up. All I'm asking for is some proof that you were in Dallas at the time of the kidnapping. Names of people you spoke to. Sales receipts. Credit card receipts. Anything to

179

prove you were there and not here."

"I didn't speak to anyone I knew." Blair squirmed in the uncomfortable metal chair. "I paid cash for gasoline, and I only bought some small items, so I didn't save the receipts."

"You saw no one you knew?"

"I just said that."

"Is there anyone who might remember seeing you. A sales person, maybe?"

"I doubt it. There were hundreds of shoppers."

"You're not helping me, Blair."

"Why should I? I don't have to prove anything to you. I was in Dallas, whether you believe me or not." Blair felt clammy perspiration on her hands. She wiped them on the folds of her silk skirt.

"I do believe you, Blair." Frank paused a moment, then said, "And the time I waste arguing with Lauzon is time away from finding the real suspect." He thumped the sketches on his desk.

Blair slumped in her chair. "I'm sorry, Frank. It's just that this whole thing has made me crazy. The honest truth is that I just don't have any proof. All I can tell you is that I left Austin around noon, drove to Dallas, and left there right after ten. I was home between two and three."

"Why didn't you spend the night?"

"I had to get back. I have only one funeral director working on Sunday. I have to be available."

"I see." Frank's tone changed. "You ran into your ex-husband recently. Tell me about that."

"There's nothing to tell. I was making a death call at St. Mary's. We chatted a few minutes. He was there to see Charmaine and the baby."

"His wife and father are upset by that. Why?"

"They hate me. It's as simple as that."

"Did you and Myles argue that day?"

"No."

Frank nodded, then shoved a piece of paper her way.

"Take a look at this. Do you recognize it?"

Blair put her hands into the pockets of her jacket and clenched them into fists. It was a copy of the currency transaction report.

"Where did you get that?"

"One of my investigators turned it up."

"How? Why?"

"Just answer my questions. Do you recognize it?"

Blair tightened her fists. "Of course I recognize it. It's a C.T.R. Don't play games, Frank."

"It says you withdrew twenty-five thousand dollars from your bank account last Friday—a week ago today. Mind telling me why?"

Things were happening too fast. She had no time to think, to evaluate. "A friend needed the money."

"A friend in Dallas?"

Blair scrambled mentally. "Right. So I took it to him."

"You said you didn't see anyone who knew you."

"I lied." She was surprised at how flat her voice sounded when, inside, her heart was racing.

"Who was this person who needed money?"

"I'd rather not say."

"You'd rather not say. Why?"

"Look Frank, it's not a crime to lend a friend some money." Her voice was getting higher and louder.

"Why cash?"

"He asked for cash," Blair snapped.

Frank leaned forward and put both forearms on his desk. "Why?"

"None of your business." The words were nearly a shout.

"Well, some people are making your whereabouts that night their business. And if they find out you gave some man twenty-five thousand dollars in cash, they might just think it was because he had done a job for you."

"What are you talking about?"

"Kidnapping," Frank barked.

Blair gasped in horror. "You can't believe that."

"No, I don't." Frank's tone was compassionate. "So tell me this man's name, and let's clear up this mess."

"I—I can't. It would cause him trouble."

"Blair, you were willing to drive to Dallas in an ice storm to help this man. Wouldn't he want to help you now? Wouldn't he want to verify that you were with him when Tiffany Lakeman was abducted?"

Adrenaline was beginning to flow now. Blair's thoughts were crisper. She faked an embarrassed little smile. "You're right. Of course he would help me. But I should talk to him first. If he agrees, I'll have him contact you. But, please, Frank, keep his name out of this if you can."

"I can't promise."

"But you'll try."

A blond young man tapped on Frank's cubicle and stuck his head around the corner. "Sergeant, got something for you."

Frank excused himself and returned a few seconds later. He sat on the corner of his desk this time, close enough for Blair to smell his cologne and to see fine red lines in his eyes.

"When you made the death call recently at St. Mary's, what floor did you go to?"

"I don't remember. It was . . . four, I believe."

"Did you use the stairs?"

Blair chuckled. It felt good. "It's a little hard to manipulate a cot on a staircase, Sergeant."

"I guess it would be. Have you been back since?"

"No."

"I've heard differently."

"Well, then you've heard wrong. Wait. My friend Liz. I went there to see her and the baby."

"When?"

The cubicle grew smaller with each of Frank's questions. "Saturday. The day Tiffany was abducted. But it was before noon, Frank. Ask Liz."

"I will."

182

Blair sagged against the chair. "Don't bother. It won't do any good. Liz was asleep when I got there. I didn't wake her. I just looked at Clay and left."

"So you went to the nursery."

There it was again. The deep, black hole. *God, help me. How do I get out this time?* "Yes, I went to the nursery."

"See Tiffany Lakeman?"

Blair leaned forward and cupped her face in both hands. She mumbled into them. "Yes, I saw her."

"What did you do then?"

Her face rose slowly from her palms. She glared at Frank. "I broke through the glass door, snatched Tiffany out of her crib and ran off with her."

Frank leaned forward. His face no more than a foot from Blair's. "I'll ask again. What did you do then?"

Blair lowered her eyes and looked at the floor. "I left after five minutes or so."

"On the elevator?"

"No. The stairs."

"From the fifth floor? Why?"

"Because I heard Charmaine's voice. She was coming up behind me. I didn't want to run into her, all right? The stairs were closer."

"Why didn't you want Charmaine to see you? You had a right to see your friend's baby, didn't you?"

"Charmaine hates me. I didn't want her to jump in the middle of me right there in the hospital. So I got out of there."

Frank nodded his head several times. For an instant, Blair thought he was going to reach out and touch her hand. She found herself wishing he would tell her everything was going to be okay.

"Blair, please get in touch with your friend in Dallas. I want this cleared up." His tone was gentle. "I want people off my back about you, and I want to get off yours. I'm really not such a bad guy."

Blair stood and managed a smile. "You couldn't prove it by me."

Frank Traxill probably was a nice guy, but Blair left his office hoping she never had to look into his penetrating blue eyes again.

26

Flying. Now that was the way to get around. El Paso to Dallas. Nonstop. Four drinks and you're there. The cab ride from the airport to the Holiday Inn seemed longer to Lenny than the flight, but there were no drinks in the cab.

The *Do Not Disturb* sign still dangled outside the door to his room. He was going to kick some tails if he found out those nosy maids had been in there. Of course the satchel was in April's room, locked inside her suitcase, so that should still be safe. But Lenny had some white powder valuables stashed here and there in his own room.

"April." He slapped the door adjoining their rooms with an open palm. "You decent?" It was only nine o'clock. She probably wasn't in bed yet. Most likely she was in the shower. It seemed like every time he turned around, he heard the shower running.

"Come in."

Lenny eyed the room with mock suspicion. "You ain't snagged you a boyfriend and stashed him in here somewhere while I was gone, have ya?" He leaned against the dresser. April was lying on her bed with a book across her stomach—or where a stomach ought to be. "You look like you been in some concentration camp instead of the Holiday Inn. You eat anything while I was gone?"

"Of course I ate."

"Well, you look like a sack of bones. You think Blair's gonna want some danorixec daughter?"

"It's *anorexic*, and I eat plenty." Hesitantly, she said, "Have you called her yet?"

"Give me time. I just walked in the door. Gotta unpack first." Lenny pulled out a plump wallet and tossed a ten on the foot of April's bed. That ought to get a spark out of her, he thought. She always looked at money like it was crawling with maggots. "Go downstairs and get me a cheeseburger and a beer. Aw, hell, you can't buy beer. Just get me a burger. I'll take care of the other."

"You could call room service."

"Oh, it's room service now, is it? Well, ain't you something?" Lenny kicked the sole of April's tennis shoe. "You haul it downstairs, Princess April. I'm not paying room service prices."

With April out of her room, Lenny opened the closet door, noticing first how sharp he looked in the mirror. The suitcase was right where he'd left it. With a tiny key, he unlocked it and removed the satchel. Then he tossed the suitcase back on the shelf, and returned to his room.

The money was still in the satchel. Safe and sound. The letters were there, too. The one to Brandi had slipped to the bottom. He liked that name, Brandi. It had more zip to it than April. Naming the baby April had been Jewell's idea.

Getting a birth certificate for a two-year-old had been a piece of cake, even for dumb old Jewell. She had done it all herself. Somehow she had gotten hold of some other kid's birth certificate, used Liquid Paper on all the typewritten words she needed to change, typed in lies about April and then photocopied it. Bingo. Perfect. April's kindergarten teacher hadn't said a word about it being a photocopy instead of a certified. Not one solitary question had been raised in the entire eleven years. Amazing.

Lenny wished getting a new identity had been that easy for

him. Becoming Lee Pickens had been a little harder, a lot riskier and a helluva lot more expensive. But it was done now. Lee Pickens had gotten his birth certificate, a social security card and a driver's license in El Paso all in the same day. Not bad. Tomorrow Lenny would sell the Buick to some salvage yard. He would rent a car for a few days. Then late Tuesday, before his little rendezvous with Blair, Lee Pickens was going to buy something a successful man in Texas couldn't do without. "A dual cab Chevy truck with a telephone right there at my fingertips. Alriiiight."

Lenny snapped the satchel shut and hung it inside his pea coat in the back of his closet. "When I wheel into El Paso, you Mexican parrots better hold onto your feathers. You're gonna make Lee Pickens one rich hombre."

Minnie felt guilty for taking another weekly check from Professor Lauzon after working so little. He was staying with Myles and Charmaine, so there was almost nothing to do at his house but water the plants and keep the dust wiped away.

If only the police would find Tiffany. Then those poor, broken-hearted people could start piecing their lives together again. But with each day that passed, any trail the police might find would get colder and harder to follow. That horrible woman who took Tiffany was probably states away by now. Looking at the sketches of her had made Minnie's skin crawl. The woman had finally started to look familiar to her. Of course, she had not mentioned that to anyone, because it was a ridiculous thought. The sketches had been shown on television news reports for most of this week. And if you saw a stranger's picture a dozen times a day for five solid days, you'd be bound to think the person looked familiar.

Minnie stayed on her knees a little longer than usual this evening. Having made her peace with Roseanne, she felt better about asking God to see Myles and Charmaine and Professor Lauzon through this awful time. Then she prayed that God would make all the detectives alert on the job so they would find that woman in her white uniform and her hair net—and Tiffany, of course.

It was still dark around Roseanne's house. Maybe Minnie had been wrong about why her shades were down. Roseanne had dropped by to say thanks for the banana bread, so Minnie knew she wasn't still angry with her. To Minnie's delight, Roseanne had stayed only a minute.

"I've been at home all this week with the flu," Roseanne had explained; and, in fact, she hadn't looked well at all. "You know, Minnie, sometimes the Spirit has a mission for you and the only way it can speak to you is to get you off by yourself."

"I suppose," Minnie had answered. "Now you better get on back home and go to bed. Rest and liquids. That's what they say."

On the way out the door, Roseanne had said, "I'm praying for Myles and Charmaine." Then she had added, "The Spirit is telling me what to pray."

The words had sent a chill down Minnie's back.

Roseanne took a corn dog out of the oven and stuck the end of it in a bottle of mustard. Inez had taught her to make corn dogs from scratch. Inez was the woman who ran the halfway house where Roseanne had stayed the first few months after her release from the state hospital. There was no comparison between Inez's corn dogs and those gummy, rubbery things the hospital had served.

Roseanne had lied to Minnie about the state hospital. But if Minnie had known Roseanne was a former patient and not a former employee, she would have shied away from her. It wasn't the kind of thing you told people about. Like that sweet Blair Emerson. If she had known Roseanne was a patient, she would never have entrusted her with her precious silver pin.

Blair. Every day, Roseanne read the obituary column and clipped out the notices mentioning Blair's funeral home. She

188

must have hundreds of clippings now, all neatly stored in a big manila envelope that she kept in her straw bag. All those families listed in the clippings knew now what Roseanne had known for months: that Blair Emerson was gentle and kind and thoughtful.

But Roseanne knew something those people didn't know. Blair had been wronged, greatly wronged, by Charmaine Lauzon. And Roseanne had been selected to help right the wrong.

For over a week now, the Spirits had directed Roseanne's every thought. It had started after her argument with Minnie Erskin over Charmaine Lauzon. All Roseanne had said was that she was praying for Charmaine; but Minnie had gotten so angry and spiteful. Why couldn't Minnie see how much Charmaine needed Roseanne's prayers?

Roseanne had spent the night after the argument meditating, entreating the Spirits to tell her what she could do to illuminate Charmaine's soul. Then all day Saturday, she had fasted and meditated, sometimes in the garden, kneeling before the burlap-wrapped rose bushes. At other times, she had studied wise writings of the Mystic Masters. The book of writings had been given to her by a woman at church.

For as long as she lived, she would remember that glorious first night at a fellowship meeting. Roseanne had heard the word *Karma* before, but until she sat at the feet of the lovely blue-eyed woman, she had never known what it meant.

"God intends for you to be happy," the woman had said, holding Roseanne in her gaze. "If you are not, then you may be sure you have broken God's laws, either in this life or in a previous life, and that you are now suffering the penalty for this sin." Then she had related a story about a woman whose daughter had been born with cerebral palsy. The blue-eyed woman had said that this was a karmic problem, that the afflicted child had been the woman's younger sister in another life. In that previous life, the woman, in a jealous fit, had pushed her sister over a cliff. The incident had left her sister crippled for life.

189

Then the blue-eyed woman had explained the mystery of Karma. The mother of the palsied child had faced a critical decision. If she shirked her karmic responsibility and institutionalized her afflicted child, then the unpaid debt of past sin would have to be worked out in subsequent lives. But if she chose to love and take care of her child at home, then a heavy debt would be paid, and the woman could reach perfection and godliness.

After the meeting, Roseanne had cautiously approached the blue-eyed woman and confessed to a lifetime of sin. "And sometimes I just can't help doing it."

"You can learn easily by heeding advice from the spirits of more advanced souls who have encountered the same problems." She had stroked Roseanne's cheek and said, "And you can learn to hear their voices with practice and prayer."

Right away Roseanne heard from the other world. At first she had been frightened by this voice who called itself the Guiding Spirit. But it had befriended her, causing fliers to slip from newspapers so Roseanne would know where to get the lowest prices on food for her rose bushes, training her eyes to find countless coins in the street, delaying the bus so that she would have time to talk about the Spirit to waiting passengers.

But because Roseanne had been faithful in recognizing these minor miracles, she now witnessed greater ones. For *two* spirits, not just one, spoke to Roseanne now. The Guiding Spirit spoke from inside her head, just to the right of her brain. The second, the one she called the Free Spirit, floated outside her body and spoke to her most often when she was in her garden.

The Guiding Spirit had told Roseanne that, with one brave act, she could work off some bad Karma of her own, and at the same time, make Charmaine realize how wicked she had been to steal Blair Emerson's husband. Then the Free Spirit had told her to dress in her kitchen-help uniform and climb five flights of stairs at St. Mary's Hospital.

The security guard at the hospital that Saturday night had hardly noticed Roseanne at all. No one had paid attention to her once she was inside either—not the nurses or orderlies or aides. The Guiding Spirit had told her it was safe to slip into the warm, dimly lit room where little angels slept and squirmed and cried. The Free Spirit had told her just where to find Tiffany Lakeman. Roseanne's eyes had widened when her gaze fell on a tag attached to the end of a plastic crib. *Tiffany Lakeman*. The tiny baby was wrapped in a pink blanket, the color of Roseanne's favorite flower: the Tiffany rose. She praised the Spirits, then lifted the baby—petal-like blanket and all—from her crib.

Since that night, the Free Spirit had spoken only from the corner of the garden where the pink Tiffany bushes grew. Roseanne knelt there several times a day, waiting for the Spirits to tell her when her mission was complete. Some day—some day soon, Roseanne hoped—Charmaine would give up Blair's husband. And then Roseanne would return Charmaine's child.

Roseanne turned off the kitchen light and walked down the short hall to her bedroom. The room was pitch black. She sat down on her bed and let her eyes adjust to the darkness. She had emptied and cleaned a firewood box and dragged it into her bedroom to use as a crib. She eased her fingertips down the inside of the box and felt for the soft blanket wrapped around her angelic guest.

Caring for a baby was an unfamiliar mission for Roseanne. The first time she bought formula, she had asked lots of questions. The man at the pharmacy had been very helpful. And, at first, everything went well. Tiffany had slept most of the time, crying only when she was wet or hungry. But the last couple of days, she had fussed and cried and several times had thrown up her formula.

Roseanne inched her fingers upward along the blanket wrapped around precious little Tiffany. Gentle curve of a chin. Velvet soft lips. A tiny, warm nose. She cupped her palm over Tiffany's forehead. It was warm. Very warm.

191

27

It was five o'clock Saturday afternoon. Inside the deserted church, Blair slipped up the side aisle and chose a pew toward the front. The building's thick stone walls sealed out the world and its distractions. On her knees, she let her jangled nerves settle and focused on the cross behind the altar.

Blair reflected on what had brought her to the church: a need to unload, to sort through things. How natural it had seemed to come here. She remembered how differently she had felt the months after Brandi's disappearance. Then she had avoided the church, refused to go anywhere near it. It wasn't that she had stopped believing in God, but Brandi's disappearance had shaken Blair's seldom-tested faith. *Why, God? Why Brandi? Why don't you help us find her?* The questions had haunted her, but in those early weeks and months, she hadn't had the strength to explore them.

When she finally did seek answers, she had done so with a passion and a vengeance. But she ran headlong into brick walls. There had been no answers, no reasons. Only the loss. Brandi was gone.

The realization that she would never understand had been long in coming and difficult to accept. But after long months, the sharp edge of pain had begun to dull, and the focus of her questions had mysteriously shifted. She had gradually stopped asking *why* and started asking *how*. How can I survive? How can I live when part of me is dead? And then, almost despite herself, she began to move on.

The pain was still there. It would always be there. So would the emptiness that couldn't be filled. But somehow she managed to integrate them into her life and work around them. She never stopped thinking about Brandi, never stopped wondering who had taken her and why. But Blair's life ceased to revolve around those painful unknowns. Like a stranger, she watched herself begin to live again and marveled at an inner strength that she didn't know she had. *Is this how it works, God? Is this how you heal? Is this your answer?*

That same miraculous inner strength was evident in the lives of certain people she met at the funeral home. Blair was constantly amazed at how otherwise ordinary people, who had been traumatized or victimized, managed to survive with dignity and to trust God through it all.

Still on her knees, she turned her thoughts to the problems and worries at hand. Somehow she had to prove that she was in Dallas the night Tiffany disappeared. There had to be a way, had to be something she was forgetting. "Help me remember." And the money. When would the bonds sell? It had to be soon. And then there was Liz. "She knows, Lord. And I've hurt her with my lies."

Blair's body sagged forward. She rested her forehead on the backs of her hands and let the worries, the fears pour out.

"Father, am I doing the right thing?" Her voice cracked with weariness. "If April is Brandi, help me get her back." Blair pressed her lips together, trapping a keening moan in her throat. "But if she isn't, help me live through what's ahead."

Long minutes later, Blair raised her head and slid up onto the pew. Her hands were lead weights in her lap. Fatigue oozed from every pore. When finally she dragged herself to her car and started home, she felt drained, but also strangely purged. "April is Brandi," she said aloud, her voice strong with conviction.

A smutty darkness hung over the city. Street lamps pushed at the gloom. As she stared through the windshield, she began to fantasize about her reunion with Brandi, a process that lately had become almost as constant as breathing.

Sometimes, in her fantasies, Blair would be parked near a crowded shopping mall. Teenage girls wearing jeans and sloppy sweaters would leave the mall in pairs or small groups. Blair would ignore them; she knew Brandi would be alone. Then, Brandi would appear, her eyes searching, her hands stuffed into pockets of a denim jacket, a plaid scarf draped around her neck.

Other times, Blair would imagine herself creeping through a roadside park along Interstate 35, miles from nowhere. Brandi would step out from behind a grove of oak trees or a bank of phone booths. Denim jacket. Plaid scarf.

Though the setting of her fantasies varied, one thing remained constant. Brandi always wore jeans, a denim jacket and plaid scarf. But she never had a face.

Blair patted the foot of her bed. Celtic hopped up, circled around a couple of times and curled into a c-shape. His chin rested on his front paws. As a puppy, Sandy had done the same thing on a bean-bag bed in Brandi's room. Would Brandi remember Sandy? What happened to memories when they weren't rehashed and replayed as a child grew older? Did they fade until there wasn't even a trace or an impression? Or were the memories from the first two years of Brandi's life stored in her subconscious, ready to be called up when safety permitted? Did the hugs, the kisses, the cuddling feed her even now?

Blair flicked off the ginger jar lamp on the bedside table. It was after midnight. The room was black for a few minutes. Then the dresser, the chair in the corner, the cluttered bookshelf took shape. Indistinct forms slowly took on familiarity. Blair told herself it would be that way for Brandi as she adjusted to her new home—to her real home.

Sleep was fitful. Over and over Blair reviewed the trip to Dallas, searching for some way to prove she had been there when Tiffany had disappeared. Frank was trying to clear her. She had to give him the proof he needed before word of Dr. Lauzon's suspicions reached the paper or the news. Where had she been at eleven o'clock? An hour south of Dallas, creeping along the interstate, thankful for the sandy surface on the road, tire chains humming.

"Tire chains. The man in Waco." Blair sat up in bed. Celtic padded across the covers, startled from his sleep. "He would remember taking off my chains. What time was that?"

Road conditions had stretched the usual three-and-a-half or four- hour drive between Dallas and Austin to almost five hours. Waco was halfway between. That would mean she had been in Waco at about twelve-thirty. The man had been on the phone when she drove up. Would he remember the time?

"I'll call Frank first thing Monday morning." Blair lay back against the pillow. "He'll know how to get in touch with the man."

Two hours later, Blair awoke from a vague and troubled half sleep. If the man at the service station couldn't recall the exact time she had been there, if he said it could have been as late as one in the morning, then he would be of no help at all. Tiffany had been abducted sometime around eleven o'clock. Even with the bad road conditions, it would have been possible for Blair to drive from Austin to Waco in two hours. She could only hope that the man could swear there had been no baby in her car that night.

28

Roseanne shuffled through the wet, winter-layered leaves beneath the oaks in her backyard. Minnie had just driven away, so it was safe to go to the garden now and kneel before her Tiffany rose bushes. There she would cleanse her soul and wait for the Free Spirit to speak.

The soil was cold beneath Roseanne's knees. Wind whipped strands of hair across her quivering lips and into the moisture seeping from her closed eyes. Like weeding her rose garden, she plucked worldly thoughts from her mind, one by one, and tossed them aside. Finally her mind was free, ready to receive word from a higher plane.

When nothing came, Roseanne shifted her weight from one knee to the other and lifted her face, wrinkled now with worry, to the slate gray sky. She breathed in the frigid morning air. A chill ran down her back, dividing her in half. Fear on one side. Faith on the other. Faith whispered that the Spirits would not desert her. Fear shouted that she had failed in her mission and the Spirits had departed.

Tiffany's cries had awakened Roseanne just after midnight. The baby's fever had spiked, and Roseanne had held a prayer vigil. After two hours and ten minutes, Tiffany had calmed, finally drifting into restless sleep. Roseanne had collapsed into bed, exhausted.

This morning, when she had lifted the cool, limp little angel from her pillow in the firewood box, Roseanne had rejoiced that the baby's fever was gone. Her cheeks, her forehead, had been cool.

Too cool.

Deathly cold.

The frozen soil made Roseanne's knees ache. The pain spread in both directions. Up her thighs. Down her calves to her ankles. Sharp teeth of the wind chewed at her ears and nose. Still she waited, keeping her mind empty like the vast, cloudless winter sky. When no voices whispered, Roseanne begged the Spirits to speak to her, to deliver her, to guide her.

We are here.

Roseanne's blue eyes grew round, expectant. They rolled down in their sockets until she was looking at the mummy-like bush.

Your mission is complete.

Roseanne held her breath. If it were possible, she would have stopped the pounding of her heart while she listened.

Bury her shell.

Still on her knees, eyes fixed and staring, Roseanne leaned forward. The scent of burlap, the smell of soil and decomposing leaves were incense on the altar. "Bury her? Where?"

With the innocents gone before her.

"With the innocents?" The pressure in Roseanne's head was nearly unbearable. "Where are they?"

With a kind and gentle one.

The wind lowered its voice to a whisper. *Kind.* Roseanne's pulse slowed. *Gentle.* The chill seeped from her body to mingle with the frozen soil. There was silence in her soul.

Bareheaded and without a coat, the knees of her pants stained brown, Roseanne trudged up the street to the corner store. She handed coins to the clerk, took a paper from the middle of the stack and walked home again.

Eagerly she leafed through the paper. *Innocents gone before*

197

her. She knew just where to find the obituary column. *A kind and gentle one*.

There were very few death notices today. Roseanne ran her fingertip down the left-hand column. "No," she whispered, when she read the name of the funeral home. The second notice was brief, only a few lines. It wasn't the right one either. One by one, Roseanne scanned the notices, rejecting them as the spirits directed her. When only a few notices remained, Roseanne's eyes widened. Her ink-smudged fingers paused above the words *Emerson Funeral Home*.

The letters in the obituary notice vibrated before Roseanne's eyes. *Maria Antonelli, age sixteen, of Austin died Saturday. Maria was born in Amalfi, Italy, and was living in Austin while her father attended the University of Texas. She was the only child of Tony and Norma Antonelli.*

A wake service will be held at seven o'clock Sunday evening at Emerson Funeral Home. The funeral will be Monday morning at ten o'clock at the Church of the Good Shepherd.

Roseanne touched Maria Antonelli's name with a trembling fingertip. The Spirits whispered again. *The innocent one.*

Emerson Funeral Home—Blair's funeral home—was a twenty-minute walk from Roseanne's house. The moment Roseanne saw that familiar name in the obituary notice, she knew it was there that she would carry out her mission.

The evening was so bitterly cold and her mission so urgent that Roseanne took a cab. The driver spoke very little English. He stared blankly when Roseanne asked, for the second time: "Take me to Emerson Funeral Home near the university." Finally she gave up and said, "Eighteenth and Lavaca." She would have to walk from there.

Roseanne had ridden in cabs a few times, so she knew what to do and how much to tip. On the sidewalk now, she hooked the handles of her straw bag on her right shoulder. Leaning into the wind, resisting its force and the worries that weighed her down, Roseanne walked three blocks to the steps of

Emerson Funeral Home. Would Blair be there? She hoped so. Not that Roseanne would say anything to her. But she could at least see Blair from a distance.

Her knees shook badly when she climbed the steps. The door opened before her. "I'm here to attend the service for Maria Antonelli."

"This way, please." The nice-looking, brown-haired young man stepped toward double doors to his right. He opened one. "The service is just beginning. The memorial book is inside if you wish to leave your name."

"Thank you." The door closed silently behind Roseanne. She went immediately into the chapel and slid into a pew near the back.

Fewer than fifty people were there. Some knelt and recited prayers. Others sat silently. Maria Antonelli lay in a pale blue, open casket. From where she sat, Roseanne could see words and something that looked like birds stitched in the lid. Maria was hardly visible.

Two people sat in the front row on the right. They were dressed in black and huddled against each other. Maria's parents, Roseanne guessed. The people clustered on the left were teenagers, an equal number of boys and girls. Noticeably absent was the usual number of older people. No uncles or aunts. No grandparents. All back in Italy, Roseanne decided. How sad to be so far away from family. She knew how lonely that could be. She had a sister in Utah who never wrote or called.

When the service ended, the pastor stepped over to the family. Leaning on a railing in front of the pew, he whispered words of comfort that Roseanne wished she could hear. Then organ music resumed, floating ghostlike from speakers in the rear. Some mourners exited down the center aisle, heads down. Several faces were shiny with tears. Others joined the parents at Maria's casket.

Roseanne picked up her straw bag, stepped out of the pew and paused a moment in the aisle. A shiver of fear ran through her, but she inched her way forward. Finally she was standing at the edge of the cluster of people around the casket. Maria's mother was sobbing. Her father was somber and silent. No one noticed her. Gradually the mourners drifted from the chapel. Finally Maria's parents left too, taking their pain but leaving their precious Maria.

Roseanne inched her way toward the casket. Her heart was pumping wildly. There was a ringing in her ears. She was three feet away from Maria Antonelli. Then two. Then one. The beautiful child held a little white Bible in her hand. The lace collar on her ice-blue dress fit loosely around her thin neck. The casket lid was divided in half. The foot portion was closed. On it lay a spray of white carnations. Two blue ribbons flowed from a bow nestled in the flowers. *Precious Daughter*. A piece of fabric lay beneath the spray and draped over the edge of the lid, grazing the backs of Maria's folded hands. Roseanne knew the purpose of the fabric. It was to prevent people from peeking inside. Roseanne had been told that dead people were dressed only from the waist up.

Gently Roseanne slid the straps of the straw bag from her shoulder and set it on the carpeted floor. Then she bent forward, and with quivering fingers reached past Maria's folded hands and eased up the velvet fabric.

Roseanne leaned her head into the casket and peered toward the foot end. To her surprise, she found that Maria's legs were covered by folds of her dress and that she was wearing satin slippers. Gently she let the fabric fall back in place, then glanced around the chapel.

No one. She was alone.

The straw bag was deep. Roseanne leaned toward it, stuck both arms inside and felt the soft blanket wrapped around the silent angel. Tenderly she slid both hands beneath the precious bundle until her fingers touched. She was easing her arms out of the bag when a door to her left opened. Roseanne gasped and dropped the bundle back into the bag. She staggered backwards when a young man stepped toward her.

"I'm sorry. I didn't mean to startle you."

He was staring at her bag. Roseanne grabbed it up. He told her that he had thought everyone was gone, but Roseanne knew he was lying. He was a messenger from the Evil One, sent to thwart her mission. She stared into his devil eyes. Her tongue felt thick and tingly, but the Spirits helped her, gave her words to say. "I won't be but a minute. I was one of Maria's nurses. That's why the uniform. I just wanted to say goodbye to her alone."

"Take your time."

His smile was different now. He eyed her suspiciously while he picked up tissues from the pews and flower petals from the carpet. It was no use. He did not intend to leave, and she could tolerate his stares no longer.

Roseanne's knees shook so badly she could hardly make it down the aisle to the back of the chapel. Above the pounding of her heart, she heard the Free Spirit whisper: *Rise early tomorrow. Complete your mission in the morning.*

29

Sunday had been sunless and somber. Now the lightning of a winter storm dazzled the blue-black sky. Sharp pellets of rain against her bedroom window kept Blair's nerves on edge. She flinched when the phone rang, then snatched up the receiver. "Hello."

"Hi, Blair. It's Kent."

She gathered her composure. "How did the wake service go?"

"Fine. There were quite a few people here. Maria's parents held up well, considering. Blair, the reason I'm calling is that there's been a change regarding Maria's burial."

"Oh?"

"Her parents have decided not to bury her here. They want us to fly Maria's body back to Italy as soon as possible. Mrs. Antonelli is going home with her."

"That doesn't surprise me."

"I told them that securing the permits will take a few days."

"Good. We'll have Jane start the process in the morning." Blair stroked Celtic's back, trying to calm her jagged nerves. "Are you getting ready to lock up?"

"Already done it. I was just—Oh, one other thing, Blair. Something happened tonight that I didn't quite know how to handle."

Kent explained that he had walked in on a woman who looked as if she intended to put something in Maria's casket. "I had been kind of keeping an eye on her since she got there. She seemed really nervous and...I don't know...kind of odd. Anyway, I didn't ask her what she was doing or anything. I just hung around in the chapel hoping to discourage her. It seemed to work. She finally left."

"I think you handled it well. People shouldn't place anything in a casket without the family's permission."

"I'm glad you approve. Well, I guess that's it. Get some sleep."

"Will do. Good night."

Blair roamed the house. Repeatedly she returned to Brandi's room. Touching the curtains and the bedspread. Opening the closet and drawers that would soon be filled with Brandi's things.

The phone drew her back to the bedroom.

It was Lenny.

"Well, well. We meet again."

The sound of Lenny's voice sent chills down Blair's spine. "I'm...glad to hear from you."

"I'll just bet you are. Have you got my little Christmas gift ready?"

"I have most of the..."

"You better not tell me you ain't got that money together."

"No. I'll—I have it. All of it."

"You better have it. If you want the kid, you better not try to jerk me around."

"I wouldn't, Lenny. I want Brandi back more than anything in the world. You know that." Her voice choked with urgency. "I'll get the cash tomorrow. I promise. Just tell me when and...and where...and I'll bring it all. A hundred and twenty-five thousand, just like we agreed."

"You'd better be damn sure you have it—all of it."

"I will. I will. It's just that raising that kind of money . . ."

"Save it. I'm giving you until Tuesday night. Eight o'clock."

"Thank you."

"You know where the School Book Depository is? Where Kennedy got shot?"

"Yes."

"Park in front of it and wait there."

"Right. Eight o'clock. Tuesday night. I'll have the cash ready. Will . . .will you bring Brandi there?"

"Just bring the cash," Lenny snapped. "You'll get her. How it happens is up to me."

30

Frank's phone call from Blair that morning had lasted no more than two minutes. He had immediately contacted the Waco police department and gotten Chubby Elledge's name. Less than an hour later, Elledge was on the phone, telling Frank that he did remember taking tire chains off a late model sedan early Sunday morning a week ago. "There weren't many cars out that night. The few customers I did have kind of stand out in my memory."

"Tell me everything you remember." Frank slid a note pad in front of him and took a quick gulp of coffee.

"Well, I was on the phone when she pulled in, talking to my wife. After fifteen years, she still worries about me getting clubbed on the head. I call her on the hour from nine until when I leave at two. Then she has a snack..." Chubby Elledge cleared his throat. "Anyway, I was talking to her when the car drove in. I think I ..."

"Excuse me. What time was that?"

"About one o'clock. Maybe a little after."

"Go ahead. Sorry."

"Well, I told my wife I had to go, that a customer was driving up. I walked around the sedan and asked the woman driving how I could help. She asked if I would take off her tire chains. I told her I'd be glad to. Then she went next door to the cafe. I didn't have no trouble getting the left chain off, but the right one was in a bind. So I pulled the car into one of the bays, raised it off the ground a tad and yanked the chain right off."

"So you got into the car."

"Right. To pull it into the bay."

"Was there anyone else in the car?"

"Nope."

"You're sure."

"Sure as I'm sittin' here."

"No one? No children or babies?"

"Babies? Naw. There wasn't no babies." Chubby Elledge cleared his throat again and went on. "So I lowered the car, throwed the chains in the trunk like she had asked, and backed the car out."

"Wait," Frank interrupted. "You opened the trunk? What was in it?"

"Aww, let me think. Nothing much. A box for the tire chains. A real good spare. That's about it, as far as I remember."

"Then what happened?" Frank asked.

"Well, she come back from the cafe, asked me what she owed me. I told her nothing, but she gave me a ten anyway. I thanked her and wished her an early merry Christmas. Then she drove off."

"Which direction?"

"South."

"Toward Austin?"

"Well, Austin's south of Waco, but I don't know that's where she was heading."

"True. Mr. Elledge, did you notice which direction she was traveling when she pulled into the station?" *Come on, Chubby. Don't let me down now.*

"From the north."

Frank smiled. "You're sure."

"Sure I'm sure. I seen her blinker come on and watched

her pull in."

"She was going from north to south."

"That's how the interstate runs along here."

"Right. Mr. Elledge, can you describe the woman for me?"

"Oh, I can try." Chubby Elledge sucked air between his teeth, making a clicking sound. "I'd say she was in her late thirties. Medium height. Brown hair, fixed real smooth. A right pretty woman."

"What was she wearing?"

"Shoot, I don't know. Could have been pants, could have been a dress. No, wait. She had on pants and boots. I remember now. And a coat, of course. It was colder than a well-digger's nose that night."

When asked if he would recognize a picture of the woman, Chubby answered, "I think I would. I hope she ain't in trouble or something."

"I think you probably just got her out of it."

"Well, I'm glad. Seemed like a nice woman to me."

"Did she say anything else to you?"

"Yeah, something about Christmas and how this one was going to be the best she'd had in years."

Blair's answering machine was on when Frank called her. He left a request that she call him at the station.

When he hadn't heard from her by noon, he drove to the funeral home. He told himself he needed to take a look in the trunk of her car, just to verify Chubby Elledge's statement; and that was true. Mostly, though, he wanted to see what Blair Emerson looked like with a smile on her face.

When Blair wasn't at the funeral home, Frank returned to the station. From there he called Myles Lakeman. "I spoke to a man in Waco this morning, Myles." Frank related his conversation with Chubby Elledge. "Please reassure your father-in-law that Blair was not in Austin at the time of Tiffany's abduction. This is proof enough for me that Blair is in no way involved."

"I'll tell him."

207

"And, Myles, don't give up hope."

"I don't want to hear it. I've heard it before." Exhaustion weighed down Myles's voice. "Some lunatic ruined my life with Blair. Another one's doing it with Charmaine." A brief silence. "You know, she actually blames me."

A dial tone buzzed in Frank's ear.

At first Lenny thought he would stay off coke for a few days, just to make sure he was thinking good and clear. But he found out in short order that that dog wouldn't hunt. Not even eighteen hours passed before he was ready to break out of his skin.

The pea coat was hanging in the back of his closet. Lenny unbuttoned it and removed the satchel from beneath it. The manila envelope on top contained his new identification. He dumped the contents on the desk. The picture on his new driver's license brought a smile to Lenny's face. He looked damn good in that fake mustache—like a thin, blond Burt Reynolds. He ran a finger along his upper lip. The stubble there would thicken soon enough. Then he wouldn't need the fake mustache he had in his suitcase.

He removed from his wallet everything with Lenny Bond's name on it and slid it all into the empty manila envelope. This afternoon he would burn the stuff, and Lenny Bond would be history. "Now," he said with the taste of satisfaction sweet on his tongue, "Lee Pickens is gonna buy himself a Chevy truck." Lenny removed several stacks of bills from the satchel, noticing the two letters from Blair Emerson when he did. *Insurance policies.* "I'm so smart I impress myself." He returned the satchel to its place beneath his pea coat and popped the top on a cold beer.

April heard Lenny stirring around in his room. Minutes later he pounded on the connecting door. "Hey, Bones, you decent?" Her mumble must have sounded like *yes* to him, because he opened the door. "You know reading all the time will make you cross-eyed. You want to be skinny *and* cross-eyed?"

"Yeah, Lenny. Sounds good. Who would care anyway?"

"Whoa. Ain't you got a burr under your saddle," he mocked.

April didn't look up from her book. She had paid full price for it, four ninety-five plus tax, in the gift shop downstairs. But without something to read, she would go crazy waiting around for that stupid Blair to make up her mind—or to let some creep do it for her.

"I'll be back tonight, Bones. Got some rat-killing to do."

Rat-killing. How disgusting. Why couldn't he just say that he had some place to go? April still didn't look up, not even when Lenny said, "Well, it's been a real pleasure talking to you," then turned, slammed the door, and left.

He didn't lock the door, though.

April hurried to the window, watching for Lenny to appear three stories below and get into his car. When he drove away, she pulled her gloves from beneath her mattress, slipped them on and went into Lenny's room.

She'd had it with them. Lenny and Blair both. Who needed them anyway? All she needed was another fifty dollars. Maybe she would even take a hundred. After all, Lenny owed it to her for getting out of his miserable life.

That morning, she had called the bus station again and found out what time a bus left tomorrow night for Virginia Beach. Blair had twenty-four hours more, and then April would split. What choice did she have? She had overheard Lenny on the phone telling someone he was leaving for El Paso early Wednesday morning.

The satchel was in Lenny's closet, hanging beneath his pea coat. April opened it and reached inside, discovering that several stacks of bills were gone. Her mind panned her options. With so few stacks left, the money would be easily counted. Did she dare do it? Yes. She couldn't get halfway across the country with no spending money.

She set the satchel on Lenny's bed and spread the top open.

209

With protected fingers, she separated the stacks and found three in small bills. She took a combination totaling ninety dollars.

The letter with her name on it was still in the satchel. She had wondered about it a lot. When she eased it out, a second envelope came with it. She turned it over. *Brandi*.

Something stirred far back in April's mind. She lay the envelopes side by side on Lenny's bed. Same handwriting. Identical envelopes.

"I wonder who Brandi is."

31

Following her typical Monday morning routine, Blair left the funeral home at nine-thirty to make the bank deposit. "I'll be back shortly, Jane," she offered, feigning her usual disinterest in the task while her heart raced. In less than an hour, she would leave the bank with one hundred and twenty-five thousand dollars in cash. Her broker's check had reached her account late last week. All the money was there now.

I'm ready, Lenny. Tuesday night. Eight o'clock.

She felt like a bank robber when, after completing her regular deposit, she handed the teller a withdrawal slip, and told him she wanted the money in cash. Again, she was escorted to a private office where the teller and a man, whose name and position Blair didn't catch and didn't care about, went through their complex and lengthy routine.

A bank guard walked with her to the parking garage, carrying on an easy conversation about the cold weather. Blair gripped the handle of her briefcase. So many stressful days and sleepless nights had left her almost giddy. *It's a good thing Lenny asked for such a small amount. I wouldn't have been able to carry a million in cash.*

In the parking garage, the guard watched her from the elevator while she opened her trunk. Leaning into it, Blair placed the briefcase containing the pouch of money inside the trunk, then closed the lid.

It's almost over, Brandi.

Blair nodded to the guard, saw him reach for a button and heard the whoosh of the elevator when she turned away. Her knees felt wobbly when she walked toward her car door, head down, fists clenched.

Then a hand gripped her shoulder.

A sharp jab in her back.

Blair froze in mid-stride.

"Not a sound," a voice growled.

Fear shot through her like an electric current. Lenny.

"Turn around slowly and walk to that car over there."

Another jab in her back. Blair pivoted slowly. Lenny was so close behind her that she could feel the warmth of his breath in the cold garage.

"Slowly. Very slowly toward the car. Not a sound out of you."

His voice. Low. Precise. Refined. Not at all like he had sounded on the phone. What was he doing? How did he know she was there? Where was he taking her? To Brandi? Please. To Brandi.

"Go around to the driver's side."

A whiff of cologne.

"Open the door."

A car engine groaned up a nearby ramp. Did she dare scream, struggle to get free? No. He might panic and shoot her.

"Hurry. I'll shoot you right here if I have to."

She paused for a split-second and glanced toward the passing car. Then it was gone.

"Get in. And slide all the way over. I'll drive." He was standing so close that Blair had difficulty opening the door of the Cadillac.

"Get in, I said."

At that moment, Blair caught an image in the shaded window of the blue Cadillac. It numbed her with terror.

212

"Dr. Lauzon." Her fingertips flew to her lips. She gasped when he jabbed her ribs hard with the pistol barrel. "Why are you doing this?"

"Shut up or I'll kill you this moment."

32

The white envelopes sold in the Holiday Inn gift shop were a different size from the ones in Lenny's satchel. April bought a box anyway. If she replaced both envelopes after she read the letters, Lenny would never notice. He was out doing who-knows-what, but April couldn't be sure how much longer he'd be gone. She had to hurry.

The satchel was in its place beneath the pea coat. April slipped on her gloves and opened it. She removed the envelope marked *April*, took it to the desk and placed the plain white envelope beside it. She practiced her name, trying to duplicate the smooth, neat strokes and loops. But copying someone else's handwriting was more difficult than she had thought. The effort resulted in several ripped envelopes.

She tried tracing her name onto the envelope, but she couldn't see the letters clearly through the thick paper.

Finally she took a piece of sheer paper from inside the desk and laid it over her name. She traced it easily. Then she laid that paper on the blank envelope and pressed over the letters with a pen. In seconds she had imprinted her name clearly on the envelope. Writing over the impression was simple. She was pleased with the results.

Her heart was racing now. Lenny could walk in at any

214

second. She repeated the procedure for the envelope to Brandi. By the time she finished, she was nauseous and light-headed. Her thoughts lurched back and forth between reading the letters now and risking getting caught, or waiting until later.

Wait. He'll go out again. And there'll be more time, less chance of getting caught.

April's legs trembled as she walked across the room and put the letters back in the satchel. Soon she would find out who had written her a letter and who in the world Brandi was.

She returned to the lobby. At a pay phone, she gave the operator a number in Virginia Beach. Inserting the coins seemed to take forever. "Becky. Hi. It's me."

The voice on the other end squealed. "April! What happened to you? Why didn't you say goodbye? Where are you?"

"It's a long story." April watched the steady flow of people entering the lobby. "Listen, Becky, I've only got a minute. I can't stand it with Lenny. There's a chance I may split. Can I come to your house?"

"Sure . . .if you don't mind living in New Orleans."

"New Orleans?"

"Yes. My aunt got my mom a job at some fancy hotel in the French Quarter. We leave tomorrow. But, April, it'll still be okay. Mom's crazy about you."

"How will I find you?"

"We'll be at Aunt Bonnie's house for a few days. Write down her name and number."

"Just a minute." April dug out a pencil and a scrap of paper. 'Okay. I'm ready." She scribbled the information hurriedly. "Got it. Now listen, Becky, things are crazy here. I don't know for sure what's going to happen, but I'll be in touch."

"Call soon. I miss you. And be careful, April."

April hung up and smiled to herself. This was great. Perfect. If Blair didn't want her, she would go to New Orleans and Becky. Then Lenny would *never* find her.

215

33

Water lapped at the boathouse. Sitting on the cold wooden planks inside, Blair shivered like Celtic in a thunderstorm. Wrists taped tightly behind her back. Legs extended. Ankles crossed and bound. A gag in her mouth. Tape stretched across her lips.

This can't be happening.

The lake house was secluded. No one had seen them since they pulled onto City Park Road. There was no one to hear her. No one to help. She was on her own, and she had just over twenty-four hours to figure a way out of this—and get to Brandi.

On the frantic ride out of Austin, Blair had pleaded with Dr. Lauzon, trying to convince him that she had been in Dallas the night of Tiffany's disappearance, begging him to talk to Frank Traxill, telling herself at the same time that Frank surely had talked to the station attendant in Waco by now. He had seen her drive up, been in her car, her trunk.

Dr. Lauzon, blue-red in the face, had shouted, "That man probably doesn't make twenty thousand dollars a year. He would say anything if you paid him enough."

Then he had come across hard with his forearm. Blair had twisted away in time to avoid taking the blow on her face, but pain had shot through her left shoulder.

A life jacket lay next to her on the floor, her stiff cold pillow through the nightmarish hours. Standing in the door opening, Dr. Lauzon had said, "I'll be back tomorrow. If you wish to live through our next visit, you will tell me what you did with my granddaughter."

God, would he really kill me?

Blair shifted her weight carefully, banged her sore shoulder on the floor nevertheless. She lay on her side, drawing her legs up tight to trap her body heat and to shield herself from the cold. If only she could free her hands. But it was impossible. The tape cut into her wrists. Once she had rolled to the door and kicked against it with her feet, but the structure was sturdy and defied her feeble battering.

Why hadn't she screamed in the parking garage, taken a chance on being heard? But at first she had thought he was Lenny, and it had all happened so fast. And the pistol. He might have shot her.

Exhaustion finally quieted her thoughts. She closed her eyes and drifted into anxious sleep.

Sleep brought with it dark images.

Lenny. Pacing back and forth in the shadows of the School Book Depository. Cursing her. Finally squealing away in his car to tell Brandi that her worthless mother hadn't even shown up.

Brandi. Head turned away from Lenny's angry raving. Hands stuffed deep into the pockets of her denim jacket. Her featureless face streaked with tears.

34

The drive to Blair's house was filled with foreboding. Eldon Sumner fought back ugly images of what he might find there. It was eight o'clock Monday evening. Jane had called him, looking for Blair, saying she had not seen her since early that morning. "She doesn't answer her phone or her pager. I called Liz. She hasn't talked to her or seen her today."

"Where was she going when she left the office?" Eldon had asked.

"To the bank. Just like she does every Monday morning."

The bank. She didn't return from the bank. Could this have anything to do with the money she needed?

Fortunately Blair had left duplicates of all her keys with Jane. Eldon rang the bell several times before using the one to the front door. "Blair." He peeked around the door edge. "Blair, are you here, honey?"

A creeping uneasiness followed Eldon into the entry and down the short hall to the den. Over and over, he called Blair's name, willing her to answer.

The house was freezing cold. Clearly the heat had been off all day. The door to the den was closed. "Blair, it's Eldon. Are you here?" He eased open the door and gasped loudly when something streaked past him. "Celtic!" Eldon sagged against the door frame. "You scared me to death."

The confused and frantic dog ran through the house yelping wildly, searching for Blair. He finally gave up his search and ran to the back door, looking imploringly at Eldon. He let Celtic into the back yard and waited until he came in again.

The sight of a dry water bowl increased Eldon's worry. Blair was in trouble. Otherwise, she would have kept in touch with Jane. And whatever it was, it had kept her from coming home today. She never deliberately would have left Celtic unattended.

The light on Blair's answering machine blinked red. Eldon played the messages. Most of them were from Jane, there were a couple from Liz. One message left early that morning was from a man named Frank Traxill. Even if the message had not mentioned the police station, Eldon would have recognized the name from the papers.

He called Liz first.

"So she's still not home?" Liz asked anxiously.

"No. And she hasn't been here either. Do you have any idea where she could be? Did she mention anything to you?."

"No, not really. Well, she did say something a few days ago about . . .Dallas."

"Dallas?" Eldon stretched the long phone cord to the limit, putting food and water in Celtic's bowls. "You think she might be in Dallas?"

"I'm not sure, Eldon. I know she had to go up there recently to . . .help a . . .a friend of hers."

"But why wouldn't she have told Jane she was leaving town?"

"I . . .I don't know."

"Liz, are you keeping something from me? Is Blair sick or in some kind of trouble?"

"No, no. It's nothing like that." Liz spoke rapidly, anxiously. "I suspect that this guy—this friend of hers—called and needed her. Wherever she is, I'm sure she's okay, Eldon."

"Well, I'm not sure. I'm not sure at all." Liz's polite reassurances and vague non-answers only made Eldon more anxious. "One other thing. There's a message on her machine from a cop named Traxill. Do you know anything about that?"

"I have an idea, yes." Liz quickly relayed the matter of Dr. Lauzon's accusations. "But it's nothing for you to worry about, Eldon. Really."

"Well, I am worried, Liz. I'm worried sick. And if we haven't heard from Blair by morning, I'm calling the police."

Eldon hung up the phone and reached for a notepad. *Blair, call me the minute you get home. No matter what time. Everyone's been looking for you. Eldon.* Then he weighted down the note with a salt shaker, lifted Celtic into his arms, and walked wearily to his pickup truck.

Just before dawn Eldon dialed Blair's number. He knew she wouldn't answer. She hadn't answered the entire long night. He dressed hurriedly, and waited for the nurse to arrive. To his relief, Maryruth was still in bed when he left. He took Celtic with him, otherwise Maryruth might wonder why the dog wasn't with Blair.

He drove to Blair's house. It was quiet and cold and empty. *Where are you, Blair?* Quick calls to the funeral home and Liz netted nothing but more anxious thoughts. Now it was time to call the police.

"Frank Traxill, please." Eldon picked up the note he had left Blair and stared at it. "Sergeant Traxill. My name is Eldon Sumner. I'm a close friend of Blair Emerson's."

"Yes, sir. Can I help you?"

"I hope so. I'm trying to find Blair. In fact, I'm at her house now. I found a message from you on her machine. Have you talked to her?"

"No, I haven't."

"Do you mind if I ask why you called her?"

"Well, it was in regard to an investigation."

"Tiffany's disappearance."

"Yes, sir."

"Her friend Liz told me about Lauzon's accusations. That old fool." Eldon spit out the words. "I hope you didn't believe him."

"I didn't. He's been like a volcano, Mr. Sumner, but I imagine he's calmed down now that Blair's been cleared. That's why I called yesterday, to tell her everything was okay."

"Sergeant Traxill, I think something has happened to Blair. In fact, I know it."

"What is it? What's happened?"

Eldon heard concern in the man's voice. "I'm going to be absolutely honest with you because I want your help. Blair's been getting together a very large sum of money. Now you don't know Blair, but she's a very responsible person."

"I believe you. Go on."

"It's not like her to...to borrow money without reason. Or to fail to keep in touch with her secretary. And I know this sounds silly, but Blair has a dog..." Eldon paused to control his quavering voice. "Yesterday evening I found Celtic— that's Blair's dog—closed up in the den. No food. No water. Sergeant, Blair loves this dog. She would *never* go off and leave him like this."

"Sounds like she didn't plan to. Is her car there?"

"No, it's gone. Blair left here Monday morning, went to the funeral home and then to the bank. And no one has seen her since."

"Which bank?"

Eldon sighed. "Oh, it's at Seventh and Lavaca."

"Texas Commerce."

"Yes. That's it."

Less than an hour later, Frank was standing in the parking garage of Texas Commerce Bank. Blair's locked car was parked near the elevator on the second floor.

Frank had popped the trunk of more cars than he cared to think about, but the task always brought with it a niggling sense of dread. Especially this time.

But when he jimmied the trunk lid and it popped open, Frank breathed a little easier. Except for the items Chubby Elledge had described and a briefcase, the trunk was empty. The briefcase lay in the middle of the floor. Frank opened it. It contained a large leather pouch. Frank lifted the pouch from the briefcase while another detective looked over his shoulder. He released a long shrill whistle when Frank opened it.

The money, stacked and banded, was easy enough to count. Texas Commerce Bank had done it. One hundred twenty-five thousand dollars.

Frank stared at the bills. What was Blair going to do with all that money? Did someone find out about the "friend" in Dallas, maybe threaten to tell his wife?

Frank closed the trunk. "Have this car examined bumper to bumper."

Eldon Sumner was waiting for Frank when he got back to the police station. "Mr. Sumner, you were right about Blair. She was raising a lot of money. We found cash in the trunk of her car. Do you have any idea why she needed a hundred and twenty-five thousand dollars?"

35

Blair struggled across the boathouse floor and wriggled beneath a torn boat cover. Despite the musty-smelling canvas, she lay there shivering. A narrow slit of light on the floor was fading, and with it her hopes. Even if she were set free right now, she could not make it to Dallas by eight o'clock.

Somehow she had to be at home when Lenny called to curse her out for failing to show up. And he *would* call to find out what had happened. He had to.

But how could she get home?

She had prayed, hoping that God would show her the way out. But the only plan that surfaced was so repugnant to her that she was not sure she could go through with it.

Blair huddled beneath the canvas cover. Every muscle in her body ached. And she was thirsty, terribly thirsty. She had to get out of here.

There was only one way out.

Somehow she would convince Dr. Lauzon that if he killed her, he would never see Tiffany again. He had to believe that she was his only link to his granddaughter, that she was no use to him dead. But could she do it? Could she admit to abducting Tiffany? Could she confess to being everything he had called her yesterday. Yes. There was no other plan.

But what if, in his fragile mental state, Dr. Lauzon lost control, didn't believe her when she swore Tiffany was still alive?

Footsteps on the pier sent Blair's heart pounding. The door burst open. "All right, you hard-hearted tramp," Lauzon hissed. "Who has my granddaughter?"

Two distinct images burned in Blair's mind. One was the eerie stare in Dr. Lauzon's eyes. The other was the glint of the pistol he pointed at her head.

Lauzon lunged at Blair. With the side of his shoe, he kicked her hard in the ribs. Her body arched in pain.

"You went to Dallas that night. Myles says you have proof." He drove his shoe into her side again. "You gave my granddaughter to someone. You tell me who has her, and you tell me now."

Blair let out a muffled scream. With one jerk, Lauzon ripped the tape from her mouth, taking tender skin with it. He snatched the gag from between her teeth. "Now you talk." Spittle flew from his mouth like little sparks. "Tell me or I'll kill you this minute."

Blair swallowed the blood that trickled onto her tongue. "I did it," she gasped. Several seconds of heart-pounding terror passed before she could speak again. "I did it. But I'm sorry. It was wrong. Terribly wrong." Blair gagged on the blood and the bitter taste of terror. She choked it all back and said, "But I won't tell you anything more unless you let me . . ." Blair's head erupted in blinding pain when cold hard steel slammed into her face, cracking against bone, ripping the flesh on her cheek.

"You will tell me." Lauzon's face twisted in rage. His eyes blazed.

Blair bit down on her lip to hold onto consciousness. *God, help me.* The garish face blurred before her eyes. She tried to breathe deeply, to fight for consciousness. "I won't . . . tell you . . . unless . . ."

"Unless what?"

" . . .unless you take me . . .to Myles."
Blair's head rolled to the side.
A black curtain fell across her eyes.

36

Roland Lauzon parked his car in the driveway of Myles and Charmaine's house. His breathing was frighteningly labored. He was panting by the time he reached the rear of the house and entered through the back door. Myles's car was gone and the house was quiet.

The door to Charmaine's bedroom was closed. Roland peeked in. She was curled beneath a blanket. Small, heart-wrenching sobs escaped from her lips. Roland eased the door shut. "I'll get her back for you, my love. Trust me."

Outside the bedroom, he steadied himself against the wall, summoning strength for the short walk to the guest room and his medication. The walls closed in around him.

He took a few steps, then a sharp pain shot through his head. As he sank to his knees, Roland squeezed his eyes shut and pressed both palms to his temples.

He struggled to his feet and shuffled down the carpeted hall. His medication was on the night stand in the guest room. He reached for the bottle, but his unsteady hand sent it skimming across the hardwood floor. He sank to the edge of the bed. Nausea washed over him. He buried his head in his hands. "What do I do? Do I take Myles to the boathouse? Do I let this evil woman tell him that Tiffany is still alive? If she is telling the truth and her accomplice is holding Tiffany, then Blair Emerson is our only hope." Another thought crossed his mind. "But if Blair Emerson is lying and Tiffany is dead, then she must die. And it must be at my hands."

Roland lifted his head, caught his withered reflection in the mirror. "No. She will not talk to Myles. I will not let her get his hopes up, only to crush them. Blair Emerson will take me . . . and no one else . . . to my granddaughter. If she refuses, then I will know she is lying, and she will pay for what she has done."

It was seven o'clock in the evening. All day April had waited for a chance to sneak into Lenny's room, read the two letters, and return them to the satchel in the new envelopes she had prepared. But Lenny had hung around all day, drinking beer like the disgusting drunk that he was. She was sick to death of his beer and his drugs and his stupid cracks about her weight and her books. And she was fed up with Blair, too. "They can both drop dead."

April bolted upright from her bed when she heard a door close. It was Lenny. He was finally leaving. Now was her chance. She quickly slipped on her gloves.

The connecting door was unlocked. April opened it. Lenny's suitcase lay open on his bed. He had tossed his underwear and some shirts into it. Other clothes were piled on the bed.

April hurried to the closet. She shoved the empty hangers to one side. "No." The pea coat was gone. The satchel with the letters, too. Lenny had emptied the closet.

A pile of towels lay in a soggy heap on the floor of Lenny's bathroom. Bits of his blond hair littered the countertop. Shaving lather clumped in the sink. "Gross." April turned away. "The satchel. Where is it?"

Every drawer in the dresser was empty except for hotel clutter. Had he taken the satchel to the car? April looked nervously around the room. The night stand. She hadn't

227

looked there. The drawer was deep enough. She yanked it open.

The satchel was there. She pulled it out and laid it on the bed. Quickly, she spread open the top. Money. Lots of it still. She plucked out the first envelope she saw. *April*. She ran a stiff, nervous finger under the flap. She was digging in the satchel for the second letter, the one to Brandi, when she heard a hacking cough and footsteps on the concrete stairwell.

Lenny.

She snatched the empty envelopes from her back pocket, sealed the one with *April* written on the front, and stuffed it into the satchel. Then she jammed the satchel back into the drawer, kicked it shut, and ran to her room.

Breathless, April peeled off her gloves, listening for sounds of Lenny in the next room. She looked down at the envelope she had stolen and then felt the edges of folded paper inside it. *April.* As soon as Lenny left to meet Blair, she would read it. For a moment she worried about what Lenny might do if he found out she had swiped the letter. Then she decided she didn't care if he did find out. The letter was meant for her. It had her name on it.

She was still curious about the letter to Brandi, though. Now she wouldn't have a chance to read it. She looked down at the name she had traced onto the empty envelope. *Brandi.* Then she tore the envelope into little pieces and dropped them in the trash can.

Lenny threw the last of his clothes in the suitcase. He had settled up with the hotel. Now all he had to do was take care of the little matter of the letter and head for Deally Plaza.

He removed the satchel from the night stand, and fished out the letter with *Brandi* written on the front. He stuck it in his back pocket, then rapped on April's door with his knuckles. "You in there, kid?"

"Just a minute."

A minute was about all the time he had. He would meet

Blair at eight, get the cash and then tell her to hightail it back to Austin and wait for April's call around midnight. Then he would speed away in his new Chevy truck, and when he figured he was in the clear, he'd call April and tell her where to find the letter and how to reach her mother. By the time she and Blair talked, Lenny would be on the way to Laredo. He had told his partner he needed a base of operations other than El Paso, just in case Blair or her ex-old man decided to launch a dragnet for one Lenny Bond, last known heading for El Paso.

"Bones, open up. I got places to go, people to see." The door eased open. April was as white as a ghost. "I got something to tell ya." Lenny looked casually around the room. Where was her backpack? "Looks like things are gonna work out for both of us, kid. I hope so anyway. I'll call you after I see Blair—probably around nine—and let you know what's what. But, like I said, things are lookin' good."

"Are you sure?"

"Yeah, I'm sure. I'm all packed and ready to leave for El Paso. That's how sure I am."

"If she says no, when will you be back to get me?"

"Uh. Awww. About nine-thirty, I guess." Lenny took a step toward her and pulled out his wallet. "Here's some money. You might need it." He forced the bill into her hand. He knew that would send her flying to the bathroom the minute he left the room. Then he'd slip back in and find the backpack.

Lenny tousled April's hair and paused to look at her a moment. "Talk to you later, kid." He turned away, walked halfway to the door and stopped. With his back to her, he said, "You made Jewell real happy, you know that? Happier than I ever did." Pause. "Things are gonna be better for you now, April."

37

Kent Willhoite was scheduled to work until nine-thirty Tuesday evening. The Billings and Thurman visitations both had been held that evening, leaving him with no time to take care of Mrs. Antonelli's request. But almost everyone was gone now, so he stepped into the office and asked the receptionist to take care of the front door. "Any word from Blair?"

"Not a thing."

"Where could she be?" Kent frowned and shook his head. "I'll be in Maria's stateroom for a few minutes."

The room was dimly lit with one lamp. Music drifted down from overhead speakers. The pale blue casket at the far end of the room was closed. It had been locked since just before they left for the church service on Monday.

Kent had received his embalmer's license only a few months ago. He had worked for Blair for a year before attending mortuary college. And during that year, he'd decided that the funeral business was where he belonged. People like Norma and Tony Antonelli were one of the reasons why.

There were still aspects of the work that got to him from time to time. Burying children was one of them. Opening caskets that had been closed for a while was another. Despite that, he was curious to see the condition of Maria's body a full four days after her embalming.

He approached the foot of the casket and unscrewed a small, metal key cap. He dropped it in his pocket and inserted a casket key, a small crank designed to activate the casket's internal locking mechanism. With the palm of his hand, Kent rotated the key, easing up on the lid with his other hand.

Maria's face appeared as Kent raised the lid. It was as he remembered it: beautiful in its youth and thinness. Leaning over her, Kent examined her features in the dim glow. Her lips and eyelids showed not a hint of dehydration. No discoloration was visible on her face or hands.

"There's no reason your family back home shouldn't see you to say goodbye," Kent spoke softly in the silence.

The afghan that Norma Antonelli had crocheted lay on a nearby table. Kent unfolded it carefully, revealing rows of pastel pink and blue. Hours of work. A Christmas gift. "Spread it over her legs," Norma Antonelli had said tearfully. "No matter how many blankets I put on her, she always said she felt cold."

With the afghan draped over his forearm, Kent raised the lid on the foot of casket. The fabric overlay had been neatly folded over Maria's legs. If he placed it under her feet instead, he could spread the afghan over Maria's legs just as her mother had asked.

A split-second after Kent lifted the overlay, his gentle brown eyes narrowed. He recalled the peculiar red-haired woman the night of the wake service. She had intended to put something in Maria's casket. He knew it. She had been there again Monday morning, carrying that same straw bag. He had kept an eye on her until she finally left.

Kent intensified the overhead lights and examined the casket bed. He pulled the folds of Maria's dress to the side and felt alongside her legs.

"Nothing here," he whispered. "But there would have been if I hadn't been here. I saw it in that woman's eyes."

231

38

In the darkness of the boathouse, Blair's misery and hope-
lessness deepened. The green glowing digits on her watch
rolled past eight o'clock. Lenny was there now, watching the
School Book Depository, maybe from one of the knolls in
Deally Plaza. Cursing. Threatening. Was Brandi with him?
No. She would be somewhere else, far enough away to buy
Lenny time to disappear before she and Brandi could talk.
For two weeks she had lived for that moment, for their first
words.

Where are you, Roland Lauzon? Come back, you lunatic.

Tears drenched Blair's face. She willed herself not to cry; it
made breathing so difficult. But the agony over once again
losing Brandi tore through her, destroying the fragile hope
she had pieced together since Lenny's first call.

She rolled onto her side and lay there while the sobs and
shudders subsided. Pain jabbed at her ribs where Roland
Lauzon had kicked her, pounded in her head where he had
slammed the pistol. Blair steadied her breathing, dug deep
for control. She couldn't escape. She had tried that. Her only
plan was somehow to persuade Lauzon to take her to Myles.
For now, she would hoard her strength.

The wind picked up. Each mournful blast sent more

232

shivers through Blair's body. It was so cold. She lay on her side, moaning each time she rolled over to relieve the numbing pressure on her shoulder. Sometimes she fancied she heard the lock rattle or footsteps coming down the pier. Each time, she tensed and pushed herself onto her elbows.

It was her imagination. Every time.

Late in the night, she gave up hope that Lauzon would come for her. But why? Why hadn't he taken her to Myles, or brought Myles to her if he was afraid she might try to escape? There were any number of reasons, each more worrisome than the previous. An accident on the dangerously winding City Park Road. A fatal stroke. Or maybe Tiffany had been found and Lauzon had decided to let Blair die and come back later to dump her body into the lake.

Or maybe Tiffany was dead and Lauzon was coming back tomorrow to kill her.

"Stop it," she told herself. "Save your energy. Plan. Don't lose hope or you'll die."

Tomorrow. Yes, tomorrow. Lauzon and Myles would come for her. Myles would believe her. Then he would take her home and Lenny would call.

He *will* call. I have what he wants, Blair reminded herself. He has what I want. And Roland Lauzon will come back. I'm his only hope.

39

At home, Kent reached for the remote control and flicked on the television. He yawned widely and pulled at the knot in his tie. Local news anchor, Stephanie Williams, opened the ten o'clock broadcast on a somber note. "This holiday season began tragically for the family of Tiffany Lakeman, the infant girl who was abducted from an Austin hospital. Tonight police investigators are searching for this woman, who was seen at the scene of the abduction." A picture flashed on the screen just above Stephanie Williams's left shoulder.

Kent's eyes widened. He leaned toward the set and turned up the volume.

"This unidentified woman is being sought as a possible suspect in the case. Hospital personnel say she was wearing a white uniform and a bulky coat, and was carrying a multi-colored straw bag. She is a white female, approximately . . ."

Stephanie Williams continued the description of the woman, but Kent stopped listening. He was writing down the telephone number that had appeared on the screen.

Suddenly a sickening realization came. His stomach churned as he thought about the straw bag, the way the woman had reached inside it with both hands. Was it possible? Had that crazy woman carried a *baby* to the funeral

234

home that night? Had she actually intended to put the baby's body inside Maria's casket?

Kent reached for the phone and jabbed out the number. "I need to talk to someone about the disappearance of Tiffany Lakeman. I saw the woman you're looking for."

Lenny parked his Chevy truck next to a dumpster at a truckstop fifty miles south of Dallas and killed the engine. For several minutes he sat there fuming. "What the hell happened to you tonight, Blair Emerson?" For two solid hours, he had hidden in the shrubs at Deally Plaza swiveling his head around like some hoot owl. "Why didn't you show up?"

He rolled down the window, tossed the last of Lenny Bond's personal effects into the dumpster and walked to a bank of payphones nearby. His burning gut told him that Blair Emerson wouldn't answer. Nothing short of death could have kept that woman away from the School Book Depository tonight.

Just as he expected, he got her answering machine. He doused his anger with common sense and said, "Blair, this is your buddy, Lenny. I'm mighty sorry we missed each other tonight. Tell you what, though. Just to show you there ain't no hard feelings, I'm gonna give you your Christmas gift anyway. It'll probably be there tomorrow. I'll get mine from you later. Don't get any funny ideas about holding out on me now," he laughed—just in case someone else listened to the message. "I'd hate to have to show up at your house some day soon and take back the present I'm sending you. Be talkin' to ya. Bye."

So what if his plan got a little kink in it. No big deal. He'd still get the money. It would just take a little longer than planned. It was tempting to make Blair sweat a little, but he couldn't just go off to Laredo and leave April in the Holiday Inn indefinitely. And he sure couldn't take her with him. There was nothing else to do but give April a call and tell her to look in her backpack for Blair's phone number.

He was out of change, but before he went inside the truck stop to get some, he would throw away the satchel. He dragged it from behind the seat and took out the remaining money. There was hardly enough left to get Lee Pickens off with a ping, much less a bang. But he would take care of that little problem soon enough.

He peeled off a few bills and put them in his wallet. Then from the cab of his truck, he hurled the empty satchel into the dumpster. He was stacking the remaining bills in the deep, lighted glove compartment when he spotted the envelope with April's name on it.

"No need to keep this now." He tore it in half. "Hey, what's the deal here?" He blew a puff of air into both halves of the ripped envelope. "This sucker's empty. Where the hell is the letter?" He knew there had been one in it. He had read it himself, all that junk about Blair not wanting April back. What could have happened to it?

"April." For some time now he had suspected her of taking money from his wallet. A buck here. A buck there. What if she had been nosing around, stumbled onto the satchel and found the envelope with her name on it? Who else could have taken it?

Lenny locked the glove compartment quickly, trotted to the truck stop cashier and back to the pay phone. He dialed the Holiday Inn and told the operator to ring April Bond's room. How was he going to explain to her why Blair would write a letter like that?

"What do you mean there's no answer? Try again." *Hell's bells, April, get out of the bathroom and answer the phone*. The ringing continued. Finally the operator came back on the line. "Hey you. Connect me with the front desk." Where could that crazy kid be? It was eleven o'clock. "Hey, man, this is Lenny Bond. Send somebody up to check on my daughter. She ain't answering the phone."

Lenny turned up the collar of his leather coat and stamped the soles of his expensive boots to keep warm. His breath clouded like smoke. *What happened to you tonight, Blair Emerson? You must have been in a car wreck or something. But being the nice guy that I am* ... "Yeah, I'm here. What do you mean she's gone? All her stuff, too?" Lenny slammed the receiver down, cursing loudly. He trotted back to his truck and started the engine. "Damn." Lenny shook his head and slowly lit a cigarette. "You weren't ever supposed to see that letter, April. Never. That *other* one is for you, kid."

Heading south on the highway, Lenny felt as if somebody had sliced open his belly. Headlights from other cars decreased in number until, three hours south of Dallas, he cruised the dark stretch of road alone. "How'd things get so messed up?" He lit another cigarette and twisted the top off a beer. "There's no telling where that poor kid's heading right now. Probably not Virginia Beach. She'd be afraid I'd find her there."

Lenny chugged the beer and tossed the bottle out the window. "I hope you hold onto that backpack, April. Or you may never get back to your mama."

40

It was mid-morning on Wednesday. Frank Traxill rang the doorbell at the Lakeman house and stepped back, waiting. This was the part of his job he hated most. He desperately hoped that Myles, and not Charmaine, would open the door. It had been a sleepless night after he talked with Kent Willhoite. The young man had said several times that he could be mistaken about the woman's intentions, but neither he nor Frank really believed that he was.

The front door opened, and Myles mumbled an empty greeting. He was dressed in wrinkled clothes, and a heavy growth of beard darkened his face.

Frank followed Myles to the den. A log in the fireplace split and tumbled from the grate as Myles dropped into his recliner. Frank sat on the raised hearth, so close to Myles that his knees almost touched the chair arm. "I had a call last night, Myles. It was from a man who recognized the technician's sketch of the suspect. He doesn't know her name, but he saw the woman we've been looking for Sunday night and again Monday morning. She was at the place where he works."

"Where is that?"

A long pause, then, "Emerson Funeral Home."

Tired brown eyes widened. "Blair's funeral home?"

"Right. The suspect attended a service there Sunday night and came back again the next morning. She claimed to be one of the deceased girl's nurses."

"And?"

"Kent Willhoite—the funeral director—gave us an excellent description of the woman, all the way down to her red hair and blue eyes and straw bag. The family says the woman was never a nurse for their daughter." Frank paused before adding, "They had never seen the woman before."

"Then why was she at the funeral home?"

Frank had anticipated the question and had actually rehearsed answers to it during the night. But there was no smooth way to say what had to be said. "Myles, I hate worse than anything to say this . . . and we could be wrong. I wouldn't mention it to you except I think you deserve to know the truth." Frank took a deep breath before continuing. "After the service, the suspect waited until everyone was gone. When Willhoite walked into the chapel, the woman was reaching into the straw bag with both hands as if she was taking something out. She stopped suddenly when he walked in on her."

For several seconds, Myles simply stared. Gradually his eyes narrowed, his forehead creased and his body slumped forward. He buried his face in his forearms. "Oh, God, no."

"Myles, we don't know for sure . . ."

With his face still buried, Myles's voice sounded deep and far away. "*I* know."

There was nothing Frank could say, no way he could argue with Myles, no reason to. His gut told him Tiffany Lakeman was dead and the red-haired woman had tried to bury her with the Antonelli girl.

"Myles." Frank gripped his shoulder. "If this is the woman who took Tiffany, then she must live right here in Austin. Someone will recognize the sketch. Someone knows this woman. And we'll find her. That I promise you."

Myles raised his head and looked at Frank. "Don't give me

239

your promises. I don't want your lousy promises." He struggled to his feet. "Some lunatic wanted to make sure that my baby's body would never be found, and she came close to doing it. If that guy hadn't been at the right place at the right time, Tiffany's body would have been buried in that casket." Myles was shouting now. His voice was hoarse and strained. "So don't say anything to me about promises."

Sleet pelted against the guest-room window. Roland Lauzon's shallow breaths clouded the pane as he stared out at the driveway.

He had been standing there earlier when Frank Traxill drove up, had watched him get out of his car and approach the house. Then Roland had slipped down the hallway and stood outside the door to the den.

The shock of hearing what Traxill had to say stunned Roland. Tiffany was dead—that's what Traxill had come to tell Myles. Tiffany was dead. Murdered.

Roland had wanted to burst into the room, shouting his outrage. Traxill was a fool. Worse than a fool. That story about a red- headed woman. Even an imbecile could have seen who was behind that disguise. Blair Emerson might have fooled those idiots, but not Roland Lauzon.

Roland rested his forehead against the cold pane and began to sob. "Tiffany. My precious child. I tried to help you, my love. But I was too late. Too late." He made careless swipes across his face. "You will pay, Blair Emerson. You will pay."

It wasn't yet two o'clock in the afternoon. Waiting until just before dark would mean less risk of being seen on the road to the lake house. Myles's Mercedes was parked behind Roland's car in the driveway. That might pose a problem later when he was ready to leave. Asking Myles to move it would raise questions. Somehow he would have to get Myles to leave in it, to go somewhere. Or else he'd get the keys and take the Mercedes himself.

Blair Emerson had fooled not only the police, but also her imbecilic employee with that ridiculous uniform and red wig.

But Roland knew the truth. She had finally confessed. And some day everyone else would know the truth about Blair Emerson, local murderess and mortician, who had nearly committed the perfect crime. Yes. In a few days, her body would float to the top of Lake Austin. The authorities would rule it a suicide.

Everyone's best interest would be served. The taxpayers of Texas would be spared the expense of convicting Blair Emerson for murder. Myles and Charmaine could rest in the knowledge that justice had been done. And Tiffany would be avenged.

Most importantly, Roland Lauzon would have the supreme pleasure of watching Blair Emerson die.

Minnie had spent the morning wandering around a house that was far too small to wander in. After lunch she dragged out the ironing board and set it up in front of the television. From a hall closet, she removed a box labeled *Christmas*. Her daughter had asked her to bring her red tablecloth when she came for Christmas dinner.

There was nothing much on television. Still the racket was preferable to silence. Would the police ever find little Tiffany? How could Myles and Charmaine bear up under all this agony? Charmaine was strong in some ways, but this was her child. Minnie had spent only a few minutes with Professor Lauzon last night, when he told her to take the rest of the week off. But she could tell by looking at him that he was nothing less than a dynamite keg. And poor Myles. God bless him. Life can be so cruel.

"What kind of person could do such a horrible thing?"

Minnie turned up the volume on the television. A news brief showed the revised sketch of the woman the police were looking for. "The suspect is a white female, approximately five feet three inches tall, one hundred fifteen pounds, bushy red hair and blue eyes."

Minnie studied the sketch. It was different from the

241

previous ones. The woman no longer wore a hair net. Round face, large blue eyes. Lips narrow and shapeless. Red hair sticking out wildly.

In the few seconds the sketch was on the screen, Minnie stood as though fastened to the floor. "Dear Jesus, that looked like Roseanne Brenner." Minnie stared at the screen in disbelief after the sketch was gone. "The face. The eyes. That crazy hair." But it couldn't be Roseanne Brenner. She was loony, but not in any vicious way.

Minnie ran the iron over the tablecloth, back and forth over stubborn year-old creases. The image on the screen stayed with her, ghostlike, haunting.

Suddenly her mind lurched backward to things Roseanne had said about Charmaine having it all, about Charmaine getting what she wanted—even Blair Emerson's husband. Numerous times she had said she was praying for Charmaine. "Praying what, Roseanne?" Minnie's knees went weak. She sat down hard in a wobbly arm chair. "Roseanne handles food at the day-care center. She probably wears a hair net. And I know she wears a uniform. But why? Why would she do it?"

A sudden thought struck Minnie, hit her directly between the eyes. "Blair. She's crazy about Blair. She did it to make Charmaine pay for hurting Blair."

Minnie struggled from her chair. Could it be true? Could Roseanne Brenner have abducted Tiffany? And if it *was* true, wouldn't that mean that she—Minnie—was at least partly to blame? She had talked too much, told Roseanne far too much about Myles and Charmaine and the baby and Blair.

At her living-room window, Minnie stared out at Roseanne's house. Her windows were no longer darkened. The shades were up now. Had Tiffany been in that house? Was she there now?

Minnie gasped and stepped back suddenly. Roseanne was home. She had just walked past her bedroom window. Minnie inched forward and watched. Roseanne was taking clothes from her closet, laying them on the bed. "She's packing, leaving. I have to stop her."

Minnie dialed the police emergency number and asked for Sergeant Traxill, the man mentioned on the news broadcast. She pressed the phone hard against her chin to keep it from quivering. Helplessly, she waited, her eyes darting back and forth from Roseanne Brenner to the iron that was now scorching her red Christmas tablecloth.

41

Roseanne had awakened Wednesday morning with a sense of impending doom. During the night, the Guiding Spirit had told her that it was time to move to a new mission field, that the Enemy was drawing near. This time she was not to stand firm in its face, but flee to safety. She didn't know yet where she would go. She would trust the Spirit to direct her when she reached the bus station.

It was early afternoon and she was almost finished packing. Her pale face had taken on a look of perpetual worry. She was rolling her socks into little balls and stuffing them in her suitcase when she heard a knock on the door. She grimaced. There was no time to talk. She had to finish packing and leave before the Enemy attacked.

On her hands and knees, Roseanne crawled across the threadbare rug on the living-room floor, out of sight of whoever was standing on the porch. At a window to the right of the door, she inched aside a dusty curtain. Minnie Erskin. A Christmas gift in her hand. A friend. Or at least the closest thing to a friend Roseanne had.

She stood and opened the door. A cold, gray mist floated over the street, along the sidewalk, up the front steps. "Hello, Minnie," she chimed, stepping onto the front porch and smiling at the gift. "Who's that pretty thing for?"

"Merry Christmas, Roseanne." Minnie poked the gift at her. Her smile seemed stiff, forced. "I'm glad I caught you at home. I'm...uh...leaving tomorrow for my daughter's, and I wanted you...wanted to give you your gift. It's not much."

The package was small, about the size of the loaf of banana bread Minnie had given her earlier. The wrapping paper was red and sparkled with brilliant white stars. The red satin bow brushed against Roseanne's hair when she held the package to her ear and shook it. "That's real nice of you, Minnie. I'm sorry I didn't get you anything."

"Don't think a thing of it."

Roseanne studied Minnie's face, noted that her lips were twitching, her eyes had a nervous look about them.

"Do you have plans for Christmas, Roseanne?"

"Uh, yes. I'm going to my sister Rebecca's house." She hated lying, but the words were coming freely. They must be from the Spirits, she told herself. "I was just packing to leave. I might just decide to stay up there, too. I'm not sure."

When she heard a car approach, Roseanne leaned to the side to peek around Minnie's arm. Tires squealed when the car jerked to a stop at the curb. Two men, one short and pot-bellied, the other tall and muscular, got out and were hurrying up the sidewalk. Their forms were blurred by the heavy mist, but the tall man looked familiar. Who is he? Roseanne wondered. Where have I seen him?

"Where does Rebecca live, Roseanne?" Minnie's voice sounded strained. She threw a quick glance in the direction of the men, but—for a reason Roseanne couldn't understand—pretended not to see them. They were on the steps now. The soles of their shoes scraped on the rough concrete. Roseanne's eyes were fixed on the tall man's unsmiling face. *Who is he? What does he want?*

"Looks like you have guests, Roseanne." Minnie's voice had grown soft, almost sad. Gradually she wormed her way between Roseanne and the front door.

Roseanne cocked her head and squinted her eyes. "I don't

know these men." She stepped back, suddenly frightened. "Tell them to go, Minnie. Make them go, please." She felt a sudden chill settle on her skin, seep into her muscles.

"Roseanne Brenner?" The tall man's voice was strong and deep. He was staring at her. At her hair. Her face. Her eyes. "Are you Roseanne Brenner?" Roseanne cringed when he reached inside his pocket.

"Who are you?"

"Sergeant Traxill." He held a shiny object out in front of him. It blinded Roseanne. "Austin Police Department."

Roseanne's eyes were full blue moons. Her lips trembled. Police. That face. She'd seen it on the television. In the newspaper reports about little Tiffany. *The Enemy*. "Why are you here?" she asked softly.

"I need to ask you some questions about Tiffany Lakeman."

Roseanne felt a touch on her shoulder. For an instant, she thought it was the Spirits. But it was Minnie. Her face was wet with tears. Her lips were moving. But the monstrous roar in Roseanne's head drowned out Minnie's words. The Spirits. They were both speaking at once. Shouting. Roseanne couldn't distinguish their words, but she didn't have to. She knew that the Spirits were angry. She never should have opened the door to Minnie. She should have been obediently packing. It was her greed, her ugly greed in wanting the Christmas gift.

She looked from Minnie's face to the large hand that was now gently gripping her left arm, urging her toward the door. "There's nothing to be afraid of, Mrs. Brenner," the tall man said, his voice low and soothing. "I only want to talk to you. I want you to help me find Tiffany."

Tiffany. Suddenly the whirlwind in Roseanne's head calmed. The voices fell silent. She could hear nothing. The Spirits had deserted her sinful soul. Standing inches away from the tall man, Roseanne could only read his lips when he said to Minnie, "This wasn't your fault, Mrs. Erskin."

42

It was after four o'clock. Eldon hadn't eaten all day, and he had a severe case of caffeine jitters. In the kitchen of Blair's house, he made a turkey sandwich and took it to the table. The dry food he had poured in Celtic's bowl that morning was still there. Blair always joked that Celtic would eat anything that didn't eat him first; but for two days, he had only nibbled at his food. Hour after hour, he just lay near the kitchen door and waited.

Looking out the windows at the bleak gray sky, Eldon's weariness grew. More than forty-eight hours had passed and still nothing. Where are you, Blair? Who stopped you from getting in your car that day and leaving the bank? And why didn't they take the money?

Eldon shoved the half-eaten sandwich aside and reached for the phone when it rang. He hoped it was Frank Traxill, but to his surprise it was Myles Lakeman. "You've been in my prayers, son. Is there any news about Tiffany?"

In a voice flat and weary, Myles told Eldon that Tiffany was dead, that some woman named Roseanne Brenner had confessed to kidnapping her.

"Myles, I'm so terribly sorry. Who is this woman?"

"It turns out she's a neighbor of my father-in-law's

housekeeper. She's been in and out of psychiatric hospitals for years." A heavy dullness weakened Myles's voice. "She told the police that she never meant to hurt Tiffany. She even planned to return her."

Eldon sat at the breakfast table. His shoulders sagged. He could think of nothing to say. Myles talked on, oblivious to Eldon's silence.

"The detective that was heading up the search told me that Roseanne Brenner had wrapped Tiffany in a blanket, put her in a wooden box and buried her in her rose garden." Myles spoke as if he were relating a morbid fairy tale.

"Why did she take her?"

"We're not quite sure. Apparently it had something to do with Charmaine and Blair."

Eldon jerked to attention. "Blair?"

"And strangely enough, it was one of Blair's employees who helped the police catch her. I called the funeral home just now to speak to Blair. Jane sounded strange. Why did she say I should call you?"

Eldon didn't answer immediately. He was thinking about what Myles had said about this Brenner woman and Blair.

"Why are you at Blair's house, Eldon? Is something wrong?"

"I'm afraid so, Myles." Eldon summarized the details of Blair's disappearance and described how Frank Traxill had found Blair's car at the bank with the cash still in the trunk.

"What was Blair doing with a hundred and twenty-five thousand dollars in the trunk of her car?"

"I wish I knew. Maybe then I could help. I don't mind telling you, Myles, I'm worried sick."

"Do you think she might have left town because of Roland's accusations? I mean, that doesn't explain the money, but . . ." Myles's mind seemed to drift. "Roland . . . When I told him that Tiffany was dead, he didn't say a word . . . didn't shed a tear. I didn't have the heart to tell him that it was Minnie's neighbor who did it."

Myles groaned loudly. "I shouldn't have left Roland

alone. Now I don't even know where he is. God forbid that he should hear all the details over the radio." He expelled a long, loud sigh. "I have to go, Eldon. Let me know when you hear from Blair. She'll be all right. She has to be."

When Eldon hung up the phone, he noticed for the first time that the red light on the answering machine was blinking. He pushed the message button and listened.

"Blair, this is your buddy, Lenny. I was mighty sorry we missed each other tonight. Tell you what, though, just to show you there ain't no hard feelings, I'm gonna give you your Christmas gift anyway. It'll probably be there tomorrow. I'll get mine later. Don't get any funny ideas about holding out on me now. I'd hate to have to show up at your house some day soon and take back the present I'm sending you. Be talkin' to ya. Bye."

Eldon played the message several times, underlining phrases in his mind. *Missed each other. I'll get mine later. Holding out on me. Show up at your house.*

"The money. The money was for this man. For Lenny." Eldon dialed police headquarters. "But why, Blair? Why?"

Frank arrived at Blair's house in minutes, with Myles right behind him. He had seen Myles twice already that day. Early that morning, to tell him about Kent Willhoite's call. Then this afternoon, at the morgue. How could the man take it? Two children . . .gone. "This is a rotten time to ask for your help, Myles. But I thought since you and Blair know a lot of the same people that you might recognize this guy Lenny's voice."

"It's okay, Frank. I want to help if I can."

The three men huddled around the machine and frowned at each other as the tape played.

" . . .funny ideas about holding out on me . . . hate to have to show up at your house . . . take back the present I'm sending you . . ."

"There's no doubt about it," Eldon said. "The money Blair raised was meant for this guy. But why? What did he

249

have that she wanted?"

Maybe a picture of her and the man she's involved with in Dallas, Frank speculated. "Well, whatever this so-called gift is, something kept Blair from getting it to this guy Lenny last night." He played the tape again. "Does the voice sound familiar, Myles?"

"No. I don't have any idea who that is."

"Eldon, since Blair didn't talk to you about this man, do you think she might have talked to someone else?"

"Liz Elrod maybe. They're close friends."

Frank leaned against the cluttered desk. "Do you know her?"

"Not as well as Myles does," Eldon answered, remembering how evasive Liz had been on the phone. "I think you two ought to go see Liz, rather than call her. I can't help but think she's holding something back."

Frank nodded. "While we're gone, go through Blair's mail. See if this guy sent anything to her." He turned to Myles. "Let's go."

As they walked out the front door, Myles volunteered to lead the way. "I don't know the exact address, but Liz's house is on Greystone. I'll know it when I see it."

"I'll follow you." Frank walked past the Cadillac parked in the drive. Clumps of dried grass and weeds hung in the rear bumper. The tires and fenders were mud-splattered. "Where the heck have you been driving that thing?"

"I haven't." Myles glanced at the side of the car while fumbling in his pocket for the keys. "This is Roland's car. He took off in mine just before I came over here." Myles's forehead creased in confusion. "Sure is a mess, isn't it?"

Frank stopped. "Why'd he leave in your car?"

"I had him blocked in," Myles answered absently, opening the front door.

Something began to stir in Frank's mind, and it unsettled him. It was a familiar feeling—like a sixth sense. "Where was Dr. Lauzon going?"

"I have no idea. He's gone off several times lately. I guess

250

he just needs to be alone. He shouldn't be driving, but there's no arguing with him." Myles turned to Frank and frowned. "I hope he doesn't hear about . . . where you found Tiffany."

Frank flipped the automatic door lock on the armrest and opened the back door of the Cadillac. Upholstery. Carpets. They were as clean as new. *Lauzon hates Blair*. He moved to the front and slid behind the steering wheel. *Accused her of abducting Tiffany*. The floor mat on the driver's side was badly soiled. *Cursed me to my face for not arresting her*. The passenger's side showed only dusty shoe prints. *Decided to take care of her himself?* "Where do you supposed he was when he got the car in this shape?"

"I don't know, Frank. What difference does . . ."

"Your father-in-law blamed Blair for Tiffany's disappearance, Myles." Frank looked under the front seat, in the glove compartment, ran his palm between the cushions.

"What are you saying, Frank? Roland wouldn't . . ."

"Yes, he would." Frank got out of the car and held up a carelessly folded piece of paper. "Look at this. It was stuck between the seat cushions."

"A withdrawal ticket. Texas Commerce."

"That's Blair's bank. That's where we found her car."

Myles's jaw dropped. He lifted his face to the gray sky, eyes closed. "Roland, no. Have you lost your mind?"

"Let's hope not." Frank gripped Myles's shoulder, drawing him back to the urgency of the situation. "Where did he take her, Myles? Where would he go?"

As Roland Lauzon started the Mercedes up a winding incline less than a mile from the lake house, the car began to lose traction on the sleet-slick road. He floored the gas pedal. The wheels skidded, and the car twisted on the treacherous pavement. He jammed the brake pedal to the floor, sending the car spinning. A tree loomed in the ditch to the right. The grill of the car plowed into the tree with a grinding crash. Roland was slammed forward, then snapped back. Stunned, he put the gear in reverse and tried to back out of the ditch, but the wheels spun uselessly.

He pushed open the door on the driver's side and stepped out into the pelting sleet. Hunching down inside his coat, he picked his way awkwardly along the uneven road. Myles's words rang in his ears. "Roland, we have to talk. I'm afraid it's bad news."

Tiffany. My precious grandchild.

At the approach to the lake house driveway, Roland slipped and fell. Ignoring the pain in his knee, he staggered toward the house. A hideous image began to form before his eyes. He stared at the figure of his precious Tiffany lying on a cold table in the county morgue, her perfect face deathly white, her lips the color of bruised grapes.

Myles hadn't explained who had been responsible for her death, and Roland hadn't asked. He didn't need to. "You murdering monster," he growled, picking his way along the driveway. "I will take to my grave the pleasure of watching you die."

The cold wind and stabbing sleet made Roland's breath come in deep, sobbing gasps. His numbed fingers fumbled with the house keys. Inside he retrieved the pistol from a shelf in the entry closet. Then he left through the back door and limped across the yard toward the boathouse.

43

Blair tried to swallow but her mouth was so dry it was wasted motion. One eye was swollen shut. There was a jagged line of dried blood down her cheek. Still, she was calmer now than in the countless previous hours. She had a plan.

Somehow she would get out of this alive. It was Wednesday afternoon. This very day she would be at home to take Lenny's call, to beg him to meet her and take the rest of the money. The money. Where was it? Surely the bank had had her car towed by now.

A sound from outside the boathouse jerked Blair to a sitting position. She sent up a silent prayer for strength and stared at the door.

Rafters in the boat stall next door creaked and groaned. A motor whined. Lauzon. He was lowering the boat into the water. Blair stiffened her back and reached deep into her soul for every ounce of strength.

The key rattled in the lock. The door eased open. With one eye wide open and the other a mere slit, Blair stared at the shadowed form. Roland Lauzon's thin, stooped body was silhouetted in the opening, the gray afternoon light an eerie background.

"You thought you could fool me like you did that imbecile

Frank Traxill, didn't you?" Lauzon left the door open, took several steps toward her. "The casket. That was very clever. You came within seconds of succeeding in your perverse plan, didn't you?" Cold hatred hardened Lauzon's face. "You dared to try burying my Tiffany with that other child."

In a single motion, Lauzon yanked the tape from Blair's mouth and flung the piece against the wall. She spat out the gag. Fine lines of blood seeped from her cracked, dried lips.

Tiffany is dead. Dear God, help me.

Blair worked her jaw back and forth. The joint popped. Lauzon was grabbing at the canvas tarp, raving about Tiffany and a casket and the funeral home. What did he mean? What was he talking about? He clawed at the tape on her ankles.

"Dr. Lauzon, please. I didn't take Tiffany. I had nothing to do with her disappearance or her death. You must believe me. I know nothing about another child's casket. Please, please believe me."

He peeled back the layers of tape on her swollen ankles, banging them against the floor planks.

"Please, Dr. Lauzon, listen to me. I lied to you about taking Tiffany so that you wouldn't kill me."

The back of Lauzon's hand slammed hard into her cheek. She screamed in spite of herself.

Lauzon struggled to his feet. Swaying, he cupped his hand on his forehead. "You wanted revenge against my daughter, and you got it. Now I will have mine."

"No, please," Blair begged. "I lied to you then, but I'm telling you the truth now." Lauzon's face loomed over her. "I didn't do it. You must believe me."

"Shut up and get to your feet."

With her hands still bound behind her back, Blair struggled to her knees, but she was too weak to stand. Lauzon stuck the pistol in the waist of his trousers, gripped her upper arm and pulled. Pain shot through her shoulder. She felt the boathouse sway beneath her feet when she finally stood. If she'd eaten anything in days, she would have thrown up.

A jab in the back forced Blair forward. She barely could

drag one swollen foot in front of the other. Gradually, numbness mingled with a tingling sensation in her limbs, and her circulation returned.

Outside the boathouse, she squinted in the gray glare. The sun was setting fast. Lauzon shoved her to the left, through an open door leading to an enclosed boat stall. A sleek, white ski boat was tied to the stall with a single rope. Lauzon pressed a button on the wall and the overhead door opposite them lumbered up. The wide, gray-green expanse of Lake Austin appeared. Blair knew this part of the lake well. This side was mile after mile of gently sloping home sites, widely spaced and set back from the water's edge. On the opposite side was a towering bluff that jutted from the water like a wall of rock.

Blair looked out across the smooth, green surface. Her mind raced furiously. Lauzon was going to put her into the boat, ride out onto the lake and push her overboard. *Will he shoot me first?*

Lauzon shoved her again. "Get in."

Blair turned toward Lauzon and saw the pistol butt protruding from his belt. *If he gets me in the boat, I'm dead.* "If you shoot me, the police will catch you. Everyone knows how you hate me." Hair whipped across her face, stuck to her bloody lips. "Even Charmaine will blame you."

Roland Lauzon's voice was as cold as the glare in his eyes. He removed the pistol and pointed it at her. "Oh, I don't intend to shoot you. You're going to take us for a nice ride on the lake. And then you're going to commit suicide."

Blair looked from Lauzon's thin, stony face to the pistol, then down to the narrow, slippery edge of the ski boat which sat low in the water. *Buy time.* "I can't even get in that boat with my hands taped behind my back, much less drive it."

"You'll drive all right. I'll take care of that." Lauzon gripped Blair's upper arm and pulled her down. She cried out and sank to her knees. "Now get in the boat."

Blair squirmed to the edge of the rough, wooden planks, worked her legs around until they were hanging over a rear seat. She shrieked when Lauzon pushed her and she tumbled

255

forward into the boat.

"Move over." Lauzon then stepped down into the boat. He removed a knife from a console near the driver's seat and turned back to Blair. "If you try anything, I'll shoot you right here. Now turn around."

A knife slashed through the tape on Blair's wrists. She peeled away the pieces, then rubbed her hands and wrists. She rotated her shoulders cautiously, massaging first one, then the other through her thick coat.

She looked up at Lauzon. He was standing in the narrow aisle between the two front seats. He pointed the gun at her forehead, stepped aside, and said, "Now. Get behind the wheel." Blair looked directly into the barrel of the pistol. Her eyes froze on the gun, only inches away from her head. *His finger's off the trigger*.

"Get up to the wheel, I said."

With a shrill scream, Blair sprang forward, lunging at Lauzon. She rammed his stomach with her head, throwing him off balance. He fell backwards, taking Blair with him. They tumbled to the floor of the boat, awkwardly, clumsily. She was on top of him. The pistol, still in his hand, dug into her ribs.

With his free hand, Lauzon pounded her head and her back. Viciously. Repeatedly. His face was inches from hers. With all her strength, Blair jabbed at Lauzon's bony face and head and neck. The pistol remained wedged between them, grinding into Blair's ribs. She twisted away and grabbed at the glint of silver. But Lauzon jerked the pistol back, paused a split-second, then brought it down against Blair's skull.

44

The tires of the Plymouth skidded wildly around the sharp curves of City Park Road where it snaked through the hills above Lake Austin. Sweat collected on Frank's brow. He hoped Charmaine was right about where her father might be holding Blair. "How much farther, Myles?"

"Two miles or so." Myles gripped the armrest fiercely, locking his jaw when the car slid around corners. "It's all coming together now. The charges against Blair. Roland's absences. His strange behavior. And today, when I told him Tiffany was . . .that she had been found . . . Now I see why he didn't ask a single question." Myles pounded the dash. "Why hasn't the unit you radioed gotten back to you? He's had time to get there, hasn't he?"

The radio crackled, then Frank spoke into it: "Yeah. A gray Mercedes. That's it. I'm minutes away. I have Lauzon's son-in-law with me. Do not approach the house. Let me know if you see anyone. Extreme caution. This is a hostage situation."

45

Dazed, Roland stared down at the boat floor. Blair Emerson's body lay crumpled at his feet. Blood seeped from her hair down her cheek. When he hit her with the gun and shoved her body off him, Roland had thought she was dead. But then he had seen her breathing. She was either stunned or unconscious.

Roland stumbled around her body, reeling from the blows to his own head. He hadn't expected her to attack him. It hadn't occurred to him that she would have that kind of strength after two days without food and water.

He collapsed into the seat behind the steering wheel and took another look over his shoulder. She was beginning to stir now and make muffled noises. He had to hurry, to finish what he had begun.

Roland turned the key in the ignition. The motor started. He hadn't driven the boat in years. Awkwardly he slid the lever into gear and steered the boat out of the stall. His head throbbed. Pain stabbed at his ribs where the weight of Blair Emerson's body had ground the pistol into his side.

The rear of the boat dug deeper into the water when Roland accelerated. He steered toward the north where only minutes away, the lake widened. That was where he would do what had to be done.

Roland took one final look over his shoulder. She was still on the floor. Eyes closed. Lips parted. She looked so helpless, so battered, that for a moment he almost pitied her. Then he turned, looked out over the dark water, and forced himself to imagine what that wicked woman had done to their precious Tiffany.

46

"Stay behind me." Frank reached inside his coat, fingered the butt of his revolver and walked along the gravel drive toward the house.

The front door was locked. They tried the rear door and found it open. The house was empty.

"The boathouse." Myles trotted across the soggy brown grass sloping toward the waterfront and pounded over the slippery planks on the pier. The doors to both the storage room and the boat stall were open. "I'll check the stall, Frank. You look in there."

In a dark, musty storage room, Frank flicked on an overhead light. Life jackets. Rope. A canvas cover in the corner. Frank jerked it back. Nothing. He scanned the ten by ten area quickly, saw a wide strip of blood-stained tape near the back wall and a long strip stuck to the edge of the tarp. "That miserable scum."

He turned to find Myles standing in the doorway. Myles spoke breathlessly. "The boat's gone."

Frank raced to his car and radioed for help. Then he turned to Myles. "Any of these houses around here occupied?"

"Most of them."

"Get in the car. We're going to borrow a boat."

47

Blair raised her head inches off the boat floor. Through half-open eyes, she saw spatters of blood glistening on the shiny vinyl seat back. Her blood. A thought broke through her dull senses. Minutes from now, she would die.

The motor roared. The front of the boat lurched up and down, pounding the glassy waters. Blair struggled to her knees, braced herself against a rear seat, and looked around. It was almost dark now, and Lauzon was driving without lights. The boat was picking up speed, heading down the lake, toward the suspension bridge. And Blair knew why. The lake widened near the bridge. Swimming to shore would be impossible.

You're going to commit suicide.

Lauzon was looking straight ahead. The pistol was probably in his hand, but she could not worry about that now. With each second, they were getting farther from the shore.

Brandi. I've got to get away for Brandi.

Blair crawled to the side of the boat. She was partially shielded from Lauzon's view by the seat back. Trembling, she gripped the chrome rail on the edge of the boat and hunched forward, staring at the dark water. A thick, cold mist sprayed her face, sharpening her senses.

Quickly and silently, she struggled out of her overcoat and shoes. She took a final look over her shoulder at the retreating shore. "God, help me." Wind whipped the words from her lips and scattered them over the glassy water.

Blair put one foot on the edge of the boat, leaned forward and pushed, hurling her body headfirst into the freezing water.

48

Ignoring the cold wind that seared his face, Frank gripped the windshield of the borrowed ski boat and scanned the lake for Lauzon. He strained to hear the rumble of another motor. Nothing. Where was Lauzon headed? Myles had suggested they try an area toward the bridge where the lake widened.

"Look." Myles grabbed Frank's arm and shouted over the roar of the engine. "There he is. Over there."

Lauzon was hunched over in the front of the boat, passing the beam of a floodlight over the glassy water. Frank tightened his grip on the windshield. *Are we too late?*

Lauzon's face was visible now. Gray hair whipped by the wind. Mouth slack. Eyes wide. He looked like he was in a trance, like he didn't see or hear them.

When they were yards away, Myles slowed the boat and shouted over the rumble of the motor. "Roland, it's me. Myles." He rose to his knees and steered the boat skillfully with one hand. "Stay where you are. I'm coming. Charmaine sent me to get you."

In seconds, the two boats were side by side, rocking and scraping against one another. Myles killed the motor. Frank anchored the boats together with a ski rope, then he and Myles scrambled from one to the other.

Frank flicked on his flashlight and shined it on the rear floor of the boat. A gray and black plaid coat. A pair of black leather shoes. He flinched when he saw blood splattered on the vinyl seat back.

Myles grabbed Lauzon's shoulders and turned the old man around. "Roland, I know you've been holding Blair in the boathouse. Where is she now? Tell me the truth. Is Blair in this lake?"

Numb with cold and fear, Blair swam just beneath the water's surface, working her arms and legs furiously. She felt as if she had been in the water for hours. *Where is he? Can he see me? Am I swimming toward the shore? The bluff?* She had no idea. It was dark now, and panic had confused her.

When she thought her lungs would explode, she surfaced. The instant her head emerged from the water, she swung it back and forth, searching frantically. *Where is he? Where am I?*

Lights blurred far in the distance, maybe two hundred yards away. Lights on houses and boat docks. Behind her, a wall of rock rose from the water. "No," she whimpered. The bluff—she was swimming toward the bluff. No way out. No one to hear her.

She quelled another rush of panic. *It's all right. I'm out of the boat. I'm alive.*

Then she saw it. A broad, cone-shaped beam of light. Lauzon. He was panning a light over the water. Could it reach this far? A quick breath and Blair slipped beneath the surface. Head sharply back, eyes open wide, she peered through the inky water. Nothing. Seconds passed. Still no light. She surfaced, gulping air hungrily.

The bluff was close now—not more than thirty yards away. *Can I make it?*

I will make it. I will. For Brandi.

Lungs aching, eyes closed to the dark and silent water, Blair fought her way toward the bluff.

Just a few more yards. Help me, God.

Standing in the bow of the boat, Frank worked the floodlight across the water, calling Blair's name. Could she still be alive? Something inside him said yes.

Myles and Lauzon were huddled together next to him. Lauzon was mumbling and sobbing. Frank spoke sharply: "Lauzon, are you sure this is where she went over?" All he got was a blank stare in return. "Answer me."

Myles raised a hand to calm Frank. "Roland, are you sure this is where Blair jumped?"

"I think so. Yes." Roland slumped forward and grabbed his temples. "She killed our baby. She had to die."

"Shut up, Lauzon." Frank's voice boomed over the silent lake. The beam of light turned the water from pitch black to a dark and deathly green. "Blair." His voice bounced back to him. "Blair."

Roland raised his head and glared at Frank. "She drowned. She's dead, I tell you."

Frank's hand shot out and grabbed a fistful of Lauzon's parka. "I told you to shut up."

"That's enough, Traxill," Myles barked, prying Frank's fingers loose. "Now, Roland, please. Not another word. Blair's an excellent swimmer. She could still be out there."

Frank turned back to the lake, working the floodlight. "Blair. It's Frank Traxill. Call out to me. He can't hurt you now. It's Frank, Blair."

Gasping and sobbing, Blair reached for a tree limb hanging over the water. She locked her arms around it and dangled there like a piece of driftwood deposited by the current.

Wind whipped down the lake, carrying sounds over the water. A man's voice. Oh, God. Lauzon. What was he saying?

"Call out to me. It's Frank, Blair. He can't hurt you now."
Frank.

Tree bark scraped against Blair's cheek. "Help me, Frank." Her voice was a whimper. She tried again and again, but it was hopeless.

265

Signal him. Make him hear you.

About six feet away, a ledge jutted from the bluff. Blair's eyes focused on gray and white shapes near the edge. Rocks.

She forced herself to release the tree limb and sink back into the icy water. She could not feel her feet and legs. With awkward, jerky movements, she inched her way toward the rocks.

Hurry. Hurry. Before he leaves.

The ledge was just above her head now. Blair reached up for it.

Don't leave, Frank.

Legs dangling below her, she held onto the ledge with one hand and blindly searched the rough, crumbling surface with the other. She clawed at the hard soil around a large, jagged rock. First one side. Then the other. The rock dislodged, tumbled off the ledge, splashed into the water. Other tumbling white shapes followed. Rocks glanced off Blair's head and shoulders, but she felt nothing.

A sound echoed across the water—a splash. Frank froze. Another splash.

"I heard something," he shouted. "It's coming from over there. Start it up, Myles. Go toward the bluff. Slowly." Frank searched the dark water, fanning the beam of light back and forth. "Blair, I heard you. Hang on. We're coming."

The beam scanned the water like a round yellow eye, probing the foot of the bluff, the low-hanging tree limbs.

Suddenly Frank shouted, "Stop the boat. There she is." Tearing off his coat, he called, "I see you, Blair. I see you. Stay there. Just stay there." Frank struggled into a life vest Myles tossed him and fastened it tight. He was a lousy swimmer, hated the water. But he pushed those thoughts aside as he kicked off his boots and jumped into the lake.

The blast of cold took Frank's breath away. He struggled awkwardly through the freezing water. Blair was hanging onto a rock ledge some thirty feet away. Breathless, he called to Myles. "Keep the light on her." Frank worked his arms

266

choppily, closing the gap between him and Blair. "Hang on, Blair," he panted, "I'm coming."

While he watched, Blair lost her grip. Silently she disappeared into the blackness. Frank stroked harder, faster. Then her head emerged. She was gasping for air and clawing for the tree limb.

Seconds later, Frank wrapped both arms around Blair's waist and buoyed her head above the water. She coughed and struggled, arching her back and pushing against him. "Easy. Easy, Blair," he gasped. "You're okay now."

The words soaked in. She went limp in his arms, and her head dropped back. The beam of light fell across her face. One eye was swollen shut. Her lower lip was split and puffy. Her cheek was scraped and bruised.

Frank cupped the back of her head in his palm, felt an alarmingly big knot. He eased her chin onto his shoulder. "You made it, Blair." He pushed off from the bluff and began paddling awkwardly toward the boat. "I don't know what kept you going. But you made it."

49

April took the letter from her backpack as the bus pulled in to a stop somewhere in Louisiana. She had no idea where she was when the door hissed open and she stepped outside.

In the rest room of a cafe named Jeannie's, April opened the envelope and read the letter from Blair one last time.

April, this is very difficult to say but I think you need to know the truth. Eleven years is a long time. Much has happened to both of us. I have a life of my own now, a life that doesn't include you. I think we would both be better off if you stayed with Lenny.

April tore the letter and the envelope into tiny pieces and watched them flutter into the toilet. Not even Becky was going to know why she had really run away from home. Home. What home?

She pressed the lever with the toe of her tennis shoe and stepped back to watch the water whoosh in and swallow the bits of paper. When the last scrap disappeared, April vowed that she would never speak or think of the woman named Blair again. Jewell was her mother. And she was dead.

It was almost seven o'clock. The cafe looked clean enough, and April hadn't eaten all day. She chose a table as far away as she could get from the Christmas tree and its blinking miniature lights. Tomorrow was Christmas Eve.

April ordered a grilled cheese sandwich and a Diet Coke. A Christmas carol floated from a speaker above the grill. *Joy to the World*. April tried to block the sound from her mind. She unzipped her backpack and dug past a box of towelettes, a little bottle of Top Job and the paperback book. Her fingers closed around the smooth cover of her diary. For now, it was the only friend she had, the only person she could talk to.

Then her fingers touched something else—something that stuck out from the pages of the diary.

50

Frank stood just inside the door to Blair's hospital room at St. Mary's. A full twenty-four hours had passed since he dragged her limp body out of Lake Austin. According to Eldon, Blair had spent most of those twenty-four hours drifting in and out of a drug-induced sleep.

Now, still pitifully weak, she begged the doctor to let her go home. The doctor jiggled the i.v. pole and smiled. "You're doing amazingly well, Blair, but by no means are you ready to be without this." Before she had a chance to protest, the doctor turned and left the room.

Frank watched Eldon rise stiffly from his chair and step to the bed. "The doctor's right, honey." His large, rough hand smoothed back her stringy hair. "You're as weak as a kitten. You do well to hold up your head." He tilted her chin and smiled mischievously. "Now if you don't need me tonight, I have a date."

"A date?" Blair managed an amused tone, despite her grogginess. "I'd say I'm feeling a little jealous, but frankly I don't feel a darn thing."

"No need. It's just Celtic. He's expecting me."

Blair's smile was faint. "Is my little buddy okay?"

"He will be when you get home."

Blair reached up and touched Eldon's face. "Thanks for everything. Tell mother I love her."

"I will." Eldon bent down and gently kissed her goodbye.

Frank stepped to the foot of the bed and offered to leave too.

"No. Please stay," Blair said. "I've been wanting to . . .to suggest something to you." Her voice was weak, but there was a touch of playfulness.

"Suggest away."

"There's a . . .a club here in Austin that you might enjoy, Frank. It's for swimmers. Year-round swimmers." Blair paused to moisten her lips. "They call themselves the Polar Bears, I think."

Frank chuckled. "Oh yeah? Well, *I'd* call them out of their minds." He walked around to the side of the bed. "Don't get any bright ideas about submitting my name for membership. I don't plan to get in water deeper than my bathtub for a long, long time."

Frank took the chair next to the bed. When Blair reached out her hand, he took it. It was cold and trembling. As quickly as her playful mood had appeared, it vanished. She fought back tears when she spoke. "I don't know how to thank you, Frank. I . . .I would have . . .died out there without you and Myles."

Her voice faltered, and tears began to flow. She let go of his hand and pulled the edge of the bed sheet over her mouth to muffle her sobs. Then she awkwardly wiped at her tears. Frank flinched when the cut on her lip cracked open and blood seeped into the sheet.

She jerked back the sheet and frowned at the red smear. "Haven't these people ever heard of fabric softener? I hate hospitals. I want to go home."

The air was thick and heavy. Frank didn't blame Blair for wanting to go home. He hated hospitals, too. The smells reminded him of the morgue. The odors in this room mingled with the sweet scent of flowers—gifts from friends and family. Frank had looked over all the gifts while the doctor

271

was examining Blair. A brilliant red poinsettia from the funeral-home staff. A Christmas cactus in an ornate brass pot from Blair's sister Charlotte and her family. Roses from her new godson and Bill Elrod. And there was a stylish little nightshirt from Liz.

Frank studied Blair's pale face. Cuts and abrasions and bruises on her cheeks. One eye still swollen and bluish-black. Her bleeding lower lip was puffy and chapped. A strip of hair just above her ear had been shaved away, and a bandage covered the stitches on her scalp. She was looking toward the window. Her eyes blinked slowly.

A Christmas special was playing on the television set suspended on the wall opposite Blair's bed. There could have been a live performance in the room and Blair wouldn't notice. What was she thinking about, he wondered. The awful ordeal with Lauzon? The guy named Lenny? The money? Eldon had told him that several times Blair had mumbled questions about her answering machine and messages, but her questions had been shushed.

Frank was considering whether or not to ask her about Lenny when he heard her whisper, "I need to go home."

He pulled his chair closer to the bed and spoke softly: "Blair."

She turned her head slowly to face him, almost as if she had forgotten he was there.

"You can tell me this is none of my business, but there's something I'd like to know. Then I'll leave you alone. I know you've been in some kind of trouble. And I don't mean with Lauzon. The trip to Dallas. The cash in your trunk. That money was to pay off some guy named Lenny, wasn't it?"

Blair grabbed his arm clumsily, rattling the i.v. pole and stretching the clear plastic tubing attached to her hand. "How do you know about Lenny?" Her voice was filled with alarm.

Frank wished he'd kept his mouth shut. "He called you. Left a message on your answering machine."

She struggled from the pillow, clawing for a button to

272

lower the foot of the bed. "I've got to get out of here. Help me, Frank. I've got to go home."

Frank stood, steadying the pole with one hand and pressing against Blair's shoulder with the other. "Wait. Now just wait."

"I can't wait. I need to go home," she demanded weakly. "He may call again. Please, Frank, help me," Blair pleaded. "You don't understand."

With both hands on her shoulders now, Frank pushed her gently back onto the pillows. "Calm down. He called once. He'll call again."

"What if I've lost her forever?" She was crying now. Her words were choked with sobs.

"Lost who, Blair? Who have you lost? I don't understand. Talk to me." Frank sat on the edge of the bed. Blair reached up with both hands and grabbed his arm. Blood seeped through the bandage that held the tubing to the back of her hand. Her words were garbled, but he managed to recognize one: Lenny.

"What about Lenny? Tell me."

The door opened slowly. Frank looked over his shoulder, desperately hoping for a nurse. But it was a priest who peeked in. The priest must have assumed he was intruding, because he disappeared, leaving the door slightly ajar. Over Blair's sobs, Frank caught snatches of a conversation in the hall. The priest was talking to someone—hopefully a nurse. Blair was terribly agitated, and her hand was bleeding steadily.

Frank carefully eased off the bed. Blair was still holding onto his arm. The door opened wider. Stark fluorescent light from the hallway silhouetted a thin, young girl who stood uncertainly in the doorway. The priest nudged her forward, into the dimness of the hospital room. Fine straight hair. A tight, nervous face. Unblinking eyes that stared straight ahead.

"Can I help you?" Frank asked, feeling somewhat foolish and helpless himself.

The girl's voice was hardly more than a whisper. "Is she Blair Emerson?"

Frank nodded. "Who are you?"

"I'm April Bond."

Frank felt Blair's nails dig into his flesh. A tremor moved up her arms to her shoulders. Her head turned until the girl was directly in her line of sight. Then Blair froze. Ceased breathing. Her eyes were riveted on the child.

Slowly, Blair released her grip on Frank's arm. Frank cringed when, without taking her eyes off the girl, Blair peeled the tape from the back of her hand and removed the tubing. Then, as if she were reaching to touch a vision, Blair extended her arms.

Confused, Frank pushed back the chair and watched. What took place next occurred in slow motion. It seemed to take the child forever to inch her way to the foot of the bed, then into the space between him and Blair. With obvious reluctance, she stepped inside Blair's open arms.

"Brandi." The name was exhaled slowly.

Frank's body stiffened. Brandi. Her daughter. Suddenly, everything fell into place. The cash. The trip to Dallas. The man who needed—demanded——money. Lenny. A damned kidnapper.

Frank felt like an intruder. He tried to squeeze past the girl, but the chair blocked his way. So he stood there, staring dumbly.

"I thought I'd lost you again." Blair's words were almost indistinguishable through her sobs. She held her child tightly, not noticing that the thin rigid arms did not return the embrace. "Oh, Brandi. Eleven years. Oh, dear God, thank you." She released her embrace and cupped Brandi's chin in one trembling hand. "Look at you. Look at my daughter. You're beautiful." Blair turned to Frank. Smiling. Crying. "My child. This is my child."

Frank felt his heart hammering in his chest. "It all makes sense now." He shook his head. "Oh, Blair. What you've been through for this moment." Frank put his hand lightly on

274

the girl's shoulder, felt her flinch and withdraw. "Welcome home, Brandi. Now I understand what kept your mother alive for the past three days."

51

Lee Pickens closed the door of a phone booth near the International Bridge in Laredo. He had a pocketful of U.S. coins and used one to get an operator. He gave her Blair Emerson's phone number and leaned against the wall of the booth. The clang and whine of a distant mariachi band were like salt on his raw nerves. "I'm gonna ring your neck, Blair Emerson, if I get that blasted machine again." After four rings, a man answered. Lenny thumbed in the coins. "Hey. Who's this talkin'?"

"Eldon Sumner. Who is this?"

Lee Pickens cleared his throat, deepened his voice and spoke precisely. "I'm a friend of Blair's from San Antonio. I wanted to wish her a merry Christmas. May I talk to her for a minute?"

"I'm sorry. Blair's in the hospital."

I knew it. "Hospital? I'm sorry to hear that. Nothing serious, I hope."

"It could have been. It's a long story. I'll let Blair explain it. What's your name? I'll tell her you called."

Lee Pickens looked across the street at a gaudy neon sign outside a bar. "Miguel. My name's Miguel. I sure would like to talk to Blair. What hospital is she in?"

"St. Mary's. You can call her there if you want to."

The man gave Lee Pickens the hospital phone number and said he was sure Blair would be glad to hear from him.

Yeah. She's gonna be beside herself.

52

April sat in a chair next to Blair's bed, careful to keep her hands away from her lips and eyes when she got nervous. Germs. They were everywhere. She had scrubbed her hands with hospital disinfectant soap twice in the hour she had been in Blair's room. Once when the nurse had put the tube back in Blair's bloody hand. And one other time when the man named Frank shook her hand as he was leaving. He was tall and handsome. April's face had reddened when he touched her and said, "I guess you've made your mother the happiest woman alive tonight, Brandi. Or do you want to be called April?"

Not once had Lenny asked what she wanted, and he had known her all her life—or the last eleven years of it. April shuddered. Lenny and Jewell had kidnapped her. They hadn't *adopted* her. And Lenny had forced Blair to write that hateful letter, the one April had flushed down the toilet last night in Louisiana. And all that money in Lenny's satchel. Blair hadn't mentioned it, but April knew she had paid it to Lenny just to get her back. Thousands of dollars for her. It was unbelievable.

Blair's voice shook her from her thoughts. "Forgive me for staring at you, Brandi. I'm afraid if I turn my back you'll disappear again."

Watching Blair struggle against tears saddened April. Though she hadn't asked why Blair was in the hospital, April assumed she had been in a terrible accident of some sort. Her face was scraped and bruised and swollen. Violet circles darkened the skin beneath her eyes. Her hair was a stringy mess—the way her own looked if she let it dry naturally after swimming.

"Frank was very sensitive to ask you about your name. I wish I'd thought to ask which you preferred."

Which you preferred. "It's okay."

"I think it's really important for us to be as honest with each other as we can, so I'm going to start now." Blair cleared her throat. "If it won't cause you a problem, I need to call you Brandi. You see, it was in April that you disappeared." Her voice broke. "Do you mind?"

Brandi. It was a nice name. Her name. Not some lie Jewell and Lenny made up. "It's okay. I can be Brandi." *From now on. Brandi.*

Blair was smiling now. Brandi noticed that her lower teeth were just a little crooked like her own. "What should I call you?" Brandi surprised herself by asking, proud of the growing confidence in her voice.

"What do you want to call me?"

"When I was little I called Jewell . . ." Brandi sucked the word back down her throat.

"It's okay, honey." Blair extended her hand. Brandi stared at it and swallowed hard. The i.v. tubing. The bloody bandage. The germs. No way. She turned her head. Finally Blair withdrew her hand and said, "So what did you call Jewell when you were little?"

"Mama," Brandi answered. "I hated it. Lenny made me say it."

"I like *Mom*. Or you can call me Blair if that would make you more comfortable." The offer had been made with a smile, but Brandi didn't believe she really meant it. "Well, you have plenty of time to decide. There are some things I'd

279

like to ask you though, Brandi, things I'm not quite clear on yet. Where were you, honey, when you found the letter with my name and phone number?"

"In a cafe somewhere in Louisiana."

"And you say you found it in your backpack? How do you think it got there? Do you think Lenny put it there?"

"I guess so."

"After you read the letter, you called Father Ochoa?" Blair prompted.

"And then a woman came for me," Brandi explained, remembering the woman's soft voice and her pudgy face. "She didn't know Father Ochoa, but her husband did. I spent the night at their house. This morning she drove me to some other town where we met Father Ochoa. Then he brought me here to Austin."

"But how did you know I was here—in the hospital?"

"Father Ochoa called the number you wrote in your letter, but he got your answering machine. Your recording gave your office number, in case the call was urgent. A man named Wayne said you were in the hospital." Brandi recalled how strangely Father Ochoa had acted when she had asked him where Blair worked. He had never answered her question. *Why didn't he want to tell me where Blair works?*

A nurse came in to examine Blair. Brandi turned away, not wanting to think about what the nurse was doing, much less watch.

It was all so incredible. Lenny and Jewell had kidnapped her—right out of her own back yard, with Blair just inside the house. It was so hard to believe that Jewell could do such a terrible thing. But Lenny's greedy plan to sell her back to Blair fit him to a tee. Lenny Bond was a nitwit and a jerk, and Brandi hoped he landed in some Mexican jail and rotted there.

To avoid thinking about the countless billions of germs and microorganisms in this one area alone, Brandi roamed the room, careful to keep her hands in her pockets. The scent of roses drew her to the window. On the wide, deep sill stood a crystal vase with what looked like fifty pink roses. They were from two men named Bill and Clay. Next to them was an open box. In the tissue paper lay a white nightshirt with pink and yellow ribbons woven into the yoke. It was from someone named Liz. The card said she loved Blair.

On a table next to the empty bed was the most beautiful poinsettia Brandi had ever seen. It was tall and full and brilliant red. Someone had spent lots of money for it, too. She read the card in the dim light. *All of us here at the funeral home wish you the quickest possible recovery. We were so worried about you.* Brandi backed away, frowning. Did Blair have friends at a funeral home? She sure hoped not. What if she invited them to dinner some night? Brandi would never be able to eat next to someone who touched dead bodies. They would be covered with germs, death-causing germs.

Then another, far worse possibility occurred to her, causing her skin to crawl. What if Blair *worked* at a funeral home? Father Ochoa knew how she felt about germs. Maybe that was why he hadn't said where Blair worked.

Plans began to form in Brandi's head. She would have to do the dishes like before. Hide her plate and glass and silverware. Disinfect the bathroom before using it. Wash her own clothes separate from Blair's. And no matter what it took, she would not let Blair touch her unless she had seen Blair scrub her hands first.

Stop it, just stop it, Brandi ordered herself. You don't know where Blair works. And even if she does work in some gross place like a funeral home, she might not be there long. Lenny never stayed with a job more than a few months.

The nurse had just left the room when the phone rang. Blair reached for it, but the i.v. pole was in the way. "Would you get that, Brandi?"

Brandi hesitated. She didn't want to touch the phone. Sick people had been talking into it. It rang again. She picked it up with her thumb and forefinger, careful to keep it inches from her lips. "Hello."

"Hey. Who's this?"

281

"This is . . .uh . . .Brandi."

"Oh, it's Brandi now, is it?" The drawling voice on the phone mocked her. "Well, I'll be damned, Sherlock. You discovered the letter."

Brandi's eyes widened. She dropped into the chair. The fingers of her free hand drew up into a fist that she ground into her thigh. *Lenny*. "Yes, I *found* it." Her tiny voice was sharp with sarcasm. The milkshake she had drunk in Father Ochoa's car churned in her stomach. She swallowed several times to keep from throwing up. "So what do you want?" Her voice had become a pathetic squeak. Its sound made her angry.

"I wanna . . ."

Works at a bar.

" . . .speak to . . ."

Old man ain't too fond of children.

" . . .Blair for . . ."

Decide if she wants you back.

" . . .a minute."

"Well you're not going to." Brandi bolted out of the chair. "You're not talking to her now or ever."

Startled by the violent outburst, Blair stared open-mouthed at her daughter.

"You're going to leave both of us alone." The words rolled over each other, gathering speed. "You're a kidnapper, Lenny Bond. And a drug pusher and a liar."

"Look, April, I didn't . . ."

"You just shut up," Brandi shouted. Her fingers were so tight around the receiver that she couldn't feel it in her hand. "You kidnapped me. You lied. You and Jewell. You lied."

"Jewell just . . . "

"Then you made Blair pay money to get me back." Brandi was leaning into the phone, yelling at Lenny Bond's face from miles away. "You just remember. I know what you look like. I know where you are. So if you ever bother us again, you'll end up in jail where you belong."

53

Lee Pickens was swept along by a river of people crossing the International Bridge into Nuevo Laredo. He headed straight for the Cadillac Bar. There he ordered a steak and two margaritas, up. He knocked back the first one before the waiter was out of sight and started on the second. A mariachi band strolled the room, but this time Lee Pickens couldn't hear them. Brandi's furious, threatening words still rang in his head. *I know what you look like. I know where you are. If you ever bother us again . . .*

Lee gulped the drink and punched the back of an empty chair next to him. Dammit to hell. That sneaky dang kid. Digging around in that satchel. Pawing through his things. At this point, he didn't give a rat's eyelash that she had seen both letters. What worried him was what else she might have seen. Like his new identification. Was there any way she could know he was in Laredo and not El Paso?

A solid slap on the back propelled Lee to his feet.

"Lee. *Cómo está, amigo?*"

"Right back at you, man." He flashed his practiced Lee Pickens smile, felt the mustache beneath his nose.

"My friend in El Paso says you're just the man I've been looking for."

"And your friend ain't lying, amigo." Lee Pickens pulled back a chair and nodded to the very dark, very large man called Pablo. They discussed the import business over dinner and more drinks. Lee began to relax, the alcohol distancing him from a skinny young girl in Austin and what she might or might not know.

By the end of the evening, he had decided to concentrate on Pablo and parrots and payoffs. He would forget about Brandi and Blair—at least for now.

54

It was after ten o'clock in the evening, and Blair kept her voice soft and low as she spoke into the phone. Liz asked her to speak up.

"I can't. I have a roommate. I don't want to wake her."

"She must be really sick to be admitted on Christmas Eve. What's wrong with her?"

"Nothing that I can see." Blair rolled onto her side, smiling. "I'm looking at her now. She's sleeping."

Brandi had been reluctant to wear the nightshirt Liz had sent, arguing that it was a gift for Blair. When Blair removed the tags and jokingly suggested that the alternative was a hospital gown, Brandi had taken the shirt into the bathroom and, long minutes later, returned with it on.

"She's wearing the gift you gave me."

"You loaned her my Christmas gift? Thanks a lot."

"She has shoulder length hair. Light brown. Her eyes are closed now, but they're big and brown, just like mine."

"How fascinating," Liz said flatly. "You *loaned* her the nightshirt I gave you?"

How Blair loved stringing Liz along, and never more than now. "She looks incredibly like I did when I was almost thirteen years old."

"Blair, read the label on the plastic bag hanging next to you. Does it say dextrose, or is it morphine? You're talking crazy."

"Want to know her name?"

"Sure. The suspense is keeping me awake."

"It's Brandi. Brandi Emerson-Lakeman."

The silence was electric. Blair could picture Liz, pinned to her chair with shock.

"Brandi? It can't be. She's there with you?"

"Yes, Liz." A sort of numbing peace had settled in, and Blair could talk now without the floods of tears. "I'm looking at her right now." Curled beneath the sheets, her thin face resting on the pillow, Brandi appeared to sleep soundly. Asleep, she looked as defenseless and trusting as she had as a toddler.

"But how? When?" A long, audible sigh trailed Liz's words. "The trip to Dallas. It *was* about Brandi. Oh, Blair."

"I wish now I had told you, Lizzie. It's just that I was so . . ."

"Oh, Blair. This is miraculous. You must be about to explode. How can you be so calm?"

"Calm?" Blair laughed wearily. "I feel like running up and down these halls, yelling like a madwoman. Lizzie, I can't wait for you to see her. She's got a precious face. And you can tell right away that she's smart and . . .and resourceful." Blair was speaking rapidly, the words seemed to tumble out. "You won't believe what she went through getting here. And she said I could call her Brandi." Blair paused. "Actually, what she said was that she could *be* Brandi."

"What a marvelous Christmas gift for you. For you both." Liz's voice broke. "Your baby. She's home, Blair. I want to hear every word of how it happened. Are you up to it?"

"Not yet, Lizzie. I can say that the man who returned her didn't do it out of the goodness of his heart."

Liz groaned. "You paid him."

"Twenty-five thousand. But before I could get the rest to him, Lauzon grabbed me in the bank garage." Blair shivered.

Suddenly the tears came again. "I can't talk about it, Liz. Not now. Besides, I might wake Brandi."

"Brandi. Oh, Blair. It's all over."

"Well, not quite. Don't say anything about this, Liz, but Lenny...he called here tonight."

"He what? What did he say?"

"I don't know. Clear thinker that I am right now, I told Brandi to answer the phone. Anyway, Brandi chewed Lenny up and spit him out. Warned him he'd end up in jail if he ever bothered us again. But, Liz, if he calls again, I'll probably give him the rest of the money...just to be sure Brandi's safe."

"Safe? Honey, do you really think that would keep her safe?... But, listen, don't worry about that tonight. Just be happy. Just lie there and watch your little Christmas miracle sleep. And in my nightshirt. I love it."

"Night, Lizzie. Kiss the baby for me."

Liz was right. She would drive herself mad worrying. And she simply could not allow Lenny, who had already stolen so much, to rob her of anything more.

Blair closed her eyes and prayed softly, "Father, I don't understand how all this happened, and maybe I never will. But I know—I just know—that somehow you worked it out. She's here. And I'm so thankful, so grateful." She looked over at Brandi. "It's been eleven years, God. Show me how to get back what we lost."

Was it going to be possible to get as close to Brandi as they once had been—as they might have been if she'd raised her? Though clearly bright and observant, Brandi seemed so distant. True, it had been only hours since their reunion, but Brandi had shown her no signs of affection, had refused to touch her hand the one time she reached for her. In fact Brandi seemed reluctant to touch anything in the room. But, Blair told herself, that could be because of the dreadful rash she had on her hands and wrists. She would have to have a dermatologist take a look at them.

Blair smiled to herself. She was doing it already, fussing

over Brandi—just like when she was a baby. What a marvelous feeling it was.

A whimpering sound from Brandi's bed pulled Blair from her pillows. The i.v. pole rattled when she eased it aside. Brandi's cheeks glistened with tears. Her head tossed from side to side. She was having an awful nightmare. Blair watched helplessly, then eased her legs over the side of the bed. Fighting her plastic leash, she wobbled toward Brandi.

Trembling, she leaned forward and touched her child's shoulder. "Wake up, Brandi. You're having a nightmare. Wake up." The struggling continued. Blair shook her gently. "Brandi. It's Mom, honey. Wake up." One word distinguished itself from Brandi's incoherent mumbling. *Liar.*

"Brandi, Lenny's gone. He can't hurt you anymore. You're dreaming."

Brandi's lids fluttered open. Her eyes, dark in her pale face, scanned the room. Fear flickered in them.

"You're okay, honey." Blair put her hand lightly on Brandi's shoulder. "You were dreaming. But it's over."

Brandi was looking at her now. Confusion had replaced the fear in her eyes. Blair ached to see her child so deeply distressed, but she smiled gently. "Everything is going to be fine. How about some warm milk? It might help you go back to sleep."

Brandi shook her head. "No. I'm okay now." Her breathing was still heavy, but a small nervous smile appeared on her lips. "I'm . . . I'm glad to be home . . . Mom."

The nervous smile was still there as Brandi's eyes moved from Blair's face down to her bandaged hand. Then with rough, red fingers, Brandi gently eased Blair's hand away and pulled the stiff white sheet over her shoulder.

288